PIERS PAUL READ was born in 1941 in Beaconsfield, England. His fiction has been awarded the Somerset Maugham Award, the Hawthornden Prize, and the Geoffrey Faber Memorial Prize. His novels include THE JUNKERS, A MARRIED MAN, MONK DAWSON, POLONAISE, THE PROFESSOR'S DAUGHTER, and THE UPSTART, all of which appear in various Avon editions. He is also the author of THE TRAIN ROBBERS, but is perhaps best known for his classic, bestselling account of the Andes survivors, ALIVE. Both works of nonfiction are available in Avon editions. Piers Paul Read now lives in London.

Other Avon and Bard Books by
Piers Paul Read

ALIVE
THE JUNKERS
A MARRIED MAN
MONK DAWSON
POLONAISE
THE PROFESSOR'S DAUGHTER
THE TRAIN ROBBERS
THE UPSTART

THE VILLA GOLITSYN

PIERS PAUL READ

A BARD BOOK/PUBLISHED BY AVON BOOKS

Grateful acknowledgment is made for permission to reprint:
Extracts from *The New Society* by E. Hallett Carr (1951)
appear by permission of Macmillan, London and
Basingstoke.

AVON BOOKS
A division of
The Hearst Corporation
959 Eighth Avenue
New York, New York 10019

The Harper & Row, Publishers, Inc. edition contains the
following Library of Congress Cataloging in
Publication Data:

Read, Piers Paul, 1943-
  The Villa Golitsyn.
  I. Title
PR6068.E25V5   1981   823′.914   81-47688
                                          AACR2

First Bard Printing, February, 1983

BARD TRADEMARK REG. U. S. PAT. OFF. AND IN
OTHER COUNTRIES, MARCA REGISTRADA, HECHO EN
U. S. A.

Printed in the U. S. A.

OP 10 9 8 7 6 5 4 3 2 1

The Villa Golitsyn

Prologue

One

Between 1963 and 1966 a state of undeclared war existed between Indonesia and the newly established Federation of Malaysia. Neither nation had the means to fight a conventional military campaign so the Indonesians – after a single attack upon the mainland of Malaysia – limited themselves to a barrage of anti-imperialist propaganda and covert infiltration of Indonesian guerrillas from Kalimantan into Sarawak and North Borneo.

The frontier between the two states on this giant island ran for a thousand miles through mountains, jungle and primeval rainforest. It was impossible to guard it with barbed wire fences, raked earth and watchtowers so Britain – the old colonial power which had undertaken the defence of the new nation – established bases from which small patrols of a single platoon would fan out into the jungle. There they would hide out for two weeks at a time, waiting and watching for any infiltrators from Indonesia.

This strategy worked well. Since the British and Commonwealth troops had the advantage of surprise, it was always the Indonesians who were ambushed and either killed or put to flight. Such minor military setbacks did not worry Sukharno, the Indonesian president, to whom the actual fighting in Borneo was an unimportant adjunct to his political and diplomatic offensives; but the more radical elements in the Indonesian army – those, that is, linked to the Indonesian Communist Party – felt humiliated that the warriors of a newly liberated nation of the Third World should be so effectively frustrated by the soldiers of a neocolonial power. They looked for a dramatic victory over the British which would push the confrontation into open war.

Early in the morning of 9 June 1965, a detachment of Gurkhas – Himalayan mercenaries with a British officer in command – set off from their Battalion headquarters for a fourteen-day patrol. Two days later they laid an ambush at a prearranged position overlooking the upper reaches of the Kapuas River. The site was well camouflaged – invisible from the air and cleverly hidden from the ground in the jungle vegetation.

At dawn on 12 June it was attacked by Indonesian guerrillas. The lookouts were surprised and strangled, and the rest of the platoon were either shot dead in their sleeping-bags or were taken alive. Those that were captured did not live for long. Forgetting the enlightened dicta of Mao Tse-tung on the treatment of prisoners, the victors went berserk. First, in a frenzy, they hacked at the bodies of the dead Gurkhas; then, with more deliberation, they proceeded to torture those that were still living. Some had their eyes put out with sharpened sticks of bamboo; others lost their ears, noses and tongues before being burnt alive.

The most refined torments were kept for the British officer, Hamish Churton. His clothes were torn from his body, his genitals cut off with a *parang*, stuffed into his mouth and down his throat, and then his lips were sewn together with the canvas thread used by the Gurkhas to repair any tears in their groundsheets. While breathing through his nose in bubbles of blood he was made to watch the torture and execution of his men until he too was dispatched with a bullet in the back of the neck.

The corpses were discovered a week later by a brother officer leading another Gurkha patrol. The green tentacles of the jungle were already reaching over the heap of charred bodies, and columns of giant ants carried off small morsels of flesh that had been bitten from the bone; but enough remained to show what had been done to the men before they died. The officer took photographs of this evidence of atrocity and then ordered his men to wrap the bodies in the groundsheets of the dead soldiers and bury them in the ground.

When the British Army Command in Labuan was told of this incident in Sarawak there was an urgent conference of senior officers. The Director of Intelligence, a Brigadier Smythe, was asked to explain how such an ambush could have taken place, but Smythe, already shaken by the pictures of Churton and his men, could think of nothing to say except that the Indonesians must have stumbled upon the platoon's position. It was a lame explanation. In so vast an area of impenetrable jungle, the odds against accidentally finding a well-camouflaged position without alerting the lookouts posted around it were small; yet it seemed even less likely that enemy intelligence could have known of its exact position in advance. Only

4

Brigadier Smythe in Labuan, and Churton himself, had had maps showing where he planned to be and the spot had only been chosen a week before he left on his tour of duty. The Command was obliged to conclude its conference without reaching any conclusions. The strategy for defending Sarawak and North Borneo remained the same.

Three months later, on the night of 30 September, events took place in Djakarta which went some way to solve the riddle. Communist officers in the Indonesian army attempted a *coup d'état*. They first made a preemptive strike against their right-wing commanders, dragging them from their beds to the Lubang Buaja training camp, where they were tortured, killed and thrown in a well; then they occupied various public buildings in the centre of the capital city.

The putsch failed. Certain key commanders had been overlooked – notably General Suharto. The Right regrouped and retaliated. The Leftist soldiers were surrounded and disarmed. A purge began. The hunters became the hunted. The army turned on the Communist Party, whose leaders fled from Djakarta to Central Java. The town house of the General Secretary, D.N. Aidit, was sacked and burned; but before it went up in flames his papers were recovered and removed to the headquarters of the Paracommandos. Among them was found a photographic print of a British army map giving the precise position of Hamish Churton's base camp in Sarawak. Written on the back, in Aidit's own hand, was the note: 'From our comrade L in the British Embassy.'

In the course of the following year, largely as a result of the unsuccessful coup by the Communists, power in Indonesia passed from President Sukharno to General Suharto. This new leader made up his mind to end the confrontation with Malaysia and make his peace with Britain. His government agreed to pay for the rebuilding of the British Embassy which had been sacked three years before; and to mark the new spirit of cordiality the British Military attaché was given the map which had been found among Aidit's papers.

The attaché realized at once that this not only explained the ambush of Churton's platoon in Sarawak, but was also evidence of a spy in the Embassy in Djakarta. Without mentioning the matter to any of his colleagues, he sent the print with Aidit's damning annotation back in the diplomatic bag to the Ministry of Defence in London, where an investigation was immediately started by the appropriate branch of Military Intelligence.

At first it was assumed that some native employee of the Embassy had been responsible, but this hypothesis collapsed because Churton's map had never been in the Embassy, and during the confrontation no native-born Indonesians had been employed there. The investigating officers were therefore obliged to look for the traitor among the British diplomats, and they were soon able to narrow it down to two of the younger men who had been sent to Djakarta early in 1964. Each had a name which began with L, and both had stayed with Churton in Labuan for the week before he went on the fatal tour of duty in Sarawak.

The first, on the face of it, was quite implausible as a spy. His name was William Ludley. He was the son of a Conservative politician – a minister for a time in the government of Harold Macmillan – and an old Cambridge friend of Hamish Churton. He was handsome, charming and rich: it seemed almost fanciful to suggest that he would do anything either to endanger his friend or help the Communists in Asia.

The second, Leslie Baldwin – whom Ludley had brought along with him to stay with Churton in Labuan – was a more likely traitor. While Ludley had gone to one of England's most celebrated public schools, Baldwin had been educated by the state. Ludley had taken his degree from Trinity College, Cambridge: Baldwin from Woodbridge Hall, Leeds. Baldwin's father was a tax inspector from Keighley in Yorkshire, but to the gentlemen in MI5 anyone from the industrial areas of northern England was the son of a coal miner. They assumed that he had only been let into the Foreign Office as a sop to the egalitarian ethos of the times, and thought it only too likely that Baldwin's sympathy with the masses from which he came should lead him to spy for the Communists in Indonesia. But just as they were about to make up their minds that Baldwin was the traitor, Ludley disappeared.

He did not disappear without notice. His father, James Ludley, died while out shooting in Yorkshire. William Ludley returned to England for the funeral, and then went straight back to Djakarta. From there he sent a letter of resignation to the Foreign Office in London, giving his new duties as heir to the Ludley fortune as the reason for curtailing his career. The Foreign Office, which as yet had not been told about the Djakarta leak, saw nothing unusual in this resignation and it was some weeks before Military Intelligence realized that one of their suspects was missing.

At first the news confused them. They thought that Ludley must have heard that he was under suspicion and decided to flee. But then they too decided that it was quite natural for a young man who had come into more than a million pounds and a beautiful house in Suffolk to leave his desk in the humid capital of an unfriendly country and return to England to enjoy a more leisured life. They could wait, after all, and if necessary talk to him in London.

They did wait, but Ludley, when he left Djakarta, did not return to England. He flew to Singapore and took a room in Raffles Hotel. He remained there for a fortnight and then disappeared.

The Foreign Office was now told, and for several months there was dread in Whitehall that Ludley, one of their prize high-fliers, would appear at a press conference in Moscow, Hanoi, Havana or Peking. Military Intelligence tried to find out what Ludley had done and who he had seen in Singapore but learned only that an English girl had joined him there, and had left with him on a flight to Madrid. Only four months after his disappearance did it occur to them to ask the London solicitors who managed the Ludleys' affairs for the forwarding address of their client. They were told that he was living near Cordoba in Argentina on a ranch which belonged to his family.

There Ludley remained for many years and there the authorities were content to let him stay. He never returned to England. Had he done so they might have called him in to answer certain questions, but it would have been hard to convict him of treason on the evidence had they brought him to court, and the scandal would have embarrassed the government and demoralized the diplomatic service. Confident in their own minds that Ludley was the source of the Djakarta leak, the responsible officers investigating the affair decided to let him rot in self-imposed exile.

Two

Ludley's treason seemed to have no perceptible effect on the career of his colleague, Leslie Baldwin. This ginger-haired, north-country fellow-high-flier, cleared of suspicion by Ludley's self-incriminating flight to the Southern Hemisphere, rose steadily through the different grades of the Foreign Service. No further breach of security came from the embassies in which he served, and if on occasions he was passed over for some of the more interesting and sensitive posts, it was not because of his link with Ludley but because of the prejudices of the snobbish selectors.

It was not until the 1970s that Baldwin's natural abilities gained for him some of the posts he deserved. When the Labour Party was returned to power in 1974 Baldwin's northern accent, which had been tempered but not lost over the years in foreign capitals, came into its own. He seemed to be a perfect embodiment of the 'new Briton' that the government wished to project abroad. He was sent to Paris in 1974 and four years later, when he was forty, was mooted for one of the highest appointments in the Embassy in Washington.

It was then that someone remembered the Djakarta leak. It was mentioned at a meeting of the committee convened to confirm his appointment. The man who brought it up – the Head of Personnel – did so only in passing, as if it could not be considered a serious objection to the appointment: but the Permanent Undersecretary, aware that the post in Washington would put into the hands of the man who held it every military and diplomatic secret of the Western Alliance, insisted that they make doubly sure that their candidate, Baldwin, was not what he called 'a hibernating traitor'.

It was therefore agreed that Baldwin should have a second clearance – not by Military Intelligence as before, nor by the Special Branch of the Metropolitan Police, but by the Security Service of the Foreign Office itself. The head of this department, a man called Edgar Fowler, was asked to go over the old ground and report back to the Committee when it met again in October.

Fowler, a man of around fifty, had trained as a barrister, and had been drawn from the legal profession into the Foreign Office about five years before to apply the law's more rigorous logic to questions of security. He was a patriotic man, obsessed with the defection of Donald Maclean and always afraid that the ideological bacillus which had raged through Cambridge in the 1930s might have infected later generations at that or other universities. Certainly, the Soviet brand of Communism had never again been fashionable as it was then; but Fowler suspected that many students in the 1960s who

8

had later found service with the British government had been outraged by what the Americans had done in Vietnam and might as a
result have offered their services to Communist powers.

In looking through the file on the Djakarta leak he was immediately dissatisfied. He accepted the evidence which made either
William Ludley or Leslie Baldwin the source of the leak, and he
agreed that Ludley's subsequent behaviour made him look like the
guilty man. He also noted that Ludley had been to Trinity College,
Cambridge, the same college as Philby, Burgess and Blunt, and there
had studied history under Edward Hallett Carr, whose philosophy of
history Fowler mistrusted; but he also knew that appearances did
not constitute proof and saw certain inconsistencies in the hypothesis that Ludley's actions established his guilt.

If Ludley had betrayed Churton's position to the Indonesian Communists, what was his motive? Certainly he could not have done it
for money, because he had plenty of money of his own. He could
only have done it from conviction, yet if Ludley had been a convinced
Communist or fellow traveller, why had he fled rather than wait to
betray other more important secrets later in his career? Had he
known that he was discovered? But if so, and he had been afraid of
arrest, why had he waited for his resignation to be accepted in
London and then lingered for a fortnight in Singapore? And had he
not, since then, continued to live in the non-Communist world where
he might either have been extradited or eliminated? It would have
been safer, if he had been afraid, to defect to Russia or China, but he
had moved to Argentina and there had lived off the substantial
investments in land and minerals made by his grandfather and now
owned by him. Was that the behaviour of a convinced Communist?
And where was he now? Not teaching English in Moscow or cutting
cane in Cuba, but living an idle life in the South of France.

Thus Fowler was faced with the same problem as the investigators
of fourteen years before – that it was impossible to establish with
certainty which of the two men had photographed the map in
Churton's house in Labuan and passed on a print to the Communists
in Djakarta. If both had been cross-examined at the time, one might
have given himself away, or immunity might have been offered in
exchange for a confession; but neither course of action had
been taken and it seemed too late to do it now. Indeed the
only prudent course of action seemed to be to report back to the
committee that Baldwin, through no fault of his own, could not be

given positive clearance and must therefore be passed over for the post in Washington.

This logical conclusion, however, went against another of Fowler's legal instincts – that a man was innocent until proved guilty. He had met Baldwin and admired him for coming so far from such an unprivileged background. It seemed inconceivable that he was either an active or a dormant spy, and it offended Fowler's sense of fair play that the dictates of logic should destroy his career. He therefore looked for other solutions and came up with only one – that William Ludley himself should be made to admit his treason. Fowler felt sure that if only he could have Ludley before him, he would quickly catch him out in a thousand inconsistencies: but how could Ludley be brought back to England? Or how could Fowler get to see him in France?

For a moment he thought of going as a journalist to see Ludley in Nice; but the questions he would ask would soon give him away. He then thought of sending someone else, someone who knew Ludley and might coax him to confess over a period of time. This idea grew on him. He did not want to pursue Ludley and prosecute him, but simply satisfy himself that Ludley was the traitor. The only difficulty now was to find the friend.

Part One

One

Simon Milson had recently returned from a tour of duty as Second Secretary at the British Embassy in Jedda. He had been married and was now divorced, with a son at a Preparatory School in Sussex and a daughter who lived with his wife. He was tall and thin with a pale complexion, strong hair and a face which in repose had a look of romantic melancholy but often broke into a cynical smile. He was thought amusing by his colleagues, charming by his mother's friends, and attractive by the secretaries in the office – all of which might have made his divorce seem strange had the rupture not happened in Jedda, where several diplomats had recently been abandoned by their wives.

He now lived alone in a flat in Pimlico. In the evenings he would sometimes dine out with his friends; but more often he would eat alone because most of those he had thought were his friends had sided with his wife. This treachery was something which reinforced Simon's pessimistic view of human nature. Sarah, his wife, had been what was once called 'the guilty party' – running off to England with a young geologist she had met in Saudi Arabia, suing for divorce, obliging Simon to sell her his share of their house in Kew as part of the settlement; and now living there with her lover, keeping Simon's children, and entertaining Simon's friends.

He had heard from his sister – who had never liked Sarah – that these friends – these false friends – would justify their preference for his former wife not just by praise of her wit and her cooking, but by dark remarks such as 'it takes two to tango'. He had also heard it said that behind his 'superficial charm' there was cruelty and coldness; that his handsome and youthful appearance and easy, sardonic sense of humour concealed a destructive cynicism, a self-indulgent melancholy, a calculating egoism: yet the only substantiation ever produced in these discussions of his character came from one of the circle who had stayed with the Milsons in Jedda, who told the story of how Simon had refused to speak to Sarah for a whole day because

13

she had given him a broken fried egg for his breakfast.

For a time after the divorce Simon had gone out with other women, but it was only for form's sake. Never quite as lecherous as a modern man is meant to be, the rupture with his wife had doused what remained of his desire. He felt angry with all women for the harm done to him by one, and looked upon their bodies as baited traps. There were plenty of unattached women of the right age who were happy to go out with him, but with icy courtesy he kept his distance. In time, of course, these ladies – even those as lustless as he was – felt injured that he did not make a pass; so to save himself the embarrassment, and the women the humiliation, Simon now spent most evenings eating alone in front of the television – fish fingers or fry-ups with the egg invariably broken.

For lunch he usually went to the Travellers' Club in Pall Mall, which since his divorce – and without an overseas allowance – had become an extravagance but was necessary all the same to his self-respect. His father had worked hard in the dull business of manufacturing office furniture to give his son a good education – by which he had meant a public school and Cambridge University. He had been proud when Simon had got into the Foreign Office, and although he was now dead, it was in deference to his father's wishes that Simon continued as best he could to lead the life of an English gentleman.

A club, like an umbrella, seemed to Simon a necessary appurtenance for this life. Perhaps because he had been serving abroad at the time, he had never been affected by the democratic spirit which had swept over English manners and morals in the 1960s, leaving dukes in jeans and debutantes in dungarees. He even looked askance at those of his friends in the Foreign Office who wore corduroy *blousons* in their spare time to demonstrate their commitment to the Common Market. Simon dressed as he had always dressed – in grey, pin-striped suits during the week, and in tweed jackets and twill trousers at the weekend. He liked to think that the people he mixed with – particularly those in the Travellers' Club – dressed in the same way, and was therefore irritated, one day in the early summer of 1979, as he sat drinking a glass of vermouth before lunch, to see a man of around his own age wearing an open-necked shirt and a sky-blue suit.

The man was slim with blonde hair, and he had on his boyish face the kind of selfconscious, flirtatious expression which Simon associated with homosexuals. He therefore looked away from this offensive intruder just as the intruder raised his plucked eyebrows and crossed the room towards him. To his horror Simon realized that this technicoloured pansy had been in his house at school.

'Aren't you Milson?' he was asked. 'Simon Milson?'

'Yes.' Simon half-rose from his leather chair.

'You probably don't remember me. We were at school together.' Simon stood up altogether. 'Of course . . .'

'Fifteen, no, almost twenty years ago.' He spoke in a soft voice with a trace of an American accent.

'Yes. You're Hope, aren't you?'

'That's right. Charlie Hope.'

Simon did remember Hope, the pretty boy of his year, but he was reluctant to renew the acquaintance of someone in an open-necked shirt and sky-blue suit who, he now realized, was lunching with one of the Club's better-known queers. It was not his style, however, to snub anyone so he listened as Charlie Hope babbled on as if it was only a month or so since they had met. He said he was in films or advertising or films for advertising and had just come back from Los Angeles where he now lived 'on and off'. 'And what do you do?' he asked Simon. 'Didn't you go into the FO?'

'Yes,' said Simon. 'I've been abroad a lot.'

'Are you married?'

'Divorced.'

'Really?' He looked almost pleasantly surprised. 'No one in LA stays married for long, but I thought that over here . . .'

'The wave of the Californian future has even reached our shores,' said Simon caustically, glancing at the naked throat of his former friend.

Charlie Hope laughed nervously. 'Marry late,' he said. 'That's my advice.'

'And do you intend to take it?' asked Simon with a trace of malice in his voice.

Charlie returned a bland, almost innocent smile. 'Yes. I'm getting married in November.'

Simon winced in anticipation of some reverent description of a gay betrothal, but to his astonishment Charlie said: 'She's divorced too.'

'What's her name?'

'Carmen.'

'Any children?'

'No, thank God. I wouldn't want someone else's kids.'

'And you're actually getting married?' asked Simon incredulously. 'Is it back in fashion in California?'

Charlie blushed. 'Not really, no, but it makes it simpler for her to come over here, and for me to go over there. You know, visas and that sort of thing.'

The effete old man who had brought Charlie Hope into the Club looked sourly at Simon, as if to say this conversation had gone on long enough; so the two school friends exchanged telephone numbers, although on Simon's part this was only a formality. He had no intention of looking Hope up, nor did he imagine that his pin-striped suit would appeal to Hope's laid-back life-style, but just before he moved away, Charlie dropped the transatlantic twang which he must have picked up in Los Angeles and said in just the tone he would have used at school: 'I say, Milson, do you remember Ludley?'

'Willy? Yes. Why?'

'I'm going to see him.'

'Where?'

'In the South of France.'

'What's he doing there?'

'Drinking. That's why I'm going out. I got a kind of SOS.'

'From him?'

'No. From Priscilla.'

'Is that his wife?'

'Yes. I assume so. Unless it's a case of Kenya.'

'How do you mean?'

'Didn't they used to say: "Are you married, or do you live in Kenya?" '

'Did they?' Simon did not understand what Charlie was talking about, but the host was restless and so was Simon's stomach so he simply said: 'Well, give him my regards.'

'You should go and see him. I think he's short on friends.'

'Yes, well, I will if I'm down that way.' Simon smiled and moved towards the door. The others stayed in the bar while he went through to the dining-room; but as he left his table after lunch he saw Charlie Hope tête-à-tête with the old bugger over strawberries and cream, and noticed that he had been made to put on a tie.

Two

Simon Milson had not only known William Ludley at school, he had loved and admired him with the fervour a boy of thirteen can feel for another boy four years older. When Simon had been in the fourth form, Ludley had been top of the school – Head Boy, Captain of Cricket and star of the Scholarship Sixth. Nor had Simon worshipped him from a distance, because it was part of Ludley's charm for the younger boys that he descended among them, told them to call him Willy, and shared with them the lofty thoughts that were passing through his mind.

It was Willy, for example, who had convinced Simon that there was no God. 'How can anyone with a knowledge of the comparative history of religions retain an exclusive belief in the tenets of any particular sect?' Since Willy had read the Bible and the Koran, Simon and his friends accepted this verdict on the High Anglicanism they were taught at school. Willy then went on to read Nietzsche and taught his young disciples a contempt for the Christian religion. They went to chapel with a sneer on their lips, thought that Willy was Nietzsche's superman, and envied Charlie Hope, who had long eyelashes and pretty lips, and was the one Willy chose to take on walks in the woods.

Willy had already left when Simon followed him to Cambridge, but there too he had left a legend – not on the cricket field or in the classroom but in the high jinks fashionable at the end of the 1950s. The undergraduates still talked of Ludley's parties, Ludley's claret, Ludley's girls. He was said to have come up with his own hunter and groom; to have lost three hundred pounds in one evening playing poker at Kings; to have seduced the daughter of a College chaplain; and to have kept quarter-bottles of Krug in his bathroom to rinse out his mouth after brushing his teeth – meanwhile calling himself a Marxist and affecting the views of the extreme Left.

Despite this chaotic debauchery, Willy Ludley had won First Class Honours in history. He did just as well in the Civil Service Examinations, applied to join the Foreign Office and was accepted at once. He spent a year in London and was then posted to Djakarta. It was in this period that Simon lost track of what he was doing, and after a year or so he never bothered to enquire. All at once the spirit at Cambridge had changed. Simon and his friends had started to read Marcuse and Frantz Fanon, and were embarrassed by the well-thumbed copies of *Brideshead Revisited* still standing on their shelves. Instead of discussing debutante dances in London they argued about the likely effects of the Selective Employment Tax and the American involvement in Vietnam. William Ludley was still remembered, but from long ago, as if he had been there in the 1920s, not the 1950s. When Simon came down from Cambridge and went into the Foreign Office, he was hardly aware that he was doing what Willy had done. He did not ask where he was and heard quite by chance that he had gone to Djakarta, then resigned from the service and now lived in Argentina.

Meeting Charlie Hope in the Travellers' Club, and hearing that Willy Ludley had returned to Europe and was now living in the South of France did not make Simon want to see either of them again. He threw Charlie's telephone number into the waste-paper basket as soon as he had finished the packet of small cigars upon which he had written it down; but around two months later, at the beginning of September, he received a letter with a French stamp and the post-mark of the Alpes Maritimes.

The engraved address at the top of the paper was The Villa Golitsyn, Boulevard de Cambrai, 06200 Nice; and the letter beneath, written in a firm, girlish hand, read as follows:

Dear Mr Milson,

Charlie Hope, who is at present our guest here in Nice, mentioned that you might like to come and stay with us for a week or two later this month. We would of course be only too pleased if you could come. Will has often spoken of you. He has fond memories of you from your school days together, and I should like to make your acquaintance.

With best wishes,

Priscilla Ludley

This curiously old-fashioned letter was followed on the same day by a telegram from Nice. PLEASE COME STOP NEED HELP STOP CHARLIE. Simon's first inclination was to ignore them both. He felt irritated by both the invitation and the plea from people who were stretching the meaning of the word if they still thought of him as a friend. At best he might write a letter to say that he had no more

18

leave. But as he sat eating a home-made bacon sandwich in front of *Hawaii Five-O*, the idea of a week or two in the South of France began to have its attractions. First, the only holiday he had taken that year was a week on the Norfolk Broads with his two children. It had been a fiasco. They had been bored, polite and embarrassed at his incompetence on the boat. His son was only interested in football, and seemed disappointed that Simon knew nothing about it. His daughter kept telling her brother that he would 'have to ask Steve' – Steve being the geologist who now lived with their mother. Simon knew that they both longed to go back to Dorset, where all their cousins on Sarah's side of the family were staying in their grand-parents' country house. He could see them counting the days and the hours they still had to live through before escaping from the holiday chalet.

Simon had four weeks of leave still due to him, and even if he took one of these at Christmas he would have to think of something to do with the other three. He would happily have gone without them if it would not have looked odd to his colleagues in the African depart-ment. They knew that he was divorced but not as yet that most of his friends had used it as a pretext to desert him. It was not that Simon was sorry for himself, but he did not want to be pitied – either by his colleagues at the Foreign Office or by his sister and brother-in-law who had asked him to stay at their cottage in Devon. Most of all he dreaded the solicitude of his mother, who lived alone in Kent.

It had occurred to him to take his leave and remain in London incognito, or try and rise from the sexual torpor which had followed his divorce and take some girl to Paris or Amsterdam, but he knew he never would – that he had lost the spirit for that sort of thing and would only stay in his flat eating bacon sandwiches or fish-fingers for lunch as well as supper.

All this in itself was not enough to make him decide to accept the invitation to stay with the Ludleys. What finally tipped the balance in favour of going was the effect he thought it might have on Sarah, his former wife, when it got back to her through the London tittle-tattle that he was staying with rich friends on the Côte d'Azur. The Ludleys' was a famous name and his wife was a snob: the divorce had numbed most of Simon's feelings but his *amour propre* had survived.

He therefore made up his mind to go. He wrote to Priscilla Ludley accepting her invitation and told his colleagues at the office where he was going. Thinking that it would be pleasant to travel in old-fashioned style, he booked a First Class berth on the Riviera-Flanders express for the night of 27 September and then sent a telegram to Charlie to say when he would arrive.

Three

On his last day at work before leaving for France Simon was asked by the Undersecretary to call on Fowler, the head of security. 'I don't know what he wants,' his superior said, 'but I said you would look in before you went away.'

Simon went up in the middle of the morning and was received in a friendly but slightly embarrassed manner by an upright, older man. He was offered a seat which he accepted and coffee which he refused.

'I gather that you're going on leave,' said Fowler, sitting down in his own chair behind his desk.

'Yes,' said Simon.

'And you're going to stay with the Ludleys in France.'

'Yes.'

Simon's voice must have expressed some of the surprise he felt that Fowler should know where he was taking his holiday, because Fowler made an apologetic gesture and said: 'I happened to hear . . .'

'I knew him at school,' said Simon.

'Of course.'

'And now he's living in the South of France.'

'I know.' Fowler paused. 'Have you seen much of him since your school days?'

'No.'

Fowler stood up and turned his back on Simon to look out of the window. Although ten or fifteen years older, he seemed embarrassed and confused by what he wanted to say. He turned to face Simon again, put his hands on the back of his chair, leaned forward and said: 'Do you know what E.M. Forster said – that one's first loyalty is to one's friends?'

'No. Did he say that?'

'He's supposed to have done. Would you agree with it?'

Suspecting now that this was some covert interview for a taxing post, Simon wondered what answer would produce the best impression. Then he thought of his friends, and the way they had betrayed him by entertaining his wife and her lover, and he replied: 'No. I think other loyalties come before one's friends.'

'Family?'

'Yes.'

'Of course Forster wasn't married.'

'And oneself,' said Simon. He waited deliberately for the apparent egoism of this remark to take effect, and then qualified it by adding: 'Not oneself in a selfish sense, but in the sense of one's integrity, one's professionalism.'

'Good,' said Fowler. 'I agree.' He sat down, rubbed his face in the palm of his hands, and then said: 'I only asked about that – about Forster's axiom – because I'd like you, if you can, to find out something about Ludley.'

'To find out what?'

'Well, I'll tell you, but I didn't want you to think that I was asking you to betray a friend although in a sense I suppose I am.'

'He's not a close friend,' said Simon.

'I know, but still . . .' Fowler looked more discomfited than the younger man. 'I'll tell you the whole story, or as much of it as I can. You can always turn me down.' He looked at his watch. 'Ludley joined us from Cambridge . . . You were there, too, weren't you?'

'Yes.'

'But you didn't read history?'

'No. Law.'

'My own subject. Much more sound. Deals with things as they are. But Ludley, you see, read history – and people who speculate about the past get funny ideas about the future.'

Simon said nothing but waited while Fowler seemed to muse upon the dangers inherent in the study of history, moving his lips as if sucking a moustache he no longer had.

'I can't tell you everything,' he suddenly said to Simon, 'but briefly we think that Ludley, sometime in 1965, gave a classified document to the Communists in Djakarta.'

Fowler paused as if Simon might protest at this point, but again Simon said nothing.

'As a result of this treason – a direct result – a friend of his from Cambridge, an officer in the Gurkhas, was ambushed in Borneo, taken alive, tortured, mutilated, and then killed.'

Simon raised his eyebrows; he almost smiled. 'How dreadful,' he said.

'His men were killed too,' said Fowler, 'all as a result of treachery by someone in the Embassy in Djakarta.'

'Ludley?'

'Do you think it's possible?'

Simon hesitated. 'I don't really know. I'd rather lost touch with him by then, but certainly, in the old days, Willy was capable of anything.'

'How do you mean?'

'He didn't care what other people thought of him.'

'Uninhibited?'

'More than that. He had a great contempt for what he called middle-class conventions.'

'But one wouldn't turn traitor *pour épater les bourgeois*,' Fowler said in an exasperated tone of voice; and then, in a calmer tone, he corrected himself. 'Perhaps one would. And the times – one must never forget the spirit of the times at the vulnerable age.'

'I lived through the same times, more or less,' said Simon.

'Ah yes, but you're the sound type. Not susceptible, I wouldn't have thought, to . . . ideological temptations.'

'No.'

'Whereas Ludley – he might have been?'

'Yes.'

'1965,' said Fowler. 'The Americans bombed North Vietnam in February. The marines landed in South Vietnam in March. We were backing the Malays against the Indonesians. There were British troops in Borneo. It could have seemed, then, that a decisive struggle was starting for the whole of Asia.'

'Yes.'

'Ludley, if he had been a fellow-traveller, might have thought that he could help the other side . . .'

Simon shifted in his chair. 'When I knew him,' he said, 'he wasn't particularly interested in politics, but that could have changed.'

'He was a Marxist at Cambridge.'

'I know.'

'Of course that might have been just to irritate his father. Did you know James Ludley?'

'No. Willy never introduced us to his family.'

'Nastiest man I've ever met,' said Fowler. 'The mother was a cold woman, too. She died before her husband – driven to it, more or less, by him. All of that, if you play at psychology, would explain treason in the son. A desire to take revenge on the father.'

'He never spoke of him at school,' said Simon.

Fowler looked at his watch. 'I must come to the point,' he said. 'The facts are these. A Classified, Most Secret, document – a map, in fact – was found in the hands of the Indonesian Communists back in the autumn of 1965 and was handed on to us the following year. It explained how they had been able to ambush poor Churton and his Gurkhas. It had come from a 'comrade L' in the British Embassy. Two men – Ludley and another fellow I shall call X – had stayed with Churton a week before he left for Sarawak.

'Soon after the map was discovered, Ludley did a bunk, and because of that it was always assumed that Ludley was the culprit. For various reasons, which you can probably guess at, it was decided not to pursue the matter. Ludley had resigned of his own accord and since then has always lived abroad. The problem which faces us now is that this fellow X is up for a top job – a job which demands the very highest trust – and in the back of our minds there is this nagging little thought that perhaps it wasn't Ludley after all, and that if it wasn't him, then it was X.'

'I see.'

'X is one of our best people, and until now this nagging little worry hasn't mattered because he hasn't held quite such a sensitive position.'

'There's nothing else against him?'

'No. Nothing at all. So the time has come either to give him a job which is his due, or tell him that he'll never go any further.'

'I can see your predicament,' said Simon. 'You need to be certain it was Ludley.'

'Yes. To be one hundred per cent sure of X, we've got to know that it was Ludley. There's no question of arrest, prosecution or anything like that. The scandal would do too much damage.'

'Yes.'

'But we do need to know.'

'Of course,' said Simon, 'and if I can help in any way . . .'

'I hesitate to ask you to spy on a friend,' said Fowler, 'but if, while you are staying with him, you could bear in mind that little business in Djakarta, and decided to your own satisfaction that it *was* Ludley . . .'

'Of course.'

'Your judgement would be a great help to us.'

'I'll do what I can.'

'You don't mind?'

'Not at all.'

Fowler stood up. 'There's no great urgency . . .'

'Shall I telephone from Nice?'

'No. I don't like the telephone. Report when you get back.' He led Simon to the door. 'You're absolutely sure you don't mind?'

'No. I don't mind at all.'

Simon returned to his office in a mood of boyish excitement. He had barely come across the security services before and now felt that mixture of exhilaration and self-importance which affects a man who is given a secret mission by his government. The idea that his former friend and future host might be a traitor did not upset him: little that anyone could do could shake the sardonic detachment with which he kept all feelings at bay. Nor did he feel any reflex disgust at the thought of treason itself. Simon's conservative mannerisms and opinions were only the accoutrements of an actor playing a role. He might carry an umbrella, wear a pin-striped suit and lunch at his club, but he did not feel the strong patriotic emotions which one might expect in a man of such habits and appearance. He had been born and brought up in England, but the suggestion that because of this accident of nature he should think Britain better than France or the United States would have seemed to him a vulgar prejudice. In some ways Britain might be better, but in others it was demonstrably worse; and the loyalty he felt to the British government was no more and no less than the loyalty he would extend to any other employer – the European Commission, the United Nations, a Swiss bank or an American corporation.

Nor – despite the deference he had shown towards him in his office – was Simon overawed by Fowler's position as head of security. As soon as he could he went to the reference library to find out who had been with Ludley in Djakarta. He then compared the two or three names with those of diplomats now of a certain seniority who were due for a new posting. He quickly realized that X must be Leslie Baldwin – a man he knew of but had never met.

Four

It was raining when the boat train left London for Dover. Simon was alone in his First Class compartment and sat contentedly by the window, looking out at the dank Kent countryside. Nothing in life pleased him more than a well-executed plan, and now he was enjoying the fruits of a series of correct decisions. He had been right to escape from the English autumn to an Indian summer in Nice. He had been right to stay with the Ludleys where he could expect a high standard of comfort – even luxury. The only anxiety he had felt was over the human aspect of his stay. He could hardly look forward to the pansy company of Charlie Hope; Willy himself was by all accounts an alcoholic; and his wife was almost certainly a sharp-nosed, opinionated county bitch who had only asked him to stay to make a fourth at bridge. Thanks to Fowler, however, he would have his own game to play, which would certainly see him through the two or three weeks he meant to stay in the South of France.

He ate lunch on the boat, and afterwards went up on deck. The rain had stopped: there was only a little wind from the sea. He lit a cigar and walked to the front of the boat to look at the approaching coast of France. There were not many other passengers – fewer than one might expect in late September – and he remarked on only one, an English schoolgirl who clung to her felt hat as she looked out to sea. He noticed her only because of her uniform – a brown tweed skirt, brown stockings, leather shoes and the felt hat with brown ribbon. It seemed old-fashioned on a girl of sixteen or seventeen, and that pleased Simon because the plastic fitments of the ferry had somewhat sabotaged his pretence that he was a 1930s swell going out to stay with Beaverbrook, or that other more celebrated Willy, Maugham. It also struck him as odd that an English schoolgirl should be returning to school in France.

At the Gare Maritime in Calais he found the compartment reserved for him in the Wagon-Lit coach of the Riviera–Flanders Express and settled down for the journey. At eight, as the train trundled across the dull countryside of northern France, he made his way along the corridor towards the dining car, passing the English schoolgirl sitting bolt upright in a second-class compartment. There was a hockey stick strapped to the suitcase on the rack over her head.

At dinner Simon read a guidebook to the South of France, noting on a postcard what he should try to see around Nice. The food was good: he drank a whole bottle of Burgundy, and swayed from side to side as he walked back down the corridor to his compartment. The berth had been made up in his absence and he went straight to bed. He awoke twice during the night: once as the train was shunted around Paris from the Gare du Nord to the Gare de Lyon; and for a second time to use the ingenious chamber pot which, once filled, closed to return to its native Burgundian soil what remained of the wine he had drunk at dinner.

He awoke finally at Marseilles. He raised the blind and saw people on the platform. He pulled it down again and changed out of his pyjamas into navy-blue slacks and a light-blue linen shirt. The train left the Gare St Charles and started its run along the Mediterranean coast towards Nice. He raised the blind again. A watery, yellow sun had risen to illuminate the hills around Bandol. He left his compartment and made his way along the corridor towards the dining-car. It had gone. In its place there was a buffet – a few tables and chairs, and a counter at which a bleary-faced steward handed out little pots of coffee and brioches. As he walked along the carriage to fetch his breakfast, Simon noticed the English schoolgirl, still dressed in her brown tweed uniform, sitting at one of the tables; and when he came back holding his tray, a seat at her table was one of the few that were free. He therefore sat down opposite her, saying, in English, that he hoped she did not mind.

She shook her head as if to say that she did not, and then looked out of the window. He stirred sugar into his coffee and opened his guidebook, but instead of reading it he studied the girl. She had long, untidy brown hair, ragged at the shoulders, and a fringe which all but covered her eyes. It was plain that like Simon she came from the north of Europe, because the skin of her hands and her neck was exceptionally white. Only her cheeks had some colour. When she turned from the window to drink her coffee he could see that she had a small nose. The eyes glanced at him from under the fringe. She put down her cup. 'Excuse me,' she said, 'but are you English?'

'Yes,' said Simon.

'Can you tell me,' she asked, 'where Monte Carlo is?'

'It's further along the coast,' he said.

26

'Is it before Nice, or after?'

'After Nice. Just before the Italian border.'

She bit her lower lip.

'Are you going to Monte Carlo?' he asked.

'I think so, yes, but my ticket is only to Nice.'

'Are you on your way back to school?'

'Yes, I am. Or rather I was.'

'In Monte Carlo?'

'No. In Kent.'

He smiled. 'You seem to have missed your station.'

She looked at him suspiciously from under her fringe. Two tears waited at the corners of her eyes and she blurted out. 'No, well, I sort of couldn't face it. You know . . .'

'You've run away?'

'No, well, yes, sort of . . .'

'What are you going to do?'

'My uncle Godfrey lives in Monte Carlo. At least he did. I think he still does. I thought I might go and see him.'

'Is he expecting you?'

'No.' One of the tears left the eye and set off down her cheek. 'I haven't actually seen him since, well, since I was a baby.'

Simon laughed and ran his tongue over his teeth to dislodge a fragment of brioche. 'He'll probably send you straight home.'

'I know.' The other tear now pursued its companion.

'Why did you run away?' Simon asked, touched by this overgrown child trying hard not to cry.

She shrugged her shoulders. 'You know . . .'

'I can imagine.'

'School was so *stupid*.' She spat out that word as if rage might stave off the tears. 'I mean hockey, and this uniform, and bossy monitors, and *never* being allowed out.'

'How old are you.'

She hesitated. 'Seventeen – at least I soon will be.'

'It does seem old-fashioned to make you wear a uniform at seventeen.'

'It's ridiculous. And the teaching is bad. The only point of schools is to get you into university, and no one from our school ever does.'

'Why did your parents send you there?'

'They're snobs,' she said, snorting through her nose. 'They think I'll make the right kind of friends . . .'

'What are the right kind of friends?'

'Rich people with country houses.'

'Are your parents like that?'

'No. They're dead middle-class. Daddy's an accountant but he'd like me to marry a duke.'

'And you'd turn him down?'

'Who?'

'The duke.'

She blushed. 'I don't want to get married at all.' She tossed back her fringe and blinked.

'Why not?'

She shrugged. 'Boring.'

'So what would you like to be?'

'I don't know . . . An actress, perhaps, or an engineer.'

They chatted on about her life as the train turned inland again, leaving the Massif des Maures between them and the sea. Simon found the girl, who said her name was Helen Constable, both comic and attractive – not sexually attractive but amusing and charming in a gangling way. She was determined to appear grown-up and self-possessed yet those two tears lurked in her eyes. At the beginning of his breakfast Simon had thought that she might help him pass the last hours of a long train journey; by the end he felt he should help her. Certainly he thought that we should all reap what we sow, and if this girl had run away from school she should face the consequences; but now that he had two children of his own, a sense of responsibility for children in general led him to warn her of the white-slave traffickers who might be waiting for her in Nice. He offered her his help which she accepted with an ingenuous gratitude, returning with him to sit in his compartment for the last stretch of the journey.

Five

The railway station in Nice is set back from the sea at the rear of the city. When the train stopped on the platform, Simon climbed down and then turned to take Helen Constable's battered leather suitcase, which he then carried for her towards the exit. She followed awkwardly, as if she had only just learned how to use her long legs, and she wrinkled her nose at the smell in the air of ripe fruit and French cigarettes.

Charlie Hope was waiting for Simon in the main concourse of the station. He was dressed in jeans, sneakers and an orange T-shirt. 'I'm glad you could come,' he said, glancing nervously at Simon and taking the two suitcases from out of his hands.

'I'm not sure I shall be of much help,' said Simon.

'You'll be more help than I am.'

Simon would have asked him what he meant if the schoolgirl had not been standing there beside him to be introduced and explained. 'This is Helen Constable,' he said to Charlie. 'We met on the train. I said we might help her get hold of her uncle in Monte Carlo.'

Charlie smiled at her. 'Yes, of course. We could try and call him from here, if you like, but it would be easier back at the villa.'

Helen looked at Simon.

'Wouldn't the Ludleys mind?' Simon asked Charlie.

Charlie laughed. 'They don't mind anything.'

He led them out of the station towards a white Jaguar six or seven years old, with French registration plates and a left-hand drive. He put the luggage in the boot and they climbed into the car – Simon next to Charlie and Helen in the back. 'We'll go by the Prom,' said Charlie. 'It takes slightly longer but it will give you a feel of the town.'

'What's the matter with Willy?' Simon asked quietly as they set off.

'He's drinking too much. In fact, I'd say he's drinking himself to death.'

'Can't his wife stop him?'

'It seems not,' said Charlie; and before Simon could ask him anything more, he half-turned to Helen and asked: 'Have you been here before?'

'No.'

'Well this is the Place Masséna. Note the pastel-coloured stucco. Like Turin. Nice was part of Italy, you see – Piedmont as it then was – until 1860. And these gardens are built over a river – the Paillon. In Herzen's time we'd have been driving down a river bed.'

'Who is Herzen?' Helen asked.

'A friend of Willy's,' said Charlie.

29

'He must be quite old,' said Helen, looking out of the car at the palms and shrubs of the public park.

'He was a Russian,' said Simon. 'He died some time ago.'

They turned into the Promenade des Anglais and drove west. To the left was the sea and pebble beach on which a thin sprinkling of half-naked men and women lay supine in the sun. To the right the grand hotels – Rhul, Westminster, West End and Negresco – stood behind their sentinel palm trees.

'Can't you stop him?' Simon asked Charlie.

'Drinking? No.' He laughed – a nervous laugh.

Simon turned to look at Charlie's face. It was bland: he was looking at the red light at which he had stopped, waiting for it to change to green, with his usual fixed, ingratiating smile.

'The trouble is,' Charlie added, 'that I've started drinking too. He makes you feel awfully mean if you don't join in.'

The lights changed and they turned off the Promenade des Anglais and drove inland again – under the railway line which had carried the train into Nice, and then up a steep, winding road lined with suburban villas. At the top they drove into a cul-de-sac, through two tall green gates, down fifty yards of gravel to stop at the front door of the Villa Golitsyn.

The house was not what Simon had expected. Half-hidden by cypress trees, it was tall and square with yellow stucco walls and purple shutters. The roof was of red tile, and beneath the exaggerated eaves there was a painted frieze of interwoven blue irises.

They got out of the car and Charlie fetched the suitcases from the boot. 'There's a garden around the corner,' he said, 'but no swimming pool I'm afraid. A funny sort of house to have taken, but then that's Willy . . .'

He opened the heavy, studded front door and led them into a dark hall. The floor was of black marble and the walls were covered with a green and gold paper. Because so little light came in through the shaded windows, Simon felt as if he was standing at the bottom of a pond. He followed Charlie through two double doors into a long room which seemed to cover most of the ground floor of the house. Despite the large windows and the sunny, cloudless sky this room too seemed dark because the walls were a dark red – the colour of roast beef – and the ceiling was formed by panels of stained wood. The furniture too was dark – an oak dining table at one end, and a spinach-coloured sofa at the other. Over the fireplace there was a large gilt mirror and on the walls some grim portraits of what appeared to be Muscovite grandees – and equally sombre pictures of their wives, who for all the tricks and talents of the nineteenth century painters peered squat and plain from their gold frames.

Charlie crossed the room towards the open French windows which led out onto a terrace. 'Willy?' he shouted. He disappeared into the garden. The two others waited. Simon went to a tall, glass-fronted book-case made of the same dark oak as the dining table at the far end of the room. It contained an incongruous mixture of books – uniform editions of the classics, including the memoirs of 'Willy's Friend', Alexander Herzen, mixed up with paperback thrillers and the red Michelin Guides. Next to the book-case there was a heavy roll-topped desk with brass handles, on which stood two photographs in silver frames. One was of Willy as Simon remembered him – it must have been taken in his first year at Cambridge – and the other matching photograph was of a girl a year or two younger. Simon assumed that it was of his wife.

Besides the photographs and the books there was nothing in the room to give him an idea of what Willy might have become. It had the impersonal feel of an embassy drawing-room; the only signs that it was someone's home were two postcards propped against the wall over the mantel; some newspapers and magazines on the sofa; half a dozen different bottles on the sideboard; and an unemptied ashtray on the parquet floor.

Charlie came back through the French windows. Behind him, blank against the light, there was the figure of a woman.

'Hello,' she said as she came into the room. 'I'm Priscilla Ludley. I'm so glad you could come. Will has told me so much about you.'

They shook hands. She wore baggy shorts and a man's shirt – the tails tied together over her stomach. 'You'll have to call me Priss,' she said. 'I'm afraid everyone does, although I'm not a prissy person, am I, Charlie?' She turned to smile at Charlie and saw Helen, who stood beside him. 'Who's this?' she asked, turning back to Simon with a look of amused curiosity. 'Have you brought your daughter?'

Simon introduced Helen and explained her predicament.

'I'm awfully sorry to be a nuisance,' said the schoolgirl, shaking her hair over her face as if to hide behind it.

'Don't be silly,' said Priss in a kind but clipped tone of voice. 'I'm very glad you're here. We rather depend upon people passing through for company.' She smiled – a smile which was almost

31

artificial but made with good intentions. She led Helen to the spinach-green sofa, and as the two women sat down to discuss the uncle in Monte Carlo, Simon studied her appearance.

He had not at first thought she was pretty: her figure was too slight and her features too subtle to make an immediate impression; but as he watched her now, her tall body leaning towards the younger girl, her fair hair hanging straight down from her cocked head, he saw that she was exceptionally beautiful.

She seemed to be around the same age as he was – thirty-three or thirty-four – yet the skin of her stomach and legs was as smooth as that of a younger girl. Because she was tall, had blonde hair, blue eyes and a creamy brown complexion, she reminded him momentarily of the wife of a West German diplomat in Jedda, but despite her height, her appearance was not Teutonic. Her limbs were delicate and her voice, as she spoke to Helen, was unmistakably English – soft and quick with an old-fashioned tightness of the mouth which made her sound like an actress in a pre-war film.

Every now and then she would look at Simon and address a remark to him with the offhand friendliness of someone who had known him for a long time. This familiarity unsettled him. Since the suffering of his divorce, he had protected his bruised heart with a reflex reluctance to be attracted to women, but now he felt involuntarily drawn towards Priscilla Ludley – not just by her attractive face and figure, but by the much more powerful pull of her eyes, her smile, her mannerisms and the sound of her voice. He searched frantically for a flaw, but all he could find to criticize was a trace of hard curiosity in her expression, as if she was sizing them all up for reasons of her own. Towards Helen, for example, she showed more than polite solicitude: she kept looking down at the woollen jersey and tweed skirt which covered her adolescent body and eventually said: 'You must be awfully hot, dressed like that.'

'I am, rather,' said the schoolgirl, blushing behind the screen of her hair.

'Why not come up and change into some cooler clothes?' Priss got up from the sofa and started towards the hall. 'You aren't in a hurry to ring your uncle, are you? You'll stay to lunch?'

'Yes, I mean, I'd love to, if it's not too much trouble.'

Priss turned towards Simon. 'Come up, will you? I'll show you your room.'

They climbed the curling stone staircase. 'It's a ridiculous house,' said Priss. 'It's big but there are hardly any bedrooms.' They reached the landing. 'It was the winter home of an old Russian prince – one of the Golitsyns – and nothing much has been changed since the Revolution. Poor Charlie has to sleep in a serf's attic while we have this grand suite.' She pointed through an open door into a vast bedroom, dark because the shutters had been closed against the sun. In the gloom Simon could make out a large, four-poster bed with heavy red hangings and faded gold tassels.

'There's one other room up here, which is where I've put you, Simon,' said Priss. She opened a door at the end of the landing, crossed to the window and pushed open the shutters. Daylight shone into another large bedroom with two narrow single beds and a vast painted wardrobe. 'Rather *style Russe,* isn't it?' she said, turning to Simon with another of her deliberate smiles.

'It's delightful,' he said.

She turned to Helen. 'Come and change,' she said. 'You can borrow the Prince's dressing-room. It's connected to our room but it's quite private.'

They left Simon to unpack. He felt sticky after the journey so he took a shower and changed into jeans and a short-sleeved shirt. He then went and stood for a while at his window. It looked out from the side of the house over the lush gardens of the neighbouring houses. At this level the Villa Golitsyn was overlooked by several blocks of flats, some of them quite close, and Simon wondered why the Ludleys should have taken a house in the middle of the town rather than something more secluded in the hills behind Nice.

He left his room and went down through the gloomy hall and vast living-room into the garden. There he sat down on one of the wicker chairs he found placed around a parasol. It was hot, and he faced the sun to try and brown the pasty complexion he had seen reflected in the bathroom mirror. He could hear the sound of cars and motor-cycles driving up the hill; and every now and then there was the roar of an aeroplane taking off over the bay, or a clap of thunder as a train crossed the steel bridge below. But though open to these sounds of the city, the garden itself was hidden from the view of the other houses or blocks of flats which surrounded it by the cypress trees planted close together along its perimeter; and by a large, untended olive which cast its shade onto the south side of the house.

The garden itself was gravelled in the French manner with little close-clipped box hedges surrounding rectangular rose beds. At the centre there was a shell-shaped fountain, dry now and covered with flaking moss. Behind it, to one side, was an orange tree; to the other, a lemon tree; and right at the back of the garden a tall palm, its leaves rustling in the slight breeze.

Priss Ludley came out with a bottle of wine and some glasses on a tray.

'It's very nice here,' said Simon.

'Well, it's not *calme calme,* as the French would say, and it's very unfashionable to live in the middle of Nice, but it's more or less what we wanted.'

'Where do the fashionable people live?'

'Oh, in Cannes or outside Grasse, or around St Paul de Vence: but out there you have to drive everywhere, whereas from here you can walk to the shops, the bars, the sea, the doctor – all that sort of thing. There are some steps which go down from the garden to the Boulevard.'

She spoke rapidly, nervously, automatically, as if she had frequently had to justify where they had chosen to live. 'It's a nice *quartier* too,' she went on. 'There aren't any American novelists or Dutch pansies or retired British bankers. Our neighbours are all either academics from the university, which is just up the road, or French *bons bourgeois,* with the occasional fossilized expatriate from the days when Nice was fashionable.'

'So why do you live here?' Simon asked.

She frowned. 'Well as I said, it's convenient. Will doesn't like driving.'

'No – I meant to ask, why don't you live in England?'

'Oh, I see.' She sighed. 'Lots of different reasons, really. It's simplest to say tax, because that's something everyone understands. Will came into some money – quite a lot, really. If we had stayed in England we would have had to pay ninety-eight per cent income tax.'

'As a socialist Willy should approve of that.'

She blushed. 'Yes, well, there are other reasons. The climate and . . .'

She would have gone on, but Charlie now came out of the house and sat down between Priss and Simon on one of the wicker chairs. 'I like what you've done to Helen,' he said to Priss while pouring himself a glass of wine.

Priss smiled – almost a furtive smile. 'It was all she had. None of my things would fit her.'

34

'What is she wearing?' Simon asked.

'Wait and see,' said Charlie, 'but I warn you that you won't recognize your little friend. Priss has transformed her into a twenties flapper. "Anyone for tennis?" That sort of thing.' Charlie mimicked what he had just described. Then his expression changed to one of mild anxiety. 'Where's Willy?' he asked. 'Shouldn't he be here to greet his guests?'

Priss bit her lower lip. 'He went down for some supplies.'

'Shall I go and meet him? He could probably do with a hand.' He put down his glass.

'Yes,' said Priss. 'Tell him that Simon's here.'

Charlie started towards the gate in the corner of the garden.

'If he's not in the café at the corner,' Priss shouted after him, 'try the one further along with the pinball machine.'

He disappeared down the steps just as Helen came out of the house. She was certainly transformed. Instead of a tweed skirt and blouse she was dressed in a short, sleeveless navy-blue tunic: her hair had been brushed back from her face and was held behind her ears by a hoop. She looked at Simon with a funny smile – like a child who had just raided the dressing-up drawer.

'Come and sit down,' said Priss, pouring Helen a glass of wine. 'Don't you think she looks nice?' she said to Simon.

'It's my gym slip,' said Helen, sitting down in the shade of a parasol, but stretching out her legs to catch the sun.

'It looks fine,' said Simon.

'It'll certainly do until the shops open after lunch,' said Priss.

'It's much cooler,' said Helen.

'We'll go into town this afternoon and get you some jeans.'

'I don't want to be a nuisance.'

'You're not.'

'We ought to try and get hold of her uncle,' Simon said to Priss.

'I tried the number,' said Helen. 'There was no reply.'

'He may be away,' said Priss.

'I really am awfully sorry . . .' Helen began.

'Nonsense,' said Priss. 'You can always stay here for a day or two.' She turned to Simon. 'Don't you agree? There's no point in her leaving with nowhere to go?'

'None at all,' said Simon, 'if you really have room for her.'

'She can sleep in the dressing-room,' said Priss.

Simon turned to Helen. 'Perhaps you ought to let your parents know that you're all right.'

'I don't see why she should,' said Priss sharply. 'Let the old fools sweat it out for a bit.'

Simon frowned. Helen's eyes widened with approval. 'If they know where I am,' she said, 'they'll make me come back.'

'Then it's settled,' said Priss. 'We need an extra girl. So as far as I'm concerned, Helen can stay as long as she likes.'

Simon said nothing more. He felt irritated by this sisterly conspiracy between the schoolgirl and his hostess. He realized that Helen was not his charge, but felt responsible for her all the same. It seemed only humane to inform the parents that their child was alive, and he was astonished that Priss, who was herself approaching middle age, should speak of people she had never met like a vengeful adolescent. He wondered for a moment if she had Lesbian tastes; and if that was so, whether Helen would have been better left to fend for herself. She might then have fallen into the hands of a Corsican pimp. Here at least he could keep her under his protection.

There was a second cause of Simon's irritation. He was hungry. Breakfast with Helen on the train seemed a long time ago, and he was wondering when they would get lunch when there was the sound of wire scraping on the gravel, which immediately brought an anxious look onto Priss's face. She stopped in the middle of what she was saying to Helen and turned towards the wicket gate at the corner of the garden.

At the top of the steps, panting for breath, there stood a tall, thin man carrying two bulging plastic bags. His linen suit hung loosely on his body. His face was oval and long like the effigy on the tomb of a crusading knight, and the skin of his cheeks and chin had the same texture as the dried lichen on the stone fountain in the middle of the garden. His wispy, receding hair was brushed back from his face, and at first it seemed to Simon that he was too old to be Willy Ludley, but as he approached, with Charlie a few paces behind, he realized that this was indeed the hero of his youth.

'Hello Simon,' Willy said in his old drawling voice.

'Hello Willy,' Simon replied – feeling a great wave of affection come over him in the presence of his old friend.

'Will,' said Priss. 'This is Helen. She's on her way to Monte Carlo.'

Willy turned away from Simon, and his puffy lids blinked over his bloodshot eyes. Helen drew her pretty legs into the shade and stared at her host from under the parasol.

'This is Will,' said Priss to Helen.

Helen smiled at him but Willy did not smile back. Instead he stared at her, put down the two supermarket bags bulging with bottles, and then stared at her again. 'What a perfect specimen,' he then said in a much louder, richer voice – a sound like the lower tones of a cello.

Simon smiled, because he knew at once that they were about to see one of 'Ludley's performances'.

'She's not a specimen,' said Priss irritably. 'Simon met her on the train and . . .'

'And saw at once,' Willy interrupted, 'a perfect specimen of the *puella scolastica Anglicana*.'

'Do shut up,' said Priss. She turned to Helen. 'Don't pay any attention. He's just trying to embarrass you.'

Willy reached for the bottle of wine and filled a glass. 'Am I embarrassing you?' he asked Helen.

'No, I mean . . .'

'I certainly don't mean to embarrass you.' He sat down. 'On the contrary, I meant to compliment you on your youth, your freshness and above all your uniform . . .' He leaned forward and felt the hem of her tunic. Helen did not move.

'Do stop treating her like a moth,' said Priss.

'For an old *roué* like me,' said Willy, 'nothing is as elegant and attractive as the school uniform . . .'

Helen wrinkled her nose. 'I think it's horrid, really.'

'Please believe,' said Willy, 'that your present costume is more alluring than anything a couturier could devise.' He stood to fill his glass which was already empty. 'Perhaps,' he added – and as he stooped over the bottle he looked at Priss – 'perhaps it brings back the early moments of some first love . . .'

Priss stared back into his eyes with a strange expression which Simon intercepted but could not understand.

Six

Lunch was served on the terrace in front of the house by a swarthy Moroccan woman. As they ate Simon told Willy what he had done since they last met. Willy questioned him closely on certain subjects such as the management of the Saudis' trade surplus and the attitude of the Foreign Office to the status of Jerusalem, as if still interested in international affairs. He appeared to be well informed, but when Simon asked him what he had done over the past twelve years he replied, curtly: 'Nothing.'

Simon was taken aback – not so much by the reply itself as by the sharpness with which it had been delivered – and Willy, as if regretting this impoliteness, added in a softer tone: 'I've tried a dozen things, Simon, but none of them came to much. I had a go at ranching in Argentina but . . .' He sighed and raised his hands as if the gesture would explain what went wrong.

'And here?'

'Here I thought I'd *write*.' He pronounced the word with ironic emphasis. 'People write, don't they, when they've nothing else to do?'

'And what have you written?'

'Nothing. The climate's no good for thought. Soggy. The humidity penetrates the skull. The brain becomes a sponge.'

'In most other respects it's not a bad place to be,' said Priss from the other end of the table. 'People leave you alone, as long as you've got money, and you don't feel particularly out of place because most of the people here are foreigners.'

'It's a pleasant nowhere,' said Willy. 'People come here to retire – to sit in the sun and wait to die.'

'But don't you swim and water-ski and do things like that?' asked Helen incredulously.

'No,' said Willy flatly.

'You should take some exercise,' said Charlie to his host. 'It would do you good.'

'*Je suis anglais,*' said Willy in mock-Churchillian French. '*Alors je me promène sur la Promenade des Anglais.*'

'We do try and enjoy ourselves,' said Priss to Helen with a slightly

38

forced gaiety, 'and I hope you will too.'

After lunch they went back to the wicker chairs in the garden for coffee, and then slipped off to their different rooms for a siesta. Simon took a volume of Herzen's memoirs from the living-room to read as he lay on his bed – in Herzen, he thought, there might be a clue to Willy's ideological proclivities – but before he had got very far he fell asleep.

He did not dream, but awoke an hour later in the kind of confusion that often follows a dream. He did not know where he was. His head felt heavy, his mouth sticky and the dark room seemed to shake like a train.

He got out of bed and went into the bathroom to splash his face with cold water. He looked at his watch; it was four in the afternoon. He longed for strong tea, and left his room to see if he might ask for some downstairs but as he came onto the landing Priss saw him from the hall and said: 'Could you wake your little friend? I'm going to take her into town to buy some clothes.'

'Where is she sleeping?' Simon asked.

'In the dressing-room – the door next to yours.'

He went back along the landing and knocked at the door to the Prince's dressing-room. There was no answer. He opened it quietly and went in. The room like his own was dark: the yellow sunlight of the autumn afternoon was blocked by the purple shutters. He crossed to the bed. Enough light came in through the slats of the shutters for him to see Helen's body, dressed only in her underclothes, sprawled asleep on the bed. She wore large, navy-blue bloomers.

Thinking that she might be embarrassed to wake and find him there, he turned to go back and knock more loudly on the outside of the door when suddenly he realized that the figure of a man stood behind him, leaning against the wall beside the wardrobe, silently watching the sleeping girl.

'Who's there?' Simon asked.

The man did not move.

Simon crossed to the window, pushed open the shutters and turned to see Willy still standing by the wall watching the sleeping girl. She stirred, stretched, and Willy's brow suddenly creased as if he had been struck by some painful, inner anxiety. Without looking at Simon, or acknowledging his presence in the room, he turned and left through a second door which led into the main bedroom.

Helen was now awake. She pulled a sheet over her body. 'What time is it?' she asked.

'About four. Priss wants to take you shopping.'

'OK, I'll be down in a minute.'

Simon left her to get dressed. He went into the garden where Charlie sat drinking tea. There was no sign of Willy.

'They've trained that Moroccan woman well,' said Charlie. 'She even makes cucumber sandwiches.'

Simon sat down and filled a cup with tea from the silver pot marked with a crest and coat-of-arms – presumably those of the Ludley family. 'Fill me in about Willy,' he said to Charlie.

Charlie avoided his eyes. 'How do you find him?'

Simon shrugged his shoulders. 'He's obviously not very well, physically. But in other ways he seems just the same.'

'He is, isn't he? The same old Willy. That's why it's so important to pull him round.'

'Has Priss no influence over him?'

He laughed. 'Too much and too little.'

'How do you mean?'

'Aren't wives sometimes part of the problem?'

Simon blushed – imagining that this was a reference to his own ruptured marriage. 'Yes,' he said, 'I dare say they are.'

'It's not that they don't get on,' said Charlie, his anxious eyes now looking at Simon from his weak, amiable face. 'In fact they seem much closer than most married couples. But there's something odd, and that's why I was so keen for you to come. You know more about this sort of thing than I do. I mean, frankly, although there's a lot in Willy that's the same, I don't feel that I'm the same. I mean I feel that I've moved on since school whereas he's moved back. They live out here as if it was an Indian hill station under the Raj, and that's a long way from LA.'

'But still you came to stay.'

He shrugged his shoulders: he seemed almost in tears. 'Sure, yes, though God knows what Carmen is going to make of it.'

'Who is Carmen?'

'My girlfriend. You know, the one I'm going to marry.'

'Of course. Is she coming here?'

'Yes. Any day now. She'll think it's all crazy.'

Simon leaned forward in his chair. 'Then while we're alone,' he said, lowering his voice, 'let's just sum up what the problem is and what we should try to do.'

'Go ahead.'

'Willy gets drunk. He's really an alcoholic, isn't he?'

'More or less.'

'He'll die if he doesn't stop drinking?'

'Yes.'

'So we want to stop him?'

'Right.'

'But how? Has he ever been to a clinic?'

'Yes. Priss once got him to go to a place in Switzerland. He stuck it out for a week and then shinnied down a drainpipe. The fact is, Simon, that he's unhappy when he's sober. I've seen it in his face. Life's only tolerable when he's drunk.'

'But why?'

'I don't know. If we knew why, we might solve the problem.'

'You say that the marriage seems happy?'

Charlie shrugged his shoulders. 'Yes. So far as I can judge, very happy.'

'But no children?'

'No.'

'Why not?'

'I don't know. I think Priss can't have them.'

Simon paused. 'Does he really do nothing out here?'

'He says he's writing a play about Herzen. But it's just an excuse for buffoonery – one of Ludley's performances. You know.'

'Yes.' Simon nodded. 'But why Herzen?'

Charlie shrugged his shoulders. 'He's always loved Herzen, and Herzen lived here in Nice. He's buried up by the castle.'

'Both rich. Both exiles,' Simon said. He looked up at Charlie. 'But why is Willy an exile? Have you any idea why he has never been back to England?'

'No.'

'Do any of his friends come out here to see him?'

'No. I don't think he has any friends . . . besides us.'

'Family?'

'None.'

'But what about Priss? Who was she before she married?'

'I don't know.'

'She must have some family – a mother or a sister . . .'

'To tell the truth, Simon, I sometimes suspect that they're not married.'

'What makes you think that?'

'I don't really know. I think we'd have heard if there had been a wedding.'

'Not if it was abroad.'

'Perhaps not.'

'Anyway, it doesn't really matter if they're legally married or not. They've been living together for twelve years, haven't they?'

'Yes,' said Charlie. 'And as far as I can make out, they still love each other very much.'

Priss and Helen returned at seven. Like an insect that had shed its skin to become a coloured butterfly, the schoolgirl was now an elegant young woman. Her hair had been washed, cut and was shaped like a soldier's helmet – framing her face with its firm lines, and removing the overall impression of nits and split ends. She no longer wore her gym slip, but crisp, bleached jeans, a bright check blouse and espadrilles. She came into the garden carrying a pile of parcels, dumped them on the table and smiled embarrassedly at Simon, saying: 'Priss has been most awfully kind. She's bought me masses and masses of things.'

Simon and Charlie had both stood as she approached, taking her to be someone they had not met before, and now both sat down again – incredulous that such a further metamorphosis could have taken place in so short a time. The schoolgirl who had looked as if she had chewing-gum stuck behind her ear was now a model out of a fashion magazine; and it gratified Simon that despite this new sophistication, her embarrassment seemed to acknowledge that he might approve or disapprove; that as the man who had found her on the train and had brought her to the Villa Golitsyn, he had some slight authority over her.

'You must let me pay,' he said to Priss who came out into the garden after her.

'Nonsense,' she said sharply. 'Money is the one thing we have plenty of.'

'Even so . . .'

'And I hate talking about it. It's too middle-class.' She looked irritated and sat down.

Simon said nothing.

'Do I look different?' Helen asked him.

'Quite different,' he said.

'Good.' She too sat down. 'Then the police won't recognize me.'

'We thought,' said Priss, 'that once Helen was reported missing, Interpol might send out photographs . . .'

Simon frowned, and was about to say again that in his opinion Helen should somehow communicate with her parents that she was alive, but was afraid that this too might be thought 'middle-class' by his hostess; and there was something about Priss which made him reluctant to cross her or say anything that might lower him in her estimation. In that sense she reminded him of Willy at school. It was not that no one had dared disagree with him, but no one had wanted to. They had used to guess what his opinions might be on a particular subject, and then present them as their own.

Priss now went into the house to make supper. Charlie explained that the Moroccan woman, Aisha, left the villa after clearing up the lunch and did not return until the next morning. Simon therefore went to offer to help in the kitchen, but Priss refused his services so he decided instead to go for a walk in the evening light. Helen went with him – eager to disport herself in her new clothes. They went through the gate in the corner of the garden, and down the stone steps to the street. In five minutes they had reached the Promenade des Anglais.

A steady succession of cars went back and forth in both directions. They waited, crossed at the traffic lights, and then walked beside the sea towards the centre of the town. On the other side of the road there were blocks of balconied flats, and villas of different styles from different epochs – simple, early nineteenth-century houses together with odd, crenellated, turreted houses matching the fragmented fantasy of later generations. To their right, on the far side of the Baie des Anges, they could see Cap Ferrat – vague behind the haze of the early evening. Closer and clearer were the great hotels, the Opera House, the Italianate roofs of the old town and the hill where the castle had once stood – all coloured gold by the setting sun.

With them on the wide pavement next to the sea other people walked to and fro with less purpose than the mechanical traffic – first the Niçois themselves – small, sharp-faced women with tanned, ageless faces, and their short, thick-set, strutting husbands, men with bulls' necks and self-important miens. And then the foreigners – the dowdy British; the lanky, kindly Dutch; the vigorous Germans; and the pale, green-faced Belgian pensioners, sent to Nice for their health

43

after a life of labour, only to breathe in a cocktail of carbon monoxide and damp sea air.

Helen was quite unconscious of the fumes from the traffic and noticed only the beauty of the mountains, the city and the sea. 'It's lovely, isn't it?' she said.

'It lives up to its reputation,' said Simon.

'And to think that now . . .' – she glanced at her watch – 'I'd be eating toad-in-the-hole with eighty-five other girls.'

'You like it better here?'

'*Much* better.'

Simon's face took on a look of slight perplexity. 'I know it sounds fussy,' he said to Helen, 'but I wish, if only for my peace of mind, that you would telephone your parents.'

'They'd send me back,' said Helen.

'We can dial direct. They won't know where you are.'

'Priss doesn't think I should.'

'I know, but she doesn't understand. She hasn't got any children of her own.'

'Have you?'

'Yes. A son and a daughter.'

'I didn't know you were married.'

'I'm divorced from my wife.'

'Are your children with her?'

'My son's at boarding-school, and I know how much I would suffer if he disappeared on the way back at the start of term.'

'All right,' said Helen reluctantly, 'but I'd like to do it from a public telephone. I don't want Priss to think I'm wet.'

Simon smiled. 'You like her, don't you?'

'Who wouldn't?' She looked down at her new clothes. 'He's a bit odd, though, don't you think?'

'Willy? Yes.'

'Have you known him for long?'

'Yes, or rather I knew him a long time ago. I haven't seen him for more than twenty years.'

'And what about Charlie?'

'We were all at school together, but I hadn't seen him either until I ran into him in London about a month ago.'

'He seems very nice,' said Helen, 'but not like Priss.' She sighed. 'And I like Willy too, but I hardly dare open my mouth when he's there.'

'You'll get used to him.'

'Priss said he gets drunk.'

'I think he does.'

'Well, Daddy gets drunk.'

'Perhaps not as drunk as Willy.'

'But he's a special sort of person anyway, isn't he?'

'How do you mean?'

'I think Willy and Priss are the sort of people Daddy calls *hors catégorie*.' She pronounced the word *hors* as 'horse' and *catégorie* as if it was the English word with a 'y' on the end.

'I'm still not quite sure that I know what you mean,' said Simon. –

'Well, Mummy and Daddy are really very conventional. He's an accountant. We live near Ascot. He plays golf and I've got a pony. All that. You know.'

'Yes.'

'And they're terrible snobs. Daddy rates people like hotels – with stars. One to five. He thinks he's a five-star person, of course . . .'

'Of course.'

'But once we drove past the gates of a country house and he told us how the man who had lived there – someone rich and grand and with a title – had lost so much money gambling that he had had to sell the whole estate, which had been in the family for hundreds of years. He told the story in a kind of reverent voice, like our classics mistress describing the sexy goings-on of Greek gods and heroes. Reverent and embarrassed at the same time. So I asked him – Daddy – how many stars he'd give this man who had lost all his money, and Dad just said that people like that were *hors catégorie*.'

'*Hors catégorie*,' Simon repeated in a better French accent.

'Is that how you pronounce it?'

'More or less.'

'And it means, doesn't it, that you're outside the normal way of judging things?'

'Yes.'

'Well, that's just how I feel about Priss and Willy. I'm sure they're *hors catégorie* and it's such a squash on Mummy and Daddy because they'd love to have *hors catégorie* friends but they haven't and now I have, haven't I?' She beamed at Simon triumphantly.

'Yes,' he said. 'Some *hors catégorie* and one, I hope, with a star or two.'

'Oh, you're *five*-star,' she said – intending it as a compliment.

They walked along the front as far as the Negresco and then turned into the town and found a public callbox from which they could telephone England. Simon fed all the change he had in his pockets into the machine and then dialled the appropriate numbers to reach Helen's parents on the Winkfield Row exchange. Helen listened and said: 'It's ringing.' A hard look came onto her innocent features. When Simon heard her say: 'Hello? Mummy?' he left the booth and waited next to it on the street.

A minute or two later she came out and they set off in silence back towards the Promenade.

'Did she seem upset?' Simon asked.

'No. Just cross.'

'Did she want you to go back?'

'Yes. She went on about how Daddy had paid the fees and what a waste of money it was if I didn't go.'

'You didn't tell her where you were?'

'No, but she threatened . . .'

'What?'

'She said that if I didn't come back she'd sell Pixie.'

'Who's Pixie.'

'My pony.'

The thought of the pony seemed to make Helen a little melancholy. Simon asked her if she had any brothers and sisters.

'A younger brother,' she said. 'He's still at prep school.'

'What's he like.'

'Spoilt.'

'Will you miss him?'

'No.'

It was beginning to get dark when they reached the steps up to the garden of the Villa Golitsyn. 'You won't tell Priss, will you?' Helen whispered to Simon as they approached the house.

'What?'

'That I rang home.'

'No.'

'Promise?'

'I promise.'

Seven

They were halfway across the garden when they heard the voices of two men in dispute coming from the house. They were shouting at one another in English, but with a heavy foreign accent. Simon and Helen both hesitated on the terrace and listened.

'Ve vere friends, Alexander. Ve are friends. How can you let zis ozzer lov come between ze lov we have for each other?'

'And is it a sign of your so-called love,' shouted another, deeper and less Teutonic voice, 'that you steal my wife and destroy my home?'

'Steal? Like property? Ha!'

'You ingratiate yourself into my family, pretending that you share my ideals . . .'

'Me? Ingratiate myself? Pretend?' screamed the higher-pitched voice. 'Am I not ze man who led an army into battle vile you stayed comfortably in your *Bürgerliche* drawing-room?'

'You are certainly the man who led an army into running away.'

'That . . . that is too much!'

This incomprehensible conversation was carried out in a loud, declamatory style: and Simon felt for a moment that the ghosts of nineteenth-century German émigrés were haunting the Villa Golitsyn; but as they came through the French windows into the drawing-room it was to find Willy and Charlie standing in the centre, five yards apart, each with a piece of paper in one hand and a glass of wine in the other. Both ignored their entry; indeed Willy began to recite an incomprehensible soliloquy in a harsh, toneless voice.

Simon and Helen stood looking somewhat confused until Priss came in from the hall. 'Don't pay any attention,' she said to them. 'They're just playing the fool.'

Willy's wail became a shriek of indignation. 'What?' he shouted, lurching towards Priss. 'Is that the way to encourage an artist? To call his rehearsals "playing the fool"?'

Priss dodged him and disappeared through the green baize door which led to the kitchen: Willy therefore attached himself to Helen instead, hooking his arm around her neck in a rough embrace. 'Can *you* understand?' he asked her, slurring his words. 'The delicate,

47

creative being *shattered* . . .' – he let go of her neck and staggered into the middle of the room again – 'shattered into a thousand pieces by a cruel word of feminine incomprehension.'

'That's *my* line,' said Charlie with theatrical indignation. 'That's a Herwegh line.' He raised his arms, crossed the room and threw himself into Willy's arms with melodramatic sobs. 'Vimmen don't understand uns, Alexander. Zey don't understand ze burden ve bear. Zey despise uns because no one needs poems but everyone needs zupper.'

At which moment Priss threw open the green baize door and marched into the room carrying knives in one hand and forks in the other. 'We're having ravioli al pesto,' she said, 'so I hope everyone likes it. Charlie, dear, if you can still tell the oil from the vinegar, will you please make some salad dressing. Will, you get the glasses. Helen, put on that red dress, would you? I hate jeans at dinner. Simon, would you mind helping set the table? Aisha doesn't function in the evenings.'

They all fell obediently to their tasks and twenty minutes later sat eating ravioli al pesto by candle-light. Priss, wearing a long skirt and a silk blouse, sat at one end of the table, Willy, in another loose-fitting linen suit, at the other. Charlie and Simon sat on either side of Priss, and Helen sat between Simon and Willy. They ate for a while in silence. Willy speared each ravioli with his fork as if it was a small fish and lifted it slowly to his mouth. He sat bolt upright, his gaze straight ahead. Every few minutes his right hand darted out to the bottle of wine: he topped up every glass – whether it was empty or not – and then filled his own to the brim.

Conversation soon started at Priss's end of the table. Charlie asked her where she had bought the ravioli and the two started to chat about shopping like any châtelaine with her *jeune fille de la maison*. At the other end Helen – tentatively and timidly – asked Willy whether what they had been acting before supper was part of his play. He did not answer. His fork went down for a ravioli, then rose again to carry the plump piece of pasta into his languid mouth.

'Answer, Will,' Priss said in mid-sentence.

He turned to Helen with a charming inclination of his head. 'I beg your pardon? Did you ask me a question?'

She blushed. 'Yes. I wondered, well, with that acting, whether you were writing a play?'

'I am, yes. A melodrama.'

'What is it about?'

'Herzen. Alexander Herzen. It is a work of piety, you see. We live in Nice because Herzen lived here – here in this very parish of Sainte Hélène – your patron saint, incidentally, and the mother of the Emperor Constantine. She went to Jerusalem to find the relics of Christ. I came to Nice to find relics of Herzen, the patron saint of sceptics.'

'I don't know anything about him,' said Helen.

'He was a rich, radical Russian,' said Willy, 'who fled from the despotism of the Tsar, took part – in a small way – in the triumphs and fiascos of 1848; then ran from Paris to Nice, which was then part of Italy . . .'

'Yes,' said Helen. 'Piedmont.'

Willy raised his eyebrows in theatrical surprise. 'Yes. Piedmont.'

'And what happened here?'

'Disloyalty. Betrayal. Death. He had married his cousin Natalie. Most romantic. She was like a sister to him. Their marriage was forbidden. They eloped together from Moscow to Siberia, where he was living in exile. An early, rare example of marriage based upon true love. Years of happiness. Children. Then France and, we may assume, a certain disillusionment – not only political but of the domestic sort.'

At the other end of the table the other three had stopped talking and were listening to Willy.

'Enter Herwegh,' he went on. 'German poet, romantic, revolutionary. In 1848 he had led an army of German exiles against Baden-Württemberg. Ignominious defeat. He runs first and farthest. Returns to Paris. Everyone despises him; avoids him. Herzen takes pity. When he moves to Nice, Herwegh and his wife Emma move with him. They take the top floor of the Herzens' house here in Sainte Hélène. Herzen travels, and while he is away Herwegh and Natalie . . .' Willy sat silently at the head of the table shaking his head.

'They had an affair,' said Priss.

Willy winced, then repeated: 'They had an affair. Yes. How banal it sounds. Anyway, Herzen returned. Sensed what was going on. Confronted his wife. She confessed. He was distraught; drunk; he rent his hair. He offered to leave her with Herwegh, to go to America, but she begged him to stay. *He* was the one she really loved. Herwegh must go, but Herwegh did not want to go. He wheedles and whines.

49

Natalie and Herzen are adamant. He must go. He leaves for Genoa. The husband and wife – the cousins, the siblings – are reunited. Their love has survived betrayal. Another child is born, but the ordeal has taken its toll. Natalie falls ill. The drama has damaged her delicate, nervous, nineteenth-century constitution. She hovers around death, seems to be recovering . . . when again, another disaster. Her second son and his tutor and Herzen's mother are returning to Nice from Marseilles by boat. There is a storm off the Iles d'Hyères. The boat sinks. Their bodies are never found. Natalie staggers from this second blow. Is this not the punishment of the God in whom she does not believe for the adultery Georges Sand had condoned? There is influenza in Nice. Natalie falls ill again. Herzen kneels devoted at her side. In vain. She falters . . . falters . . . and dies. He looks out over her grave at the Baie des Anges, wishing that he too could have drowned with his mother and son.'

After the ravioli there was salad, cheese and fruit. Willy ate none of these, but as it seemed reasonable to do so moved on from the wine to marc de Provence. Simon poured a glass for himself: it burned his lips and throat.

While Priss and Helen cleared the table, the men sat on the sofa and armchairs. Charlie started to tell the other two men what had happened to some of their old school friends but neither seemed interested. When Priss and Helen came back from the kitchen Simon played Scrabble with the two of them while Charlie and Willy played backgammon with the bottle of marc beside them. Every now and then Priss glanced anxiously over Simon's shoulder at the backgammon boys as if waiting. There was the occasional word of slurred dispute, then came a crash. Priss rose: Simon turned. Willy had fallen forward, unconscious, over the backgammon board. The glass-topped table had shattered under his weight. The marc would have spilt on the carpet if there had been any left in the bottle.

Charlie tried to lift Willy off the floor but he was himself so drunk that he only made things worse. He slumped, sobbing, over Willy's body: Simon had to pull him off and sit him on the sofa. Then, with Priss's help, he took hold of Willy and dragged him on to the sofa next to Charlie. One or two slivers of glass hung from his shirt but none seemed to have cut his skin. They picked them off while he breathed, gutturally, his head to one side, his mouth open.

Priss turned to Simon with an expression of some embarrassment.

'Can you help me take him up?' she asked.

'Of course.'

'Can I help?' asked Helen.

'Bring his shoes if they drop off,' said Priss.

Simon took hold of Willy's inert body under the shoulders and pulled Willy to his feet. He and Priss each hooked an arm around their necks and dragged him out into the hall and up the stairs, staggering under his weight.

'Now you see,' Priss said breathlessly as they paused halfway up the stairs, 'why I wanted you to come and stay.'

They laid him on Priss and Willy's bed – the huge four-poster with red hangings – and Simon then helped Priss to take off Willy's shirt and trousers. He lay like a corpse in a morgue – a long, bony, unexercised body.

'Damn,' said Priss, 'he's cut himself.'

There was a smear of blood beneath his ribs. She went to the bathroom and came back with cotton wool, iodine and sticking-plaster.

'Does he often pass out?' Simon asked as she wiped away the blood.

'He either passes out or goes berserk,' she said. 'It's better on the whole when he passes out.'

She spoke in a matter-of-fact tone of voice. There was no sign of self-pity or self-dramatization.

'What do you do when there's no one there to help you?'

'Leave him on the floor. Cover him with a blanket.'

'I gather that he tried a clinic.'

'Yes.'

'It didn't work?'

'No.' She pulled the bedclothes over Willy's body. 'It's very complicated,' she said. 'He knows what he's doing. He knows that he's killing himself. He just doesn't seem to want to live.'

'You would think,' said Simon, 'that he had much more to live for than most people.'

She turned from Willy and looked at Simon. 'I hope you can help him,' she said. 'Charlie means well, but he's not strong enough to help Will.'

'I'll do what I can,' said Simon, 'but I don't see how I can help if you've failed.'

She looked straight into his eyes – a cool, almost severe look, like that of a serious child. 'You're a man. He likes men. I don't think he really likes women.'

'Perhaps you should have a child,' said Simon.

She looked away. 'We can't have children.'

'That's a pity.'

'I know, I know. It would make all the difference. But he knew. We both did.'

'You don't think that if you went back to England . . .'

She shook her head. 'We can't do that either.'

'It might be worth paying income tax if it stopped Willy drinking.'

'There are other reasons. We just can't.' She looked at Simon again – a sad yet languorous look which seemed to say that there were things she could not tell him, yet appealed to him at the same time, in a more poignant fashion than her clipped words, to help not just Willy but her too.

'I'll do what I can while I'm here,' said Simon. 'I was very fond of Willy at school.'

Eight

Aisha, the Ludleys' Moroccan servant, had already washed the dishes from the night before, and had swept up the glass from the smashed table, when Simon came down the next morning. There was breakfast waiting on the table – coffee, hot milk, fresh bread and croissants. Only one of the cups had already been used.

Shortly after Simon came Willy. He marched into the room erect as a soldier on parade. His hair was brushed back: he was neatly dressed. He went straight to the sideboard, poured himself a glass of brandy, drank it down and then came to the table. 'For the vitamins,' he said to Simon with a wink. 'You can't get decent orange juice in France.'

A copy of *Nice-Matin* lay by his place. He glanced at the headlines, then turned it over and read the comic strip on the back.

'Has anything happened in the world?' Simon asked him.

Willy threw him the newspaper. 'I don't follow the news these days. Do you? I suppose you have to. Part of the job.'

'I like to know what's happening.'

'Politics are dull. Politicians are duller still. Think of Danton or Charles James Fox. Even Benes or Clemenceau. Nowadays they're all vulgar, uncultured, dreary . . .'

'Why is that, do you think?'

'Democracy. People like to see their own qualities reflected in their leaders. Oiks want to be ruled by oiks.'

'Yobs,' said Simon.

'Is that what you call them now?' Willy raised his eyebrows, as if asking after a new fashion. 'Didn't we used to call them oiks? Or is my memory going too?'

'You used to call them the proletariat,' said Simon. 'You said they were the wave of the future.'

Willy laughed. 'And haven't I been proved right?'

'Not quite in the way you envisaged.'

'What did I envisage?'

'A revolution.'

'And haven't we had one? Vulgarity has triumphed. Even here on the Côte d'Azur where the working classes are swept out of sight behind the railway line, like dirt under a carpet, vulgarity has triumphed. The grand hotels aren't grand any more: they're just expensive. No more grand dukes, just actors and Arabs.'

'Would you rather see the Negresco reserved for Communist Party leaders?'

He shrugged his shoulders. 'I don't care who goes to the Negresco.'

'You used to care.'

'Yes, I did, didn't I? I was quite a pinko.' He smiled at the memory. 'In those days it seemed quite clear that if you didn't throw a crust to the poor every now and then, they would come and snatch the whole loaf.'

'And socialism was throwing a crust?'

'That's what I always assumed.'

'And Communism?'

'That's when they come and snatch it.'

'You never went that far?'

'How could I, when I had the loaf already?'

53

In the middle of the morning they all drove across Nice to the Old Town, parked the car on the Promenade, and walked through to the market.

'Will there be any *cêpes*?' asked Priss.

'Too early,' said Willy.

'They appeared about this time last year,' said Priss, sauntering ahead of the others between the stalls of flowers, herbs and vegetables. 'I don't think I could ever live in England again,' she said, turning to Simon, who was immediately behind her, 'because there's so little to choose from when you go shopping. Here there is such a mass of delicious things . . .'

'And yet you don't seem to have grown fat,' said Simon.

'Really greedy people don't get fat,' she said, waiting until he had drawn up beside her. 'They eat small amounts of lots of different things.' Her lips were thin like her fingers: she smiled, but there was no trace of sensuality on her face. 'I always used to think,' she went on, 'that if the English ate better food, they'd be less gloomy. But they're always trying to save time, like the Americans. Instant this. Frozen that. Save time for what? To make money. Money for what? They don't know. Will would say it was the Protestant ethic . . .'

'What would I say?' asked Willy who was walking behind them.

'That Puritanism killed the Anglo-Saxon cuisine.'

'Indubitably,' he said like an actor speaking his one line in a play. He looked at Simon. 'You should come here on a Sunday morning when everyone in England is lying bored in bed reading the Sunday newspapers or sanctimoniously going to church. The market is busier than it is today. Cheerful, greedy people. They think up their sauces while they're at mass, and buy the leg of lamb on their way home. That's the real reason why we live here. It's neither Puritan nor Catholic. They manage without all the oppressive mumbojumbo that you get in Spain or South America, yet they firmly believe in the Forgiveness of Sins. The *bon père de famille* who sleeps with his secretary on her day off, or picks up a tart on the Avenue de la Californie on his way back from work, still sits at the head of the table at Sunday lunch with all the authority of a patriarch. In a Protestant country, you're either one of the Elect or one of the Damned: either way you've got every reason to be gloomy. Here they're all promiscuous, lying gluttons yet they still expect to go to Heaven.'

They came out of the covered market and stood in a group in front of the Prefecture.

'Listen,' said Priss to Willy. 'Why don't you take Simon up to the castle while we do the shopping?'

Willy sighed. 'It's a terrible climb.'

'Go on. It'll do you good. We'll meet you here in an hour's time.'

Willy and Simon set off through the narrow streets of the Old Town and then climbed the steps which led up the hill. It was warm. Simon removed his jacket. Willy, though taller than his friend, and with longer legs, lagged behind. Simon turned every now and then to wait for him. Willy's face was flushed but open and happy; and behind him there was an ever widening view of Nice and the Baie des Anges. They came to a small park laid out on what had once been the ramparts. From here they looked down upon the port – the pretty colonnades, the restaurants on the quai, and the large white ferry-boat waiting to set sail to Corsica.

'There's *Clöe*,' said Willy, pointing down at the port.

'Who's Clöe?' asked Simon.

'Our boat. She's blue. Small. Next to that cruiser.'

It was impossible to tell which of the many boats was his. 'I didn't know you could sail,' said Simon.

'We used to do a lot,' said Willy. 'We had a much bigger boat – a yacht – but it meant hiring a crew and being swindled so we sold it and bought *Clöe*.'

'Can you manage her on your own?'

'Oh yes, if I'm sober. Priss is a good sailor, too.'

They continued their climb. 'There's a place at the top where you can get a drink,' said Willy solicitously, as if his guest had complained of thirst, 'unless it's already closed for the season. We'll see.'

The café, when they reached it, was deserted. 'It's a little early,' said Willy, looking at his watch. 'Perhaps they'll open later on.' Breathing heavily he climbed the steps which led on up to the highest point of the citadel – a belvedere built above a cascade. They stood there, facing west, with the water gushing out beneath their feet. In the distance Simon could make out the Cap d'Antibes and the Esterel Hills: then, closer at hand, the airport and the part of Nice where the Ludleys had their villa. Closer still he could make out the tree-lined boulevards of the nineteenth-century section of the city which was divided from the older town by the covered River Paillon. The Old Town itself was directly beneath them – the dome of the Cathedral, the campanile of the town hall, and the terracotta tiles of the many roofs all making it seem more like a miniature Florence than a city in France.

'I've grown very fond of Nice,' said Willy with a tone of affection in his voice. 'Neither too big nor too small, with enough people to give it life, and the sea and the mountains like two lungs. It's modest, too. The state is inconspicuous – the Prefecture and the Palais de Justice tucked away between the market and the Cathedral. That's why Herzen liked it. He hated Paris, just because of its monuments to oppressive regimes – the Louvre, Versailles, Les Invalides. Here the largest buildings are those old hotels . . .' He pointed to two or three imposing buildings perched above Nice. 'That was the Imperial in the Russian quarter where the grand dukes used to stay. It's a lycée now. And that one in Cimiez was the Regina. Flats now, I think. Queen Victoria stayed there with John Brown.' He spoke quite casually as if Queen Victoria and John Brown were friends they had in common. 'We'll go up to Cimiez,' he said, 'and take a look – the Regina Hotel and the Roman arena – the ruins of two empires side by side.'

'Melancholy,' said Simon.

'What?'

'The ruins of Empire – of ours, at any rate.'

'I don't agree,' said Willy. 'It was a dreadful institution – the systematic exploitation of weaker people dressed up with sanctimonious cant about the spread of religion and civilization.'

'You're glad it came to an end?'

'Yes. I'm glad it's gone, and all our self-important posturing has gone with it.'

They turned to go down.

'Why,' asked Simon, pointing to a plaque in the corner of the cobbled belvedere, 'is this called after Nietzsche?'

'The French have a passion for giving a name to every little cul-de-sac and alleyway.'

'But why Nietzsche?'

'He must have come up here. He thought of *Zarathustra* while walking up to Eze from the sea.' Willy started down the steps towards the café.

'I would never have associated Nietzsche with the South of France,' said Simon.

'No one does. They only think of Somerset Maugham and Scott

56

Fitzgerald. But other writers came here before they did. Before Nietzsche too. Smollett started the whole thing off in the eighteenth century. I can't think why. It hasn't inspired me to write a thing.'

The café was still closed. Willy pressed his nose against the glass of the door like a child at the window of a toy shop. A middle-aged woman was sweeping the floor. When Willy rapped on the door she looked up and shook her head. He lifted his hand and elbow to mime a man taking a drink. She shook her head again. He knocked again. She shrugged her shoulders and let them in. They sat at a table and a few minutes later Willy was served with a glass of cognac and Simon with a cup of coffee.

'Some people are like camels,' said Willy with a sigh, 'but I seem to have been born without a hump. I need continuous replenishment.' He emptied his glass and called for another one. The woman brought over the bottle to fill it: there was no expression on her face, as if the exigencies of an alcoholic were part of her everyday life.

'Do you read Nietzsche now?' Simon asked Willy.

'I never read. It gives me a headache.'

'You used to read him.'

'Did I?'

'He had quite an influence on your life.'

Willy drank from his glass and sniffed.

'And ours,' said Simon.

'How was that?' He seemed a little bored.

'Well, you convinced us all that God was dead.'

'*Madame*,' Willy shouted. '*Encore un cognac, s'il vous plaît.*'

'That Christian virtues were human vices . . .'

'*S'il vous plaît, madame . . .*'

'That it was cowardly and contemptible to live on the moral capital of Christianity if you didn't believe in its tenets.'

The woman came to their table. She glanced at Simon with no expression in her eyes. She filled Willy's glass.

'You said that Nietzsche's superman was beyond good and evil; that he makes his own morality.'

Willy sipped his brandy sparingly, as if he had decided that this was the last glass. 'You're quite right,' he said. 'But how can you remember that from so many years ago?'

'It made a strong impression.'

'They were vivid years, weren't they? I thought everything was possible.'

'And permissible?'

'Yes. Possible and permissible.'

'And have you changed since then?'

He did not answer but turned to Simon and asked: 'And you?'

'Not really.'

'Is everything possible now?'

'If you set your mind to it.'

'And permissible?'

Simon hesitated. 'No, I suppose not. I think it's wrong to hurt others.'

'But that's all?'

'Yes.'

'Were you hurt?'

'When?'

'Didn't your wife leave you?'

'Yes. Yes, I was hurt.'

'I'm sorry.'

Simon shrugged his shoulders. 'It's over now.'

'It isn't easy to get on with women,' said Willy with a sympathetic smile.

'You never know what they want.'

'They often don't know themselves.'

'If you're nice to them, you're weak; and if you assert yourself, you're a bully.'

'At least you have a son,' said Willy. 'I envy you that.'

'I'd rather have a wife,' said Simon.

'One always wants what one hasn't got.'

'You've been lucky with Priss.'

'Yes.' He sighed. 'She puts up with a lot.'

'She's different from the general run of women, isn't she?'

Willy did not answer his question. 'Before Priss,' he said, 'in my last year at Cambridge, and later in London, I was very much in love with another girl. We were engaged – privately, not publicly – until someone told me that she was sleeping with another man. She apparently wanted to marry me for my money but found I was no good in bed.'

'What did you do?'

'I asked her if it was true. She denied it. She swore on the Bible, on her mother's grave, on everything, that it was a lie. Then I pretended that I'd been sleeping with other girls – that I wanted an open, modern marriage – so she admitted that she'd been sleeping with this other fellow since Cambridge, not because she loved him – she still insisted that she loved me – but because she needed him . . . needed him physically, you understand.'

Willy had turned a little pale. He shook his head. 'I tell you, Simon, it was enough to put me off love and sex and the whole damn thing.'

'Until Priss came along.'

'I knew where I was with Priss.'

They stood and went to the bar where Willy paid the bill. 'I'm very glad you came out here, Simon,' he said. 'I've often thought about you and wished you were here.'

'It was you who left us, Willy.'

'I know. And it was a mistake. I greatly underestimated the importance of friendship.'

'You could have made some friends out here.'

'No Frenchman has the qualities I missed in you.'

'What were they?'

'Your common sense. Your practical idea of right and wrong.'

'But that's just what Nietzsche despised – people living according to a conventional, Christian morality without believing in Christ.'

'But you never felt you had to live up to Nietzsche.'

'How do you mean?'

'You never felt you had to confound conventional morality.'

Simon smiled with his lips turned down. 'No. I left that to my wife.'

'That's almost conventional, nowadays,' said Willy, 'to run off with someone else.'

'Conventional, but hardly Christian.'

'No.'

'Have you?'

'What?'

'Done anything to confound conventional morality?'

'Oh yes, in my time.' He looked away. 'I'll tell you about it one day, but not now. We're late as it is and Priss hates waiting.' After saying this he strode ahead, staggering down the hill, his long legs stiff like stilts.

Nine

Willy was shouting drunk at lunch – ad-libbing lines from his *Herzen* in a preposterous German accent, knocking over the gravy-boat, and clasping 'Natalie's' (Helen's) knees under the table as she ate her pudding. Helen was embarrassed. Priss looked cross. Once or twice she glanced irritably at Simon, as if he was to blame for the cognac in the café; and since he was reluctant to be in her bad books, Simon tried to make up for his failure as a chaperone by trying to amuse her with his conversation. She did not pay much attention to what he said. Charlie joined in the conversation but he too seemed nervous of Priss and did not want to seem too friendly to Simon if Simon was in disgrace. Helen winked at him in commiseration: it was as if they were all back at school.

After lunch they had coffee, then went to their rooms for a siesta. Instead of sleeping or reading Herzen, Simon lay on his bed thinking about Willy – about the differences and similarities between the middle-aged drunk living here in Nice and the golden-haired hero he remembered from school.

At first sight they had nothing in common; but there in the café, when they had talked about Simon's divorce, Willy had talked to him with just that concern which had led Simon to adore him as a boy. People who knew him a little called it 'Ludley's charm', but it was more than charm – a deep sympathy, a concentration of kindness, that Simon had never known in anyone else. He felt, when Willy considered him in this way, like a sick child whose father or mother touches his brow and brushes back his sweated hair.

How then had it happened, Simon asked himself, that someone who had inspired such trust – whom once he would have followed into Hell itself – had changed from a hero into a drunk? The only one of his generation to have believed that a man must shape his destiny by the exercise of his will, he was now like the gnarled root of a great tree carried down by the River Var, left stranded on the stony beach of the Baie des Anges.

Why did Willy live in Nice? He had given a dozen different reasons in the past twenty-four hours – to walk on the Promenade des Anglais, to avoid income tax, because Nietzsche had lived there, because Herzen had lived there, because there was cheap wine, fresh vegetables, an atmosphere of the forgiveness of sins: but behind it all was the clear understanding that Willy lived in Nice because he could not live in England.

And why could he not live in England? Not, certainly, because he drank: there were plenty of fellow alcoholics in the British Isles. It must be because of Djakarta. He was afraid or ashamed to return to the country he had betrayed, and remorse for what he had done to a friend had led him to drink. The treason explained the drinking and the drinking confirmed the treason. The more Simon thought about it, the more probable it seemed that Willy in his twenties had only affected the detachment of a diplomat and had inwardly raged to see the American marines land in Vietnam; that he had felt humiliated by the supine support of his own government for the Americans, and had linked the struggle of the Vietcong in Indo-China with the Indonesians' undeclared war against Britain in Malaysia.

Yet to be satisfied with a hypothesis was not to prove it. Simon knew that while he was in Nice he must extract a confession from Willy which would settle the question of the Djakarta leak once and for all; and if Simon felt some slight anxiety as to whether it was honourable or not to stay in the house of a friend just to trap him into an incriminating admission of guilt, he calmed it now with the thought that by identifying the source of Willy's remorse, he might help him to give up drinking.

There was a tap on the door. Simon asked whoever it was to come in, and Helen's head appeared between the door and the jamb. 'Are you asleep?' she asked.

'No.'

'Do you want to go for a swim? Priss and I thought we'd go down to the beach.'

'Is it warm enough?'

'Oh yes. Come on. If we were in England we'd think it was boiling.'

Simon heaved his body off the bed. 'I'll be down in a minute,' he said.

When she had left him, he put on his bathing trunks beneath his trousers and then came downstairs to find Helen and Priss waiting for him in the hall.

'It's really quite nice at this time of year,' said Priss as she led the way down the steps. 'The crowds have gone, but the sea is still warm.' She seemed to have forgiven Simon for the cognac in the castle.

'Does Willy ever swim?' Simon asked.

'He used to, when we first came out here, but he doesn't like the topless girls.'

'Why not?'

She shrugged her shoulders. 'I don't know. Ask him.'

They walked down the steps of the boulevard, and on down past Les Grands Cèdres – the large block of flats which stood between the Villa Golitsyn and the sea. They crossed the Promenade at the traffic lights and went down onto the public beach. Priss pitched camp by throwing down her towel about five yards from the sea, and then flicked off her skirt and blouse and lay back in her bikini. Simon and Helen changed more cautiously, but then Priss had a slim figure and brown skin whereas the newcomers were both white and less sure of their bodies – Helen because of the adolescent plumpness which still filled out her limbs, Simon because of the slack flesh around his stomach.

Helen soon lost her selfconsciousness and went into the sea. Simon watched her splashing around like a porpoise, thinking how like her movements were to his daughter's in Norfolk that summer. At the same time, despite her childishness, and the modesty of the one-piece bathing dress that covered half her body, he saw that she was prettier than she had seemed on the train.

Pretty as she was, she did not compare to Priss, who lay next to him on the shingle. A body expresses character like a face, and while Helen's pubescence betrayed a charming but empty personality, Priss's arms and legs – her elbows, shoulders and neck – had the same strong and graceful shape as her character – the human equivalent of a racing yacht where Helen was more like a dinghy.

It was warm. Priss faced away from him, so Simon could study her figure without impropriety. Normally nothing is less erotic than a semi-dressed body laid flat on the beach, but with his emotions already engaged by her personality, Simon imagined himself next to Priss on a bed. She lifted herself up, turned, and sat for a moment with her knees near her chin, studying her toenails: and Simon, with his eyes half-closed, and concealed in any case behind his sun spectacles, had a clear view from only a few inches of the underside of her body – her delicate bosom, neither large nor small; the neat wrink-

62

ling of her concave stomach with its long, slim silver scar; and the smooth-sided canyon between her legs.

He raised his torso and turned as if to bronze the side of his body: sexual desire was an uncomfortable sensation for a man lying face-down on a pebble beach. For a moment he watched Helen frolicking in the sea; then he turned to Priss and said: 'I'm sorry about this morning.'

'It wasn't your fault. I should have warned you.'

'Even if you had, I don't see how I could have stopped him.'

'I think *you* could.'

'How?'

She turned her gaze from her toenails to look at Simon. 'He respects you,' she said. 'If you told him how awful it is for everyone . . .'

'I'm sure he knows.'

'He knows, but he doesn't care. He thinks it's contemptible to bother about what other people think of him.'

'I remember.'

'But I know that he minds about you. That's why, when Charlie said that he'd met you in London, I hoped he'd be able to get you to come out here. You see, really . . . the doctors in Switzerland said that Willy would kill himself if he didn't stop drinking.'

'Shouldn't he see a psychiatrist?' Simon asked.

She shrugged her shoulders. 'Of course, but he never would, and I'm not sure that it would be right to make him. He's always had a strong idea of what is noble and what is base. He would think it ignoble to hand himself over to an analyst.'

'Why?'

'Too passive. Feminine. Abdication of Free Will. So if I forced him to go to an analyst he would lose his self-respect. You see, I did once get him into a clinic – the one in Switzerland – and he looked quite defeated. Dead. Then he escaped. He climbed down from a balcony on the sixth floor and for two months after that he was wonderful. Really his old self. He drank a bit, but never before lunch. He was happy, cheerful, funny. Full of ideas. His escape was like a shot of some wonder drug. It made him feel fine, but it wore off. He went back to his old ways.'

'I was thinking about him after lunch,' said Simon, 'trying to decide in my own mind why he might drink so much. It isn't in his family, is it?'

'No. Not particularly.' She spoke carefully. 'His father drank, but no more than anyone else.'

'He wasn't an alcoholic?'

'No.'

'And his mother?'

Priss shook her head. 'She died when Willy was still at school, but not of drink.'

'Did you know them?'

'Yes.'

'What were they like?'

She turned away from him so that he could not see the expression on her face. Then she looked at him again. 'Would you know what I meant if I said that someone had died inside – had deliberately killed their own capacity to love and be loved because they had suffered so much?'

'I can imagine it.'

'Willy's mother was like that. Cold. Withdrawn. Even when he was a child. People thought that she was a snob because she did everything by form; but it wasn't snobbery. It was just the only structure she had left.'

'And why did she suffer so much?'

'From *him*.'

'Willy's father?'

She nodded.

'I've heard he wasn't very nice.'

She laughed – a cruel little laugh. 'I know one's not supposed to speak ill of the dead,' she said, 'but I can't say anything about him without speaking ill . . .' She spoke with a dainty vehemence.

'Was he such a monster?'

'He was charming to his friends. People loved to come and stay at Hensfield. Didn't you read the obituaries?' She laughed again. ' "Ne'er shall the like be seen again." You had to be an intimate of the family to know what he was really like.'

'You make him sound fascinating.'

'He was, in a way. He was very clever, and he used his intellect to humiliate people who were less clever – particularly Willy's mother, until she was past caring. He was very rich and assumed that everything could be bought – especially women. He was proud of his virility. His motto was: "If it moves, fuck it." ' Priss glanced at Simon as if to see whether he was shocked by what she had said. 'When

Willy was twelve he taught him how to masturbate. He used *droit de seigneur* on all the servants, and he particularly enjoyed seducing other people's wives – the younger, the better – not because he wanted to please the wives but simply to humiliate their husbands. He didn't really belong to the twentieth century at all: certainly not to the England of the Welfare State. He was more like something out of *Les Liaisons Dangereuses*.'

'You seem to have known him quite well.'

'I did.'

'So you knew Willy as a child?'

'Yes.' She turned away from him again and looked out to sea. 'I was, as it were, the girl next door.'

Helen came back from her swim and sat on her towel a few feet away from her older friends.

'Did you marry before Willy went abroad?' Simon asked Priss.

'No. After.'

'While he was with the Foreign Office?'

'No. Just after he resigned.'

'In Singapore?'

'Yes.' She looked surprised that he should know. 'We had our honeymoon in the Raffles Hotel.'

'Did he drink then?' asked Simon.

'No, no.' She smiled to herself as if remembering those early days of her marriage. 'A bit, of course, but not compulsively.'

'When did he start?'

She frowned. 'It all happened gradually. We went from Singapore to Argentina – we had a ranch there and Willy decided to try and run it by himself. He saw himself as a gaucho because of that book by W.H. Hudson. There he drank quite a lot of *pisco* . . .' She shook her head and said again: 'It happened gradually. I remember, once, in Mendoza when he had his first real fit. We were on holiday.' She stopped and looked miserable.

Simon waited for a moment and then asked: 'Do you know why he left the Foreign Office?'

'I think he was bored.'

'And why did you never go back to England?'

She turned sharply and looked at him straight in the eyes – a hard, almost wanton look. 'Why? What is there to go back to?'

'Family and friends.'

'We haven't any family or friends.'

'Are *your* parents dead?'

'Yes.'

'No brothers or sisters?'

'No.'

'And no friends.'

'None that I'd ever want to see again.'

'Then why did you leave Argentina?'

She sighed. 'We didn't miss England but we missed Europe. Argentina is very far from anywhere else. You feel terribly cut off, and get tired of all that steak and *pisco*. Have you ever been there?'

Simon shook his head. 'No.'

'One begins to long for some architecture – proper houses and old churches and ruined castles . . .'

'I can imagine.'

'And then Willy was hopeless on a horse. As soon as we arrived the ranch started to lose money, and as soon as we left it made a profit again.' She laughed and stood up. 'I'm going for a swim before it gets cold.'

She ran to the sea and threw herself into the water. She swam like an eel, her head down, her legs straight and thrashing. For fear that she might think him a sissy, Simon followed.

Ten

They got back to the Villa Golitsyn to find that a telegram had been delivered for Charlie to say that Carmen Baker, his American girl-friend, was arriving in three days' time.

Willy, who sat in the garden drinking tea from the silver teapot, seemed in a state of great excitement. 'Do you realize, Priss,' he said, 'that tomorrow we are to entertain a *film-star* in this humble little house of ours?'

'She's not a star,' said Charlie looking confused. 'She's an actress, or rather she'd like to be an actress. She's been in one or two things . . .'

'He's being modest,' said Willy. 'She's obviously a Jane Fonda — long legs, golden hair . . .'

'She's got black hair,' said Charlie.

'A raven-haired beauty. I can't wait.' He turned to Priss. 'We must lay on something special for lunch tomorrow. No ravioli-eater, this one. Caviar, larks' tongues . . .' He flourished his hands like an operatic tenor.

'She's really quite ordinary,' said Charlie.

'How can she be ordinary, *Carlo mio*, when she has freed you from the bonds of faggery and converted you to the one true heterosexual faith?'

Charlie blushed. 'In LA,' he said, 'one isn't necessarily one or the other.'

'California. The Land of the Free. Priss, my dear, why didn't we go and live in California?'

Priss shrugged her shoulders. 'You said you hated Americans.'

'Did I? Well, perhaps I do, but Carmen is going to change all that. She'll convert me too — not to heterosexuality, of course, because I'm already a believer, but to love of the USA.'

'Why don't you like Americans?' Simon asked.

'If they were all like Carmen,' said Willy, 'I would adore them.'

'You haven't met her yet,' said Charlie.

'But she won't be dressed in baggy trousers and drip-dry shirts, will she? She won't complain all the time that the Mexicans are poor and beg in the streets?' He turned to Priss again. 'Do you remember, dearest? In Querétaro?'

'Yes, but you can't judge all Americans by a busload of tourists in Querétaro.'

'And Vietnam? Can you judge them by that?' He took a sip of tea from the porcelain cup. 'Of course you're too young to remember,' he said to Helen, 'and you, Simon, you're too much of a civil servant to let emotions affect your judgement, but I remember when they were bombing and burning and counting the bodies . . .'

'But that's finished,' said Charlie. 'They left.'

'They did indeed. And now, aren't we meant to admire them for going? And to pity them for the trauma of Vietnam? How it brutalized their innocent, sensitive soul? How it damaged their confidence in themselves — the poor little things?'

'Is that why you left the Foreign Office?' Simon asked. 'Because of Vietnam?'

Willy turned and looked at him with a slightly more serious expression on his face. 'It might have made it difficult to stay,' he said, 'because one couldn't hate the Americans for what they were doing without despising our government — our Labour government — for supporting them. Back there in Whitehall it may have made sense: verbal support costs us nothing. But out there in Asia, where the generalissimos and profiteers drove past the hungry children in their Mercedes Benzes, it was difficult to keep a professional detachment if you didn't have . . .'

Simon finished the sentence for him. 'A heart as cold as mine?'

Willy smiled with slight embarrassment. 'Yes, Simon old fellow, but many's the time when I wished I had a cold heart, because with a cold heart you get things done. Emotional people like Charlie and me . . .' — he put his arm around Charlie's shoulder — 'we may feel more than you do; we may suffer and exult; but at the end of the day it's all vanity and egoism. *I* love. *I* suffer. Whereas you, with your phlegmatic common sense, you analyse, act and put things right.'

Simon leaned forward to pour himself some tea. 'But no analysis is exact if it doesn't take account of emotion, and if you cannot feel emotion, then you cannot place it in the equation.' He filled his cup with tea.

'I'm afraid it's cold,' said Willy.

'It doesn't matter,' said Simon.

'Do you take milk?'

Simon shook his head.

'If the Americans had been more cold-blooded,' said Priss, 'they would never have got involved in Vietnam.'

'Our policy,' said Willy, looking at Simon with an expression of amused mockery, 'the kind of policy made by clear-headed, cold-hearted people like you, Simon, was always to win if we could, and if we couldn't, to abandon our principles and betray our friends. *Perfide Albion.*'

As he prepared his reply, Simon sipped his tea. He choked. It was cold cognac.

'Look at Malaya,' Willy went on, grinning at Simon's confusion. 'We fought and won. But in Kenya, Cyprus, India, Burma — everywhere else . . .'

Priss glanced suspiciously at Simon. He put down his cup. Willy leaned forward to interpose his body between Simon and Priss. 'We left without a fight. Cunning to the last. Men like you in charge,

68

Simon.' He smiled. 'Tea too cold? Shall I make a fresh pot? Easily done with teabags.'

'No thank you,' said Simon. 'This is fine.'

When the sun set the air suddenly became colder. They went into the house to change into warmer and smarter clothes. Priss liked her guests to change for dinner. They came down again to find Willy in his old linen suit and a silk shirt – both faded and bought when he was plumper, but elegant all the same. He hovered around the drink; made a gin fizz; filled their glasses; filled his own; refilled his own. He went on and on about Carmen: he seemed more excited about her coming than Charlie was. Simon glanced at Priss to see if this annoyed her but she only looked bored. It was Helen who seemed slightly sulky at all this advance publicity for the American girl. She had looked happier at lunch when Willy was clasping her knees crying: 'Natalie, Natalie, stay with me. Don't leave the children.'

Priss had decided that they would go to a restaurant that night rather than eat at home. 'Luckily there are quite a few,' Charlie whispered to Simon, 'because once our Willy's been to one, he tends not to be welcome again.'

They got into the Jaguar and drove along the Promenade to the port. There they ate bouillabaisse at a restaurant on the quai. Helen cheered up, laughing at the puffy faces of the fish, drinking as much wine as the rest of them and, while they drank coffee, eating vanilla icecream with hot chocolate sauce. Willy ordered marc for everyone. Simon was about to object, in *loco parentis*, at a glass of such strong spirits for Helen when Priss turned to her and said: 'You don't really want marc, do you?'

'Not really, no.'

Willy ordered her a crème de menthe instead, and as she was drinking it Helen suddenly started laughing. 'If only the girls at school could see me now,' she said. 'Then they'd all run away.'

'To runaways,' shouted Willy, raising his glass in a toast. 'We're all runaways here.' He emptied it and ordered another.

When they left the restaurant they walked along the quai to take a closer look at *Clöe*, the Ludleys' boat. Helen skipped ahead. Willy followed, arm-in-arm with Priss. One might have said that he was propped against her except that she too leaned against him, her head resting on his shoulder. The image of the two of them, against the floodlit castle, the lights of the cafés on the far side of the port, and

69

the black glistening water, was somehow moving — even to Simon, who Willy said had no emotions.

'They do seem happy together,' Simon said to Charlie.

'I think they live for one another,' he said. 'I've never seen such a close couple.'

'Not even in California?'

He smiled. 'I wouldn't expect it there. That's why I'm glad Carmen is coming. She thinks that all love starts with a bang and ends with a whimper. But with Willy and Priss you sometimes feel that it's like a fantastic wine or an incredible lawn — that it's only got as good as that after years and years of care and a kind of maturing.'

Simon looked sideways to catch the expression on Charlie's face. It was bright — bright with admiration and a kind of hope. It struck him that Charlie still loved Willy — not with a homosexual desire but with an almost filial love for one whose strong personality had shaped his weaker one.

Simon had not realized until just now how weak Charlie was. It was evident in his face and in his movements that he had no real convictions of his own: the sky-blue suit and the open-necked shirt, being gay or straight or both, being Left or Right, in films or advertising, married or unmarried, were all matters of fashion — all things he did because other people thought they were the things to do. At the Villa Golitsyn he always had an opinion ready for a book or a play or a person, but if Willy or Priss or Simon took a contrary view, he would quickly agree with just the opposite of what he had been saying a moment before. Simon thought it quite likely that the only thing he would defend to the death was Willy — Willy who was largely indefensible.

As his children had noticed in Norfolk, Simon knew nothing about boats. *Clöe* seemed to him to be rather more than a dinghy and less than a yacht. They climbed on board and Willy showed him a dark hole which he said was a cabin which would 'sleep three'. At the entrance to this cabin there was a galley and a lavatory — designed, said Willy, so that 'a constipated sailor can cook and crap at the same time'.

The boat was not in good condition. The paint was peeling off the side and the metal fittings had a greenish veneer. A tarpaulin which had once covered the entrance to the cabin had partly blown away, and before they left Willy and Priss tried to tie it back in place. Willy was too drunk and Priss too weak, so Simon and Charlie did it for them. They then helped Willy off the boat, afraid that he might totter into the harbour.

'We must take her out,' said Willy, looking at *Clöe* with pride. 'We'll spin off to the Iles de Lerins.'

'Not at this time of year,' said Priss. 'I don't want to get caught in a storm.'

'*Clöe* can ride out a storm,' said Willy.

'*Clöe* can but we can't.'

'Are you suggesting,' asked Willy, 'that I'm an incompetent sailor?' It was difficult for the others to tell whether he was offended or only pretending to be.

'Oh no,' said Priss sarcastically. 'Only a skilled navigator could beach his boat on the *plage concédée* in front of the Negresco and have to be towed off by the *pompiers*.'

'There you are,' said Willy, turning to Simon and Charlie. 'She undermines me. It was the same in Argentina when I got on a horse.'

'Only because you looked like Don Quixote.'

'We are what we see reflected in the eyes of others,' said Willy acidly. 'You always wanted to be a boy, that's all.' He turned to Simon and Charlie. 'You admired me at school, didn't you? So I believed in myself. But from Priss – perpetual derision. So what have I become?' He shrugged his shoulders and smiled.

'Nonsense,' she said. 'I believed in you long before they did. It's just that I don't see you as a man of action.'

'But great Heavens, wasn't I captain of the First Fifteen?' He snatched Priss's handbag and set off down the quai towards the car. Charlie ran after him shouting: 'Pass, Ludley, pass.' Willy turned and threw the bag at Charlie with the same graceful twist of his body that Simon remembered from the playing fields at school. It flew through the air but opened before Charlie caught it, scattering coins, credit cards, bank notes and make up all over the cobbles.

'For God's sake, Will,' shouted Priss. 'Can't you be your age?'

Simon and Helen ran to pick up her things and Willy returned towards them, crestfallen, taking the bag from Charlie and returning it to Priss. He said nothing. She said nothing more but gave a kind of snorting sigh. There was no breeze so they recovered everything except perhaps a few of the bronze-coloured coins – ten- and twenty-centime pieces.

'I'm going to walk back,' said Willy when they reached the car.

'You can't,' said Priss.

'I *can*,' he said with unusual vehemence.

'It's too far,' she said.

'I've done it before. It takes an hour.'

'You'll pass out on the Promenade,' said Priss, 'and the gendarmes will pull you in and we'll have all that boring business over the *permis de sejour*.'

'I will not pass out,' said Willy quietly, and with a certain dignity. 'I am neither an invalid nor a lunatic. I just sometimes get drunk. This evening I am a little drunk but not *very* drunk and a walk will do me good.'

'I'll come with you,' said Simon.

'So will I,' said Charlie.

'Thank you,' said Willy, 'but I would rather go alone.' And such was the authority he still retained from the old days that none of them argued with him any more, but all got into the Jaguar and left him on the quai.

Eleven

When they got back to the Villa Golitsyn Helen went straight to bed. She was drunk, and made a comic sight trying to take her leave of the others in what she thought was the suave style of an adult but only came across as the play-acting of a much younger girl.

Simon, Priss and Charlie sat down to play a game of Scrabble. They were silent, concentrating on the game, yet because they too were slightly drunk they found it hard to piece words together from the seven letters in front of them. After only a quarter of an hour, Charlie gave up. 'I'm going to bed,' he said. 'Wake me if you need me.'

Simon and Priss were left alone and went on with the game, but soon after Charlie had left it seemed to Simon that Priss changed her behaviour. Whereas before she had sat forward, biting her lower lips, her eyes only on the board, she now sat back on the sofa, crossed her legs under her pale pink skirt, and every now and then looked up at Simon with an easy, friendly smile.

'Are you worried about Willy?' he asked.

She shrugged her shoulders. 'Yes, of course, but it's happened before.' Then she added, pointedly: 'One can't let it ruin one's life' – as if to emphasize that she and her husband were separate people.

They went on with the game, but as they played Simon started to feel uneasy in her presence. Because of what he had gone through with his wife, he resisted any feeling which might be called love; but it was difficult to suppress the attraction he felt for her. Simon, who at first had thought that Priss might feel a Lesbian attraction for Helen, and who only an hour before had agreed with Charlie that her marriage to Willy seemed happy and complete, now felt that her smile and her limbs were drawing him towards her. Only four or five feet of empty air separated them. He felt a strong impulse to move from his armchair to the sofa, take hold of her body, draw back her clothes and kiss her skin. Yet the very act which was unimpeded by any physical obstacle was at the same time impossible for him to achieve. She was the wife of his friend. They had only met the day before. Was he so sexually deprived that he should make a pass at Willy's wife under Willy's roof? Was she so desperate to escape from her alcoholic husband that she was now offering herself to the first heterosexual to come into her house? Was that why she had asked him to stay – not to play bridge but to make love? Or was it all part of the play, with Simon cast as Herwegh, the perfidious friend?

Priss looked up at him with a quizzical look on her face. 'Is "golt" a word?' she asked.

'I don't think so.'

'How annoying. There's colt, bolt and dolt but not golt.'

'It might pass for "gold" in Willy's play.'

'So will you allow it?'

'If you like.'

'Don't expect any favour in return.'

'All right.'

She leaned forward and put three letters on the board. 'Now it's your turn,' she said – and then noticing that Simon's eyes were not on his letters but on her, she said: 'It's difficult to know what you're thinking.'

'Why?'

'Your face is a mask, or rather it's two masks – the gloomy one, when no one's looking, and then the smile, the disillusioned smile.'

'It's no easier for me to know what's going on in your mind.'

She looked perplexed. 'No, I suppose it's not.'

'I can't even make out if you're happy or not.'

'Sometimes I am and sometimes I'm not. Isn't that true of most people?'

'Yes, unless there's something in particular which makes you one thing or the other.'

'Well, there's Will, of course. His moods affect mine.'

'You're very involved with him.'

She smiled wryly. 'I haven't much choice.'

'No, but if you had children or a job or . . .'

'Or what?'

'Well, friends. You don't seem to have many friends in Nice.'

'No, we don't. We had one or two, but Will always ends up insulting them, and the French are incredibly touchy.'

'Perhaps you should find a Latin lover?' he said with a slightly sarcastic smile.

'They're not my type,' she said, looking straight into his eyes.

'An expatriate, perhaps?'

She did not look away but said, quite slowly: 'It's your turn.'

For several seconds Simon sat looking into Priss's eyes, the semi-scoffing expression frozen on his face. He was paralysed by the double meaning of her words; but then he blushed and looked down again at his letters. 'I haven't really got anything,' he said. 'Not even a "golt". I think I'd better concede the game.'

'Very well.' Her expression did not change.

He stood. 'Will you wait up for Willy?'

'I might, but don't worry. It's happened before.' She smiled at him, but not reproachfully, and with that smile in his mind he went to bed.

Simon was woken by Charlie at three in the morning. 'He isn't back,' he said. 'Priss wants us to go out and look for him.'

Simon quickly got dressed and came down to find Priss sitting on the sofa where he had left her, but dressed now in an old-fashioned, dark-blue dressing-gown over a white, lace-edged nightdress. 'I'm awfully sorry,' she said. 'It's just that I worry.'

'Of course,' said Simon. 'We don't mind.'

74

'Charlie knows the likely places. I'd come too, but I think you might find him easier without me.'

There was still some traffic on the Promenade, and people stood around on the pavement outside Rhul's Casino. They parked the car in the market place and walked through into the Old Town, peering into five or six squalid cafés and bars which were still open. Willy was not to be found, and no one had seen their *ami anglais*.

They returned to the Jaguar and drove up the Avenue Jean Mededin, under the railway line and into some of the sidestreets behind the station. Here too one or two bars were still open but Willy was not in any of them. It then occurred to them that perhaps he had never left the Port, so they drove back to the quai where they had left him and looked in some of the cafés and bars between there and the Place Garibaldi. In none of them was Willy to be found.

Simon then telephoned Priss to see if Willy had come back while they had been out looking for him. He had not, and Priss told them to give him up. 'You might try the police station on the way back,' she said. 'He might be there.'

They got into the car and were driving back towards the centre of Nice when Charlie suddenly said: 'I know where he is.' He drove right around the Place Garibaldi and went back towards the port, but instead of going down to the quai he turned up a narrow lane which led up towards the castle. 'I hope you're feeling fit,' he said. 'We'll have to climb over a wall.'

'Where are we going?'

'You'll see.'

They came to a terrace about halfway up to the castle where the road was straight and wide enough to park the car. Here they got out and stood under a line of plane trees looking out over the parapet at the lights of the city below. They were like gems strewn on a black velvet cushion. Above them, less bright but more beautiful, was the near-full moon.

They turned and crossed the road. Simon followed Charlie along the side of a tall, white wall. They reached a gate through which he could see the white slabs of numerous tomb stones.

'We've got to get over this,' said Charlie. He looked over his shoulder at the Guardian's house on the other side of the road. All the windows were dark.

'It might be easier around the corner,' said Simon.

He now led the way back along the wall to a place where Charlie, by standing on his clasped hands, could climb onto the wall, and afterwards pull Simon up behind him. They both jumped down onto the gravel on the other side. Simon felt a great jolt in his spine as he landed, and for a moment gasped for breath.

'We are getting too old for this sort of thing,' said Charlie.

'I don't see how Willy could have got in here on his own,' said Simon.

'He must have a special way.'

'You've found him here before?'

'Yes.'

There were paths between the graves and mausoleums of the Niçoises which – being built at different levels of the ground – loomed above them in the moonlight. At first Charlie seemed lost, and it was only by following the wall to the main gate that he found his bearings. 'It's like a maze,' he said setting off again into the cemetery.

He climbed some steps, turned a corner, then stopped. 'There he is,' he whispered.

Simon followed the line of his outstretched arm but for a moment could only make out the rectangular and triangular shapes of the tombs. One figure, which he thought for a moment was Willy, had white wings. It was the statue of an angel.

'Where?' he asked Charlie. 'I can't see him.'

'There.' Charlie pointed again.

Simon peered into the strange light and suddenly saw the figures of two men – one standing on a pedestal, the other seated on a stone and looking up at the first.

'Who's with him?' Simon whispered.

'Herzen.'

Simon had never thought of himself as either psychic or superstitious, but in this eerie geometric maze, where shadows turned out to be black marble memorials and the figures of friends the statues of angels, he felt a twinge of fear as he was told that Willy was with a man who had been dead for more than a hundred years. Charlie, however, did not seem frightened and crept closer to the two men. Simon followed and, because the tomb was on a higher level which they could only reach by passing directly below, stopped behind Charlie to listen to what Willy was saying to his companion.

'In the light of experience,' he heard Willy say in a clear, casual and sober tone of voice, 'wouldn't you agree that we carried scepticism too far? Wouldn't you concede that people must have values, and that if you take away those they have without providing others, then someone less sceptical will step in and give people his values which may be brutal and absurd, like Hitler's, but are accepted by the people in preference to none at all?'

He stopped, as if waiting for the other man to answer, but when no answer came, he continued: 'Oh, I know, I admit it. You had more values than I did, but they were values based upon an optimistic view of human nature which you could hardly hold today. You had seen what the middle classes could do to the proletariat, but not what the proletariat could do to the middle classes. Or the Marxists to the anarchists. Or the Germans to the Jews. You knew that God was dead, but not that Man was dead too.'

Simon felt uncomfortable eavesdropping in this way, so he walked past Charlie, kicking the gravel to make his presence known. He climbed the steps that brought him onto the same level as Willy and his friend. Willy must have heard him because he stopped talking and, when Simon came into view, stood up and came towards him. His companion was left standing on the tombstone.

'Simon? Is that you?' he said.

'Yes.'

'Good. Come and meet Herzen.'

Simon stopped beside Willy and looked up at what he could now see was a life-size statue of the Russian revolutionary, standing on a pedestal and striking a somewhat pompous pose.

Willy bowed towards the statue. 'May I introduce an old friend of mine, Simon Milson, of Her Majesty's Foreign Service?'

Simon looked up at the bronze, bearded face, half-expecting it to lower its gaze like the statue of the Commendatore in *Don Giovanni*, but Herzen continued to look over their heads towards the sea.

'Short fellow, isn't he?' said Willy. 'Perhaps that's what made him a revolutionary.' He walked a few paces away and sat down on the same tomb as before, crossing his legs as if he was in Herzen's drawing-room. 'You usually find some personal detail in the lives of those Russian revolutionaries', he said, 'which explains their rebellion. If Lenin's brother had not been hanged by the Tsar, would Lenin have been what he was? If Herzen had not been short, or illegitimate, would he have turned against the government of the time? That is the irony of life. We think that our ideas are the product of dispassionate reasoning, and they turn out to be just the refined expression of our complexes, prejudices and emotions.'

Simon was not sure whether Willy was speaking to him or to the statue of Herzen, but since the statue did not reply he interposed his own opinion. 'Surely,' he said, 'our feelings lead our thoughts in certain directions, but once they have set off, they can only make progress if they keep to the common rules of reason.'

'But reason will lead you anywhere you want to go,' said Willy. He spoke sourly, like a man talking of his promiscuous mistress.

'There was a time when you thought reason the key to all wisdom.'

'The folly of youth.'

'What has replaced it?'

He laughed. 'Nothing. A chaos of doubt.'

'You don't believe in any system any more?'

'Did I believe in a system?'

'I thought you were a Marxist?'

'No.' He shook his head, then looked up at Herzen. 'An ideology can be useful. I always thought that. But that's all.'

'Useful for what?'

'There are times and places – Herzen's Russia, for example – where the injustice is so great that reform is impossible. You must have a revolution, and for a revolution you need a justifying idea. Marxism was useful in that respect. It inspired people to abandon the fatalism of the past and achieve great improvements in their wretched material conditions.'

'So you never believed in Marxism but saw it as a politically effective idea?'

'Yes. Not just in Russia, but in China and Cuba . . .'

'And Indonesia? Would it have been useful there?'

'Certainly,' said Willy. 'At least that's what I thought at the time.'

The first rays of the sun were appearing over Mount Boron, slowly replacing the light of the moon on the three flesh faces and the one of stone. Charlie, who had been listening silently to the conversation, now turned to Willy and Simon and said: 'I'm worried about Priss.'

'Yes,' said Simon. 'We'd better get back.'

'Of course,' said Willy. He stood, brushed down his trousers and with a last look at Herzen set off along the gravel path between the graves. 'I'm sorry to bring you up here,' he said, half-turning to address the two younger men. 'You needn't have come. I would have found my own way home.'

'Priss was worried, that was all,' said Simon.

'That's the worst thing about drinking,' said Simon. 'It gives women the excuse they're always looking for to treat you like a child.'

'I'm sure it's not that,' said Simon. 'If you love someone, you're naturally anxious.'

'Don't take her side,' said Willy quietly.

'Are there sides?'

'Always. "When you go to women, don't forget your whip."'

'*Zarathustra*?'

'Correct.'

'But you love her, don't you?' asked Simon.

'Of course I love her,' said Willy. 'Haven't I proved I love her? If only I loved her less.'

'You're more enigmatic than Nietzsche,' said Simon.

'Love is a bond, Simon, and bonds are constricting. You can love someone without understanding her or sympathizing with what she suffers. I often wonder if men and women ever really sympathize with one another. They think and feel in such different ways, and always at the back of their minds there is a mild contempt for what the other thinks is important. That's why I come up here – just like a pilgrim going to pray at the tomb of a saint. I can talk to Herzen because he would have understood the fears and thoughts that go round and round in my head.'

'Couldn't I understand?' asked Simon.

He stopped and pointed to a simple tombstone. 'That's the grave of Garibaldi's mother,' he said. 'Herzen helped carry her coffin up here.'

'Couldn't I understand?' Simon asked again.

'I'm not sure, Simon. You're like Priss. English and sensible. You can't see what all the fuss is about. Why bother about the meaning of life – just live it. Whereas Herzen – he was emotional, egotistical, self-dramatizing. Like me. I often feel that I must have Russian blood, or that I'm the reincarnation of a Russian – Herzen, perhaps, or a character out of Dostoievsky.'

'Why not an Englishman?' asked Simon. 'Byron, for example?'

Willy stopped and turned just as they reached the wall which enclosed the cemetery. His face, quite clear now in the light of the dawn, had an expression of cold, amused curiosity. 'Byron, did you say?'

'Yes.'

'Why Byron?'

'Rich, emotional, unhappy, an exile . . .'

'Nothing else?'

'Not that I can think of.'

'You don't *know*, do you, Simon?'

'Know what?'

He looked away. 'Never mind. Look, this is the easiest way out. Climb up onto the mausoleum of the *famille* Lorenzotto – mafiosi, I should think – then jump onto the wall and down onto the roof of the guardian's car. Charlie, did you hear? Good. Follow me.' And once again, as at school, they followed their leader.

Part Two

One

Willy was calm for a day or two after his conversation with Herzen at his grave, and Simon took advantage of this lull to sit in the garden of the Villa Golitsyn and read some of the books from the shelves in the house.

The Ludleys' library was not large. It contained Herzen, of course, as well as Goethe, Schiller, Flaubert, Sterne, and more modern writers like Scott Fitzgerald and Thomas Mann. There was also a group of history books which Willy appeared to have brought with him from Cambridge; as well as the Michelin Guides and paperback thrillers. But Simon was not looking for books to entertain him. He hoped rather to find further evidence among these different books of Willy's interests and convictions at the time of the Djakarta leak. He had admitted in the cemetery that Marxism would have been useful in Indonesia, but that did not mean that he himself had played a treacherous role to help bring about a Communist revolution.

There were, for example, no works by either Marx or Lenin in Willy's library, so Simon took down the three further volumes of Herzen's memoirs, and also two well-worn copies of books by E.H. Carr, the historian of the Soviet Union who had been Regius Professor of History and a Fellow of Trinity College at the time when Willy was studying there. With these books under his arm he went out into the garden and sat under a palm tree in the warm autumn sunshine.

Simon looked first at Herzen's memoirs. The prose was rich and generous. In Simon's mind it matched the clear, warm air of the morning; the scent in the garden of roses and gardenias. He enjoyed the writing but kept his distance from their ebullient, un-English author. He observed the high-flown ideals and passionate convictions of the Russian with the detachment of a scientist studying an exotic flower. It was relevant to the subject of his study – Willy Ludley – that a man like Herzen, in the 1840s, could remove his loyalties from monarch and nation and reattach them to the higher ideals of socialism and revolution. Certainly Herzen had never sacrificed a friend as Willy seemed to have sacrificed Churton, but he was seen as a traitor by the Russian government at the time. He had done what he could for revolutionaries all over Europe – for Frenchmen, Germans, Hungarians, Italians and particularly for the Poles when they rose against the Russians in 1863. It was plausible to suggest, Simon said to himself, that Willy had seen parallels between the 1860s in Europe and the 1960s in Asia, with the Americans in the role of the Tsarist Russians and the Asian Communists as the Poles.

He turned next to the books by E.H. Carr and saw at once that it was Carr who had led Willy to Herzen. His first book, *The Romantic Exiles,* was largely an account of Herzen's life. The others were more academic treatises on history, and in reading them Simon felt more at ease. He had left the company of a Russian romantic, and was now with an English civil servant. There was a commonsensical tone to Carr's writing. The prose was elegant but dry; the reasoning matter-of-fact. It seemed at first sight unlikely that anything at all revolutionary could be gleaned from his work, but then Simon noticed that a collection of his essays, published in 1951, was called *The New Society,* and that despite the care taken by the author to hide his prejudices, he too like Herzen believed in progress:

> If, however, I were asked to define the content of progress, I should fall back on the well worn word 'freedom'; and if I were asked to define the goal towards which we shall seek to move at the present time, I should say 'freedom for all', or 'freedom for many', in contrast with the 'freedom for some' which has been the great achievement of the recent past.

Well trained in the minutiae of ministerial statements and departmental memoranda, Simon noted Carr's use of the word 'shall' rather than 'should' – the admonition disguised as a prediction; and also the assumption of a consensus in another passage to cover up the missing link in a chain of reasoning:

> In the twentieth century hardly anyone openly contests any longer the two propositions that freedom means freedom for all and therefore equality, and that freedom, if it means anything at all, must include freedom from want.

Later the historian of the Soviet Union committed himself still further:

> The price of liberty is the restriction of liberty. The price of some

liberty for all is the restriction of the greater liberty of some.

The words might have been written by Stalin himself.

There then followed an indictment of the British bourgeoisie, more withering than that of many a committed revolutionary because of its calm and reasonable tone:

> The vast majority of the ruling groups in Great Britain, in every branch of the national life, still belong, either by birth or adoption, to the class which was the main beneficiary of British prosperity and power before 1914, and are therefore under the impression of a steep decline not only in British power and prosperity as a whole but, within the country, in the power and prosperity of the class to which they belong . . . It is on any reckoning extraordinarily difficult for groups or individuals who have enjoyed prosperity under a certain dispensation, and learned to regard the beliefs on which that dispensation rested as eternally valid, to re-adapt themselves to a world in which that dispensation has passed away for ever and its beliefs are shown to be no more than a reflexion and expression of the interests that upheld it.

And yet, said Carr:

> No inherent reason exists why we in this country should succumb to the same experience . . . if existing ruling groups can be adapted to the revolutionary changes through which we are passing, or be replaced by other groups . . .

Simon sat back in his chair. Helen came out and asked him if he wanted to go with Charlie and Willy to Cap Ferrat. He shook his head. His mind was not in the South of France but in Cambridge in 1961. What impression would these words of Carr's have made on Willy if, beneath the tomfoolery of his flamboyant, debauched life, there had been a leader looking for a cause? He had loathed his father, and all his father stood for – the Empire and the *ancien régime* – but more than anyone else he was himself one of those 'who still belong by birth or adoption to the class which was the main beneficiary of British prosperity and power . . .' He belonged to it, but he abjured it, and here was Edward Hallett Carr, the greatest historian of his university, promising him that he could adapt to 'the revolutionary changes' through which they were passing and work for the 'freedom of all'.

But how? Simon returned to Carr – to *The New Society*. Was he, in 1951, advocating no more than a vote for the British Labour Party? No. It was revolution he talked of, not reform; and not a small, parochial national or even European revolution such as that which took place in France in 1789.

> The French revolution was, in spite of its national origin and title, a European event in an age when Europe still dominated the world. The revolution of today is still more certainly a world event, and its future does not turn on the destiny of a single country . . . We see its workings everywhere today, sometimes in sharp and rugged outline, sometimes dimly and half-hidden beneath an apparently unruffled surface, in Europe, in Asia (perhaps at this moment most of all in Asia), in Africa, in the Americas. We cannot escape it: we can only seek to understand and to meet it.

Simon closed his eyes. The sun was now behind the olive tree, and the slight breeze from the sea moved the branches back and forth so that a speckled light fell on his lids. He appeared for a moment to be dozing, but beneath the closed eyes his mind was quite awake, thinking not of the book which lay open on his knee, nor of Herzen's memoirs, but of a children's story he had read many years ago where the son and daughter of a famous explorer, seeing that there was no part of the world left to discover, decide to go to the moon.

Had that been the case with Willy? The son and grandson of imperial Englishmen, had he seen that the Empire was finished and looked for a new cause? He was not drawn to the speculations of Marx or Lenin, but found in his professor of history at Cambridge someone entirely reasonable and matter-of-fact who taught that history *does* have a meaning, that it moves in a certain direction, there is such a thing as progress. 'Freedom for some' was the last port of call; 'Freedom for many' is the next one; and the 'many' to be given this freedom are not so much the European working class as the peasant masses of Asia.

Carr had offered Willy not only a cause, but a role in this 'world event', this 'revolution of today'. It might be 'extraordinarily difficult for individuals who have enjoyed prosperity under a certain dispensation' – and Willy was certainly one of these – 'to readapt themselves to a world in which that dispensation has passed away forever', but he offered the possibility to the heroic individual:

'existing ruling groups can be adapted to the revolutionary changes'.

Simon remained with his eyes closed. Why do men act? For need. From habit. From conviction. No need, no habit, could have led Willy to help the Indonesian Communists, but here certainly was a conviction which made it not only possible but likely. He had arrived in Djakarta with the belief that if his life was to have any meaning – if he was to play a part in the times in which he lived – it must be to assist the progressive forces in Asia. His nation, the old colonial power, had created a neocolonial, pseudo-nation in the Federation of Malaysia, but it was Indonesia, and the Communists within Indonesia, who were fighting for the 'freedom for many'. They needed a dramatic victory against the British forces in Borneo. Willy, staying with Churton, saw his chance. He had photographed the map and given a print to Aidit.

Then came the abortive coup. He might have realized at the time that his disloyalty to the Crown might be uncovered, but he did not run because only a coward would run. He did withdraw, disillusioned, perhaps, by the failure of the Communist conspiracy, or disgusted by the slaughter which followed. Thereafter he had lived in exile with remorse growing and gnawing like a tapeworm in his entrails.

Two

A voice spoke close to him. He opened his eyes, blinked, and saw Priss holding a tray. 'Am I disturbing you,' she asked, 'or would you like some tea?'

Simon sat up. 'Perfect timing,' he said.

She put the tray on the white table and sat down on one of the wicker chairs. 'You've been reading some very serious books,' she said, pouring tea into an elegant china cup from the silver teapot.

'It's interesting stuff,' said Simon, closing his book and putting it down on the gravel by his chair.

'I've read Herzen,' said Priss. 'It's more or less obligatory if you're living with Willy; but I've never read any of those other books. I think Willy brought them with him from Cambridge.'

'He was obviously interested in history.'

'Yes. He got a First.'

'Didn't you go to university?'

She shook her head. 'In my day, girls weren't brought up to take an interest in things like that.'

'Didn't you study anything?'

'Yes. Art. I used to paint.'

'No longer?'

She wrinkled her nose. 'No. I took it terribly seriously at the time but when, well, when I got married I dropped it.'

'Perhaps you should take it up again?'

'I wasn't much good, and out here everything's been done by Renoir and Matisse.'

'You must get a little bored.'

'I don't really because I have to look after Will. But he does.'

'Does he read?'

'Only detective stories.'

'Not history?'

'No.' She hesitated, then added: 'He sometimes reads the Bible.'

'Why the Bible? He isn't religious, is he?'

'No, not really. In fact not at all. But he says that since the Bible has formed the moral conscience of the Western world, one ought at least to know what it says.'

'But he doesn't believe in it?'

'No.' She spoke with a slight falter in her voice.

'Nor do you.'

'No.' She said this with more conviction.

'What do you believe in?'

She looked nonplussed. 'Must one believe in something?'

'Not necessarily.'

'I believe in Will, I suppose.'

'And that's enough?' Simon refilled his cup with tea to cover the abruptness of his questions; but out of the corner of his eye he saw that what he had asked made Priss look vulnerable and almost sad.

'It's difficult to believe in someone who no longer believes in himself,' she said. 'And then, well, it's difficult growing older without friends – I mean girlfriends, really – women of the same age.

One can't compare notes. One can't know whether the feelings one has, or feelings one has lost, are experiences particular to oneself, or just part of the whole process of growing older.'

'You aren't so old,' said Simon.

'I know. I keep reminding myself that I've got half my life to go. But what's gone before – and I don't know, perhaps this is being indiscreet, or disloyal to Will – but I can't pretend that I feel the same kind of love for Will as I once did.'

'How do you mean?'

She blushed. 'Well, passion, I suppose. Physical passion.'

'That side of things is bound to change.'

'But is it? I mean, did it with you?'

Simon considered the question. He tried to remember what he had felt for his wife before the bitterness which had followed her love affair with the geologist. They had certainly made love, but more perhaps to satisfy a need than to express an emotion. 'I don't think it went altogether,' he said, 'but what was left didn't stand up to her feelings for the other man.'

'I'm afraid of that happening to me,' said Priss – and she glanced at Simon and then looked away with the apparent confusion of a much younger girl.

Simon swallowed a mouthful of tepid tea. What she had said, and the manner in which she had said it, seemed so clearly an indication that *he* could be the object of this further affection that now was clearly the moment to declare himself, to take her hand or grasp her body, as he had wanted to over the Scrabble board. But again he sat as if paralysed. It was not just the thought that Priss was Willy's wife which inhibited him: it was also that the way in which she was behaving – the girlish blushes and oblique glances – was totally inconsistent with his earlier perception of her forthright character. From the very first moment when he had met her, he had noticed the way in which she had sized up the newcomers, and the invitation she now seemed to extend to him seemed only half sincere. He therefore said nothing, and did nothing, and after a moment of embarrassed silence Priss said: 'Of course it won't happen. I mean fundamentally I love Will. I can't imagine being with anyone else.' Then she added, as if to punish Simon for spurning her. 'Anyway, there isn't much chance of meeting an irresistible lover here in Nice.'

The others returned soon after six. Priss was in the big old-fashioned kitchen preparing supper: Simon was on his knees at the fireplace, blowing at twigs with which he was trying to light a fire.

'What? A fire, Milson?' Willy shouted at him. 'You are a sissy these days.'

'Priss's idea, not mine,' said Simon.

'We've been swimming,' said Helen.

'And talking to the famous,' said Charlie. He laughed and Helen laughed too.

'You should have seen Willy,' she said, talking to Simon but looking with great fondness towards the sideboard where Willy was pulling the cork from a bottle of wine. 'He went up to this English tourist who must have been a ticket inspector or something like that and asked him for his autograph. The man wrote down Fred Bloggs, or whatever his name was, and Willy got into a rage and shouted at him and said he was an impostor.'

'Why?'

'He pretended he thought he was David Niven.'

'But he wasn't?'

'No, he didn't look anything like him.'

'I think I was muddling him up with Rex Harrison,' said Willy from across the room. 'They both live on Cap Ferrat.'

'He didn't look like Rex Harrison either,' said Charlie.

'*Nothing* like him,' said Helen with another squeal of laughter.

'We also went to the Villa Ephrussi,' said Charlie.

'And there Willy was even worse,' said Helen with wide, shining eyes. 'He kept interrupting the guide. "Non, *madame, vous avez tort.*" In the end they threw us out.'

'I hate all that reverent attention for a lot of junk,' said Willy, coming towards them with glasses of wine.

'It was terribly funny,' said Helen, sinking down into the sofa with a sigh of contentment.

'And what have you been up to?' Willy asked Simon with an expression of mild mockery in his eyes.

'Reading your old school books.'

'Which ones?'

'Herzen, of course, and then Carr.'

'From cover to cover?'

'No, just dipping in here and there.'

'It's a long time since I read Carr,' said Willy, sitting down in an armchair next to the fire.

'But you read him at Cambridge?'

'Oh yes. I went to his lectures. They had a great effect on me.'

'Your reputation, when I went up, was for debauchery rather than learning.'

Willy smiled. 'I lived on two levels: the flippant where I drank a lot and had endless friends, and a more serious level where I was alone.'

'Why did you never let others see your serious side?'

'I was brought up to believe that it was ill-bred to be earnest about anything – even love. But one had to study, after all. That was why one was there.'

'Did you go to those lectures by Carr on the meaning of history?'

'Yes.'

'They seem to me – and his earlier book too – to justify treason.'

Willy looked surprised. 'Do they really? He seemed such a reasonable fellow.'

'He talks about progress; about Britain and Europe passing the torch to Eastern Europe and Asia.'

'Is that treason?'

'I can imagine someone taking it as a justification for treason – a young Burgess or Philby, for example, deciding at the time of Suez that their government was frustrating history, and so doing what they could for the other side.'

Willy gulped down his wine. 'It's so long ago, now. I can hardly remember. Was Nasser the future and Eden the past? They must have thought that at the time of Cromwell and Charles I, but the Restoration followed, didn't it? You couldn't call Charles II an unhistorical figure – or Sadat, for that matter.'

'So you didn't accept Carr's fundamental philosophy of history?'

'Dear boy, I can't remember. Perhaps I did, for a time. I remember reading those books over and over again.'

'And Carr led you to Herzen?'

'Yes, but Herzen appealed to me more because his view of life encompassed everything – love and sex as well as politics and economics.'

'But Herzen was a traitor of a kind.'

'To whom.'

'To the Tsar.'

'Yes, of course, and the Russian Revolution makes him a prophet, just as a revolution in Western Europe in the 1990s will make Baader and Meinhof into the heroes of our time.'

'Would we have thought of Herzen and Herwegh as the Baader-Meinhof gang of the mid-nineteenth century?'

'I think so, don't you? If we were law-abiding Russian bourgeois of the 1860s. After all, one of Herzen's closest friends here in Nice was Orsini, who went on to throw a bomb at Napoleon III, like a member of the Red Brigade who murdered Moro in Rome.'

'Is all judgement, then, retrospective?'

'Yes. If Ireland is united, the Republican terrorists will be transformed from criminals into heroes. If Western Europe becomes Communist in the twenty-first century, Baader and Meinhof will give their names to streets and railway stations.'

They went upstairs to change, but the conversation about politics and history continued over dinner. It was, for the most part, a dialogue between Willy and Simon; and as the evening went on Simon became merely a prompt for Willy, who, with increasingly wild gestures, expounded upon everything without saying much. Certainly Simon, who had hoped he would inadvertently say something about the Djakarta leak, was disappointed.

The other three appeared bored by Willy's impromptu lecture, and in a lull Helen asked him what had happened to Herzen after he had left Nice.

'He went to London,' said Willy. 'He buried his wife by the castle here in Nice and then set off to London, never expecting to love again. And who should join him there but his old friend, Nick Ogarev, with another Natalie, Natalie Tuchkov, Ogarev's wife. They moved in with Herzen, and Natalie II fell for him. She shifted from Ogarev's bedroom to Herzen's. She bore him a daughter; then twins. Lucky Herzen? Not at all. Not only was he tormented by guilt at sleeping with the wife of his oldest friend, he was also stuck with a hideous, hysterical middle-aged Slav whose fits of neurosis could only be calmed *par les relations intimes*. In other words, to coin a phrase, he had to fuck her and fuck her and fuck her just to keep her quiet. What a fate! To feel guilty for something you don't even enjoy! *"Se sacrifier à ses passions, passe; mais à des passions qu'on n'a pas! Oh triste dix-neuvième siecle!"*'

'There's no evidence that he felt guilty at all,' said Priss crossly.

'He must have felt guilty,' said Willy.

'Why?'

'He was doing as he wouldn't be done by. The fateful symmetry.

His best friend seduces his wife: he suffers. He seduces the wife of his best friend: his best friend must suffer.'

'But Ogarev didn't suffer.'

'How do you know?'

'He was probably glad to be rid of the hideous, hysterical, middle-aged Natalie Tuchkov.'

'A man may be happy to be rid of his wife, but still not want to see her seduced by his best friend.'

'That would be unfair and inconsistent.'

'Or perhaps he just thought that adultery was wrong.'

'Don't be ridiculous,' said Priss fiercely. 'If it was an amicable agreement that Herzen should sleep with Ogarev's wife – and it must have been amicable because Ogarev didn't move out – then no one suffered. And if no one suffered, then nothing was wrong, so why should Herzen have felt guilty?'

'Even if no one suffers,' said Willy, 'one can feel guilty. There are the norms of the society one lives in.'

'Muddled, middle-class, Judeo-Christian norms,' said Priss angrily.

'Of course,' said Willy, as if conceding a point he had conceded many times before. 'Muddled, middle-class, Judeo-Christian norms . . .'

'Based upon religious beliefs he did not hold.'

'Yes.' Willy bowed his head.

'So give him the courage of his convictions,' said Priss, 'and admit that he didn't feel guilty.'

Will reached for the bottle and filled his glass. 'How in Hell can we know what he felt?' he said with a scowl. 'People don't always feel what they want to feel or what they're meant to feel. I don't even know what Simon feels, or Helen, or Charlie . . .' He looked wearily at Priss. 'I don't even know what you feel, and we've slept in the same bed for thirteen years.'

Simon awoke between three and four in the morning. Like many of those who are calm and judicious by day, he was often awakened by nervous anxiety at night. He lay listening to the wind in the palms outside his window. A shutter below had come loose and banged against the wall at irregular intervals. He wanted the noise to stop but his body was too heavy to rise from his bed. Instead phrases drifted in and out of his mind. He repeated conversations of the day before: he thought of Priss in the garden and suddenly the idea came to him that Willy was impotent.

He opened his eyes and stared into the dark. Willy was impotent and he was drunk, but was he drunk because he was impotent or impotent because he was drunk? Another riddle. But certainly he was impotent because only impotence could explain the paradox of Willy and Priss – a couple at once close yet pulling apart. Priss loved her husband but wanted Simon to make love to her.

This thought both alarmed and excited him as he lay on the edge of sleep. The image of her desire shocked his fastidious nature, but he was not immune to the vanity which nature foists on the male of any species; and the thought that she longed for him to do to her what her husband could not overcame all the reservations he had felt until now about sleeping with the wife of a friend. He lived in an age, after all, when the right to sexual fulfilment was thought equal to the right to life itself.

He was convinced that his hypothesis was right. It explained all the oddity of her flirtation that afternoon – an attempt to disguise desire as sentiment. But did Willy know? Did he suspect? Simon remembered the look of irony in his eye when Willy had asked him upon returning from Cap Ferrat what he had been up to. Was he alluding to the fact that he and Priss alone had decided to remain at the Villa Golitsyn? Yes, he must suspect, for it would explain the unusual vehemence of their argument at dinner about Herzen, Ogarev and Natalie Tuchkov. 'A man may be happy to be rid of his wife,' Willy had said, 'but still not want her to be seduced by his best friend.' Had that referred to him? And was the very fierceness with which Priss had attacked the concept of sexual guilt a defence of her own feelings that afternoon? Or an attempt to reassure him?

He would not fail her again. What scruples he had had were gone, and with a grim smile on his face Simon closed his eyes. He drew his body into a ball, and conjured up Priss in his imagination, naked and smiling like the concubine in the harem of a sultan. With her image in his mind he fell asleep.

Three

Simon came down the next day to find preparations already under way for an expedition into the mountains. Priss, the partner of his concupiscent dreams, walked briskly in and out of the kitchen carrying delicacies prepared by Aisha. She packed them into a wicker hamper which lay open on the table while Charlie stacked bottles of wine and mineral water into a cardboard box.

'It's going to be a beautiful day,' she said. 'We must get going as soon as we can.'

They set off soon after nine. Charlie drove the Jaguar with Willy beside him while Simon sat between the two girls on the back seat. Priss, if she had been angry with him the night before – if she had felt herself a woman scorned – had forgiven him now. Her chatter was addressed to everyone in the car, but she had turned her body away from the window to face Simon, and it was only to him that she looked for a reaction to what she said. Her glances had a special expression – not flirtatious, nor merely friendly, but humorous, comradely, as if they were the two grown-ups in charge of a group of children.

Simon's feelings towards her were now quite decided and calm. Desire, admiration, affection and respect had come together in a pleasure in her presence which was certainly a kind of love. Her blonde hair, her thin face, her almost bony arms and legs, now seemed to him quite perfect: and he basked in the confident feeling that should he want them they were his for the taking.

They took the old road from Nice to Turin. The mountains were savage and steep. Their very size and suddenness was what protected the coast from the colder climate of the rest of Europe and allowed the exotic vegetation and farouche society on the narrow strip of land between Menton and Antibes. With little effort from its powerful engine, the Jaguar carried them up the Col de Brouis, and then down again among mists and majestic pine trees towards the town of Sospel. Here they stopped to stretch their legs. Willy walked only twelve or fifteen paces to a café where he ordered a glass of cognac. The others, after a longer perambulation to look at the walls of the old town, sat at a table outside the same café where Willy stood at the

95

bar. Priss looked anxiously at the three empty glasses already lined up beside her husband. 'We'd better not be long,' she said. 'There's quite a long way to go.'

'I'm beginning to see the point of our licensing laws,' said Charlie, rising from his seat to go to Willy.

'Bring him out here,' said Priss.

He came, holding his glass, and when the waiter came with coffee for the others, he ordered yet another glass of cognac.

'Don't get paralytic, please,' said Priss. 'At least wait until lunch.'

'Do you know,' said Willy – paying no attention to what Priss had said – 'I think we're being followed.'

'By whom?' asked Charlie.

'A man, a very ordinary man, a Belgian, I think, with a camera slung around his neck.'

'What makes you think he's following us?' asked Simon.

'When we went up to the castle in Nice, do you remember? He was there.'

'He's probably just following the same *route touristique*,' said Priss.

'I could see him from the bar,' said Willy. 'He was watching you.'

'Paranoia,' said Charlie.

'Yes,' said Priss. 'It's a symptom of delirium tremens.'

'What's delirium tremens?' asked Helen.

'It's when people go mad from drinking too much,' said Willy. 'They think rats and mice are running all over their body . . .' He started to scream and kick and shiver as if the rats were crawling up his chair. Helen laughed. Simon paid the bill.

They drove on towards the Col de Brouis. Charlie swung the Jaguar around the hairpin bends at some speed, so that Simon was thrown alternately onto the plump body of Helen and the less comfortable but more welcome shoulders of Priss. At the top of the pass they stopped to let the engine cool down, and then descended more slowly into the valley of the Roya.

Here the landscape changed again. The road ran through narrow gorges, and although it was now midday, it became almost dark as the sun and sky were obscured by the high mountains and overhanging rocks. Then the river itself rose out of the gorge and they found themselves in less sombre Alpine countryside. At the village of Dalmas they turned off the main road, and drove along a narrow lane flanked with plane trees past fields of sun flowers and an orchard of peach trees.

'It's lovely,' said Helen, looking out on the flat little fields at the foot of the deep valley.

'When Cavour gave Nice to Napoleon III,' said Willy, 'he had to leave out this little piece of the country because it was the King of Italy's favourite hunting ground.'

They stopped again at the village of La Brigue. 'I'll get some fresh bread,' said Priss to Willy, 'if you get the key to the Chapel.' She set off with Helen in one direction while the three men walked across the square to the café on the far side.

'What chapel?' Simon asked Willy.

'Further up the valley,' said Willy, 'there's a charming little place of pilgrimage. Look . . .' He turned and pointed to the church of La Brigue, which was larger and more ornate than one would expect in a village of that size. 'Thousands of pilgrims used to pass through here, hoping for a miracle from Notre Dame des Fontaines. They must have done a very good trade, whereas now, alas, there's only a dribble of tourists.' They went into the café. 'That's why,' he whispered, 'it's terribly important not just to grab the key and move on, but to linger a little and patronize these poor people.' And with an expression of selfless benevolence on his face, Willy ordered three cognacs from the old man behind the bar.

Neither Simon nor Charlie wanted to drink brandy at that time of day so Willy, with a shrug of his shoulders, gulped them down himself. He then paid for the drinks, was given the key, and within a few minutes of entering the café was back in the bright light of the square. Priss and Helen took longer to buy the bread, and when they finally returned to the car Willy pretended to be cross. 'If only we had known you were going to be so long,' he said – winking at Simon and Charlie – 'we would have had time for a drink at the café.'

Priss now sat in the front of the car to guide Charlie out of La Brigue. They left on a narrow road which ran up the valley into the mountains. All cultivation had now ceased. The wilder growth of pine, beech and scrub oak lapped at the side of the road, which finally came to an end at the iron gates to the Chapel of Notre Dame des Fontaines.

'Let's have a quick look at the frescoes,' said Priss. 'Then we can walk a little further up the valley and have our picnic by the river in the woods.'

The outside of the chapel seemed to Simon of no particular

interest. It was a rectangular building of white painted stucco with a loggia at the front as a shrine for a statue of the Virgin. He could see, however, that its situation made it a good point for a day's excursion from Nice. It was perched on the steep side of the mountain, with a wilderness of rock and pine above, and a fast-running torrent below. The air smelt of the pines, and was filled with the sound of the falling water.

They walked from the car to the chapel and with some difficulty unlocked its heavy door. It creaked on its hinges but together with the seven or eight small clover-leafed windows it let in enough daylight to reveal an array of thirty vivid frescoes depicting the life of Christ. Priss and Willy let their guests enter first, and remained near the door as if to watch the effect these paintings would have on them. Simon, Charlie and Helen wandered forward towards the altar and then stood, their heads bent back, to study this work by a pious, obscure genius of five hundred years before.

On the altar itself there was a small statue of the Virgin Mary. She was dressed in a blue robe while the Christ-child in her arms wore a crown on his head. On the walls behind this statue were scenes from the life of the Virgin Mary, and on each side of the chapel others from the life of Christ. The back wall held a single giant painting of the Last Judgement – the Just rising to Heaven while the Damned went down to punishment in Hell. Their torments were vividly depicted, with some sinners strapped naked onto spiked wheels while others sank into a sea of flame, but the most awesome treatment of the suffering of a sinner was not among these Damned in the next world, but of one suffering remorse in this one – a separate panel on the left-hand wall showing the suicide of Judas Iscariot. He dangled by a rope from an orange tree. His hair was tangled and matted, his face contorted, his eyes demented, his swollen tongue stuck out from between his teeth. His body, half-clothed in a smock, had been disembowelled: his innards dangled free beneath his chest, and from among the liver and the spleen a tiny naked man – his soul – was claimed by a horned, hairy demon with an eagle's claws, bat's wings and a rat's tail.

'Nasty, isn't it?' said Willy, coming up behind Simon. They both stood in front of the painting.

'Very strong,' said Simon dryly, discomfited by the violence of the image before his eyes. 'The painter must have been the local butcher.'

Willy shook his head. 'You have to be more than a butcher to understand despair.' He turned away and started walking towards the door.

'It seems odd,' said Simon, 'that Judas suddenly lost the courage of his convictions and killed himself.'

'Remorse,' said Willy, stopping in front of the Last Judgement.

'Perhaps,' said Simon. 'But Peter also betrayed Christ and felt remorse, but he didn't kill himself.'

'He didn't despair.'

'So the sin of Judas was not that he betrayed Christ but that he despaired of forgiveness?'

'Yes,' said Willy. 'Despair was the sin.'

'And the suicide set the seal on his despair?'

'Yes,' said Willy, 'I think so. That's why suicide was always thought such a serious sin.'

The place Priss had chosen for a picnic was about quarter of a mile further up the valley. They walked there – Simon carrying the hamper, and the others the bottles of wine. Despite the altitude and the time of year, it was warm. Following Priss they clambered over rocks and trees by the river bank, passed through a narrow gorge and eventually reached a small plateau of soft dry grass. There was shade from the pine trees which surrounded it, and a view to the other side of the valley. They were isolated in the wilderness of the mountains: there was no sign of the hand of man.

Priss opened the hamper and laid out the food while Charlie put bottles of white wine and mineral water to cool in the stream. The others lay back, resting after the climb, breathing in the pure air and eyeing the *pâté en croute* and cold chicken laid out on a white tablecloth. When it was all spread before them, Priss told them to start, and with a minimum of polite reticence, they fell on the food and drink.

For a time there was silence: each concentrated on satisfying his appetite. In place of the white wine, which was not yet cold, they opened a couple of bottles of red Bergerac wine and when these quickly emptied, two more. The white wine was opened for the apple tart, melon and grapes. After that they drank coffee from a Thermos. Priss had thought of everything. Nothing had been overlooked.

Simon, now that his stomach was full, was reminded of his other appetites, and he studied Priss as she cleared up the picnic. He wondered if she would show the same methodical efficiency when she made love: that she would, with him, he did not now doubt, for every now and then, as she scraped scraps of bread and melon rind from the plates into a supermarket bag, she glanced at him with an intent and apprehensive expression, and when she had more or less cleared everything away, she came to him and said in a low but normal voice: 'How about a walk?'

'Yes.' He got to his feet.

She turned to the others. 'We're going on up the mountain,' she said. 'Do you want to come?'

Charlie blushed. 'I think I'll sit this one out,' he said.

'What about you, Will?' she said, turning to her husband, who lay on the grass with his eyes closed, apparently incapacitated by the wine. He opened one eye, then closed it, but said nothing.

'Helen?'

'I don't think I could,' she said. 'I feel a bit woozy.'

'We ought to leave at about four, or half-past,' said Priss, 'so if you wander off, make sure to be back here by then.'

They set off. Priss led the way on, over the boulders which flanked the mountain stream. Simon clambered after her, his eyes searching for footholds, and for roots or rocks which he might grip with his hands. He did not find it easy to keep up with Priss. She was sure-footed and fit, and perhaps had drunk less wine than he had; but her very health only made her more desirable. There was something tomboyish about her in her jeans and shirt, but that did not diminish her attractiveness either. The thought that she might remove the shirt and jeans with the same method and efficiency as she showed in climbing the mountain made Simon tremble, and he was only afraid that the climb would take so much of his energy that when the time came he would acquit himself badly.

He saw, however, that she had stopped and was standing on a flat rock in the sunlight, watching him climb up behind her with a look of amused mockery on her face.

'Hard work, isn't it?' she said.

'Yes,' he replied, stopping and panting just beneath her. 'I'm not in condition. It's what comes from working in an office.'

'We can have a rest,' she said, springing from the rock onto the bank. She disappeared from Simon's view and he tried to follow her, but for a time could not see how to climb onto the rock. He clambered towards the side of the river where the torrent, in spring, had gouged out the earth from the bank; and he squeezed past the roots from the tree above. When he got onto the small plateau further up, a grassy patch like that where they had eaten their picnic, he saw Priss lying on the far side, her head resting against a bank of moss at the base of a pine tree. He crossed to her, still panting. She smiled up at him.

'Are you all right?' she asked.

'Yes.'

'I don't want to give you a heart attack.' Again the slight mockery, her mouth turned down – a mannerism she must have learned from Willy.

'I'm out of condition, that's all.' He lay down beside her and stared at the sky.

'I'd like to live in the forest,' said Priss. 'Animals are so free, so uncomplicated.'

Simon had recovered his wind. He propped his body on his elbow and brought his face closer to hers. 'If we want to,' he said, 'we can be uncomplicated too.'

She blinked as she refocused her eyes on his. 'Yes, I know,' she said.

He brought his lips down to touch hers, and she lifted her arms to embrace him. He too then clutched her body and kept his mouth pressed to hers in a long, languorous kiss. He drew back to breathe. Her eyes were shut – clenched shut – but he had no time to study her expression, for as if from a nervous spasm her hand came up from his shoulder to the back of his head and entwining the fingers in his hair brought his face back to hers.

They kissed again. Half oblivious from emotion, half anxious about technique, Simon moved his left hand to her throat. She clutched him tighter. He went further. Nothing stopped the designs of his left hand. Indeed the way in which she clung to him encouraged its predatory progress down her body until suddenly her heavy, amorous breathing cracked into a cry of alarm, and her tight grip reversed itself with such strength and intensity that her whole body jack-knifed and sprang back from his own onto the grass.

There for a moment she lay shaking and sobbing like the victim of a crude assault. Then she sat up again, and with her clothes still in disarray, wept on Simon's shoulder. He said nothing. He sat, one arm propping up his body which now supported hers; the other – the right – was timidly placed on her shoulders as if ashamed of what the left had done.

In time the sobbing subsided. She sniffed, wiped her nose on her wrist, and in a matter-of-fact manner rearranged her clothes. 'I'm sorry,' she said at last.

Simon said nothing. He could think of nothing to say.

Her eyes were on the buttons of her blouse. 'It's . . .' she began; then she looked up, shook her head, and said: 'I don't know how to explain.'

'You needn't say anything,' said Simon.

'No, you see I thought I could go through with it. I wanted to because it's so unfair to you.' She stopped.

'You don't have to worry about me,' said Simon, not quite meaning what he said because he still felt the ache of his frustrated passion.

'I just couldn't,' she said, shaking her head and looking down at her feet.

'I had hoped that . . . that you liked me,' said Simon.

'Oh, but I do, I do.' She turned and looked at him, her eyes still holding tears. 'I do like you, more than anyone except . . .' Her voice tailed off. 'Except Will.'

'I understand,' said Simon. 'It's just that I thought you wanted to. I would never otherwise . . .'

'I did,' she said quietly. 'I did want to, and I want Will to have *her*.'

'Who?'

'Helen. I thought that if we went off together, they might go off together, except that Will's so drunk.'

Simon looked nonplussed, and seeing the baffled expression on his face, Priss went on: 'She could have a baby, you see, and I know that if he had a son he would stop drinking.'

Suddenly Simon thought he saw into the scheme in this woman's mind. 'So my role,' he said sourly, 'was to make Willy jealous enough to father a child by Helen?'

She looked up, alarmed by his tone of voice. 'Oh no, I do love you,' she said, clutching his hand. And then she added, in a quiet confidential whisper: 'I've never said that I loved anyone other than Will', as if that accolade was worth more than any amount of copulation.

'I never meant to take you from Willy,' said Simon.

'I know,' she said, 'I know. But I've only ever slept with him and just now I couldn't . . . I couldn't bring myself to do it with you. It felt wonderful at first but then . . . terrible.' She shuddered and was silent for a moment. 'But it's an awful way to behave, I know. You have every right to be angry.'

'I'm not angry.'

'You're very good,' she said.

'No,' said Simon, 'but I'm old enough to know how these things happen.'

She smiled and stood up. 'We'd better get back.'

'Yes.'

They went to the stream, where she bathed her face in the cold water.

'Do you think that Willy fancies Helen?' asked Simon.

'Yes. Don't you?'

'There's a big difference in age.'

'That's what he likes – her youth. He never really fancied *women*, you see – wide thighs, big busts and that sort of thing. You're all a bit like that, aren't you?'

'Suppressed queers,' said Simon.

She smiled. 'That must be it.'

'Except Charlie.'

'Except Charlie.'

'And does Helen fancy Willy, do you think?'

'She seems to like him.'

'Yes, but holding hands is one thing. Going to bed with him is another.'

'I think she would,' said Priss – the creasing of her brow revealing how much she had thought about this before. 'At that age what one wants more than anything else is to be counted as a grown-up – to escape the stigma of being a child.'

'Perhaps.'

'She'd sleep with you or Charlie or Will just to be accepted as one of us. I'm sure of it.'

'And have a child?'

Priss frowned again. 'It would only take nine months out of her life. I'd look after it after that.'

'And what would happen to Helen?'

'She could go home.' She gave Simon a hard look, as if defying him to say that he disapproved of her scheme. 'She wouldn't want the child, would she?' she asked. 'Not at seventeen?'

'No. I dare say she wouldn't.'

They set off over the rocks by the side of the stream. Again Priss drew ahead, leaping from stone to stone while Simon, with wobbly knees, clambered, slithered, sat and dropped down the mountain, using both his hands and feet. Every now and then Priss would wait for him to catch up with her, but as soon as he had done so she would smile and move on.

The sun had moved down in the sky behind the tops of the mountains when they got back to the site of the picnic, so although it was only four the light was dim and at first there seemed to be no one there. Then they saw Helen and Charlie standing in the stream, both with their jeans tucked up to their knees.

'There you are,' said Charlie, avoiding both their eyes. 'I was beginning to think you might be lost.'

'It's only four,' said Priss. 'I said we'd be back by four.'

'What have you been doing here?' Simon asked, looking at the barrier of rock built across the stream.

'We wanted to make a pool and swim,' said Helen, 'but it still isn't really deep enough.'

'And we've missed the moment,' said Charlie, wiping his hands on his jeans. 'It's too cold now anyway.'

'Where's Will?' asked Priss.

'I don't know. He went off soon after you.'

'Where?'

Charlie still did not look into her eyes. 'I don't know. In that direction.' He waved towards the woods. 'I thought he might have met up with you.'

Priss bit her lower lip. Simon glanced at her anxiously, but if she saw his look she paid no attention. 'He must have gone back to the car,' she said.

They gathered up the empty wine bottles and the picnic basket, and set off back down the stream to the track which ran along the valley. Above them they could see the shafts of pink sunlight which shone from one side to illuminate the peaks on the other. They were all now tired, and the effects of the wine had worn off to leave them with heavy limbs and dizzy heads. They spoke little: only Simon, at one point, drew close to Priss and said: 'He can't have seen us, can he?'

She shook her head. 'I don't think so. He would never have made it over those rocks.'

He was not at the car. They packed the bottles and hamper into the boot and then looked towards the darkening pine forest all around them.

'I hope to God he hasn't passed out somewhere up there,' said Priss.

Charlie shouted for him but there was no reply.

'Perhaps he's in the chapel,' said Helen.

'Has he got the key?' asked Priss.

'Yes,' said Charlie. 'We left it with him.'

Simon volunteered to go and see. He walked to the gates and when he reached the door of the chapel saw that it was ajar. He pushed it further open. The interior was almost dark. There was a pool of light around four or five votary candles which burned by the altar, but it took Simon a few moments to accustom his eyes to the gloom. He blinked, crossed to the aisle and there saw Willy – his tall figure still and silent as a statue in front of the painting of Judas.

'Willy,' he said, 'it's time to go.'

His voice echoed in the empty church but Willy made no reply. Neither by word nor gesture did he acknowledge that Simon was there, so Simon walked towards him and saw, as he came closer, the marks of two rivulets of tears which had run from his eyes over the flaky skin of his cheeks.

'What's up?' he asked without thinking – and when Willy still did not reply, the thought came to Simon with an accompanying sour unease that Willy had indeed followed them up the valley, had witnessed what had transpired, and was now, in contemplating Judas, thinking of the friend who had betrayed him. 'Willy, I'm sorry ...' he stuttered. 'I didn't mean, that's to say ...' His apology petered out.

Will did not appear to be listening. He no longer wept but his eyes remained on the fresco. Then he sighed and said, quite quietly: 'There's nothing to be done.'

Still thinking that Willy was referring to his attempt to seduce his wife, Simon said: 'That's very decent of you, Willy.'

Now Willy turned and looked at him. 'Decent? What's decent about it?'

'Well, not holding it against Priss or ...'

'She's blameless,' he said. 'Women always are. They follow where we lead. You can never blame them.'

'Then it's decent of you not to hold anything against me.'

'You? What has it got to do with you?' He looked surprised – almost annoyed – as if a servant had presumed too great a familiarity.

Simon turned towards the dark interior of the church for fear that his confusion might show itself on his face. 'You looked upset,' he said, 'and I thought it might be because Priss and I went off for a walk together.'

'Don't be a fool, Simon. I didn't want to climb that bloody mountain.'

'Then what has upset you?'

'Thoughts, just thoughts.'

'Of the past?' Simon had recovered his composure: he looked at Willy with an alert curiosity.

'Yes.'

'That act you mentioned earlier – the sin against conventional morality?'

'That act, yes.'

'Was it also an act of betrayal?'

'Betrayal? Yes, in a way.'

'One can always confess a sin,' said Simon in a quiet, coaxing tone of voice.

Willy laughed, then coughed, and the sounds were again amplified in the hollow church. 'No, dear boy,' he said. 'I can't confess because I can't repent, and I can't repent because I'm not sorry. That is what leads to despair. To feel acute remorse yet know that one would do what one did all over again.' He glanced at Judas for the last time, and then walked down the aisle towards the back of the chapel.

'But what was it?' Simon asked, coming after him. 'What did you do that you would do again?'

Willy stopped by the fresco of the Last Judgement, and for a moment Simon thought that he was about to answer the question; but if he had heard it, he ignored it and instead he pointed to the depiction of Christ sitting at the right hand of the Father. 'Do you think he is up there, Simon, waiting to judge us for what we have done down here?'

'No,' said Simon. 'It's a myth, a fable.'

'I hope you're right,' said Willy, 'because we'll look such fools if you're wrong, going down *there*' – he pointed to the picture of Hell – 'for all eternity.'

Four

Like Willy, Simon had formed a picture in his mind of Charlie's American girlfriend, Carmen Baker, envisaging a lithe, blonde Californian nymphet with a boy's buttocks squeezed into skin-tight jeans. The girl whom Charlie brought back from the airport the next day was so different from this image that had Charlie not been standing behind her, Simon would not have believed it was the same person. She was short, plump and dark with a large bosom and wide thighs — the bosom squashed by a tight black tee shirt, the thighs shrouded by a padded, patchwork skirt.

'Hi,' she said as Charlie presented her to his friends just as they were sitting down to lunch at the Villa Golitsyn.

'How nice to see you,' said Priss, coming around the table to greet the new arrival and guiding her to the empty chair next to Simon.

'Charlie has told us so much about you,' said Simon as she sat down.

'And *me* about *you*,' she said.

The leather-faced Aisha offered Carmen a dish of stuffed peppers.

'Oh God,' said Carmen, 'I don't know if I could eat a thing.' She looked at her watch. 'It's something like four in the morning for me.'

'Did you come straight from America?' asked Priss.

'Straight from LA to Paris, and then on from Paris to Nice,' said Carmen. She spoke and smiled in a deliberate, almost exaggerated, way — as if on stage. She had bright brown eyes but a bad complexion, and the skin on her upper lip was as smooth as the surface of an egg, as if the hair was regularly removed by a cosmetician.

'I'm an expert on jet-lag,' said Simon. 'I used to fly back and forth between London and Jedda.'

'What should one do?'

'Don't drink alcohol on the plane.'

She laughed — a stage laugh. 'Too late, I'm afraid.'

'Don't go to sleep after lunch. Stay awake until it's time to go to bed over here.'

Despite her stated lack of appetite, Carmen was eating the stuffed peppers. 'Well, you'll have to think of some way to keep me awake,' she said, 'because otherwise I'll just collapse.'

'A swim,' said Charlie.

'Isn't the water kind of polluted around here?' she asked. 'I read an article in *Time* which said that the Mediterranean was just a cesspool.'

'It's not too bad,' said Priss dryly, 'especially if you drive out to Cap Ferrat or Cap d'Antibes.'

'I'd like to see things,' said Carmen. 'Isn't there that Matisse chapel somewhere around here?'

'In Vence,' said Charlie.

'Can we go see that?'

'Of course.'

'And there's a nice little Matisse museum up in Cimiez,' said Priss.

'Great,' said Carmen. 'I'm really hungry for the whole Côte d'Azur experience.' She put down her knife and fork: the stuffed peppers had gone into her stomach.

Willy, who had said nothing since Carmen had arrived, now covered his face with his hands and started to make odd sounds which might have been groans or sobs or the hiccups of suppressed laughter.

'Let's go and have coffee in the garden,' said Priss quickly, rising from her chair.

The others all obeyed but Willy remained seated – his face still covered by his hands.

'Is he all right?' asked Carmen, who seemed to sense that Willy's behaviour was somehow directed at her.

'Don't pay any attention,' said Priss. 'He likes to disconcert people when they arrive.'

Carmen looked baffled. 'Oh, I see,' she said.

'Ask Helen,' said Charlie, coming to lead his fiancée into the garden. 'He tried to embarrass you, didn't he?'

'It's only a joke,' said Helen in the casual tone of someone who was already an old hand at the Villa Golitsyn.

They went out into the garden. Simon waited with Willy. The sounds stopped. The hands remained over the face but a space appeared between the third and fourth fingers of the right hand, and a bloodshot eye peered out. 'Has she gone?' Willy whispered.

'They're in the garden.'

The hands came down from his face and reached for the bottle of wine. 'Now tell me,' said Willy in a quiet, reasonable tone of voice, 'you who know so much about human nature. What strange, unresolved complex from his childhood compels a blonde little fairy like Charlie to fall for an old bag like that.'

'She didn't seem old,' said Simon.

'But a *bag*. You don't dispute that, I hope?'

'One shouldn't judge by appearances.'

'And how else should one judge? One look at me – a drunk. One look at you – a civil servant. One look at her – a bag.'

'But a bag of what?'

'Californian pretentiousness. Or, in her patois, a bag of bullshit.'

'We shall see.'

'Shall we? Must we?'

'I think so. For Charlie. Don't you?'

'Make an effort?'

'We owe it to him.'

'Yes,' said Willy. 'Dear Charlie.'

Willy did make an effort that afternoon, and again that evening at supper. Carmen received many a broadside of Ludley charm, and responded by relaxing, preening and laughing 'hilariously' just as she must have been taught to laugh 'hilariously' at her acting school in Hollywood. The others watched, fascinated not – as she may have supposed – by her wit and charm, but by Willy's controlled performance. Charlie, originally anxious, seemed relieved that some sort of rapport had been established between his host and his girlfriend, and only Helen looked irritated that the newcomer should have so much of Willy's attention.

The evening passed without incident. Charlie and Carmen retired early on the pretext of Carmen's exhaustion – although Charlie by this time looked more tired than she did, and Carmen, before leaving the room, gave a stagey 'wanton' chuckle as if to intimate that there were *other reasons* for wanting to go early to bed.

The others followed soon after. Willy had drunk less than usual and climbed the stairs without assistance. Simon and Helen both went to their rooms at the same time as the Ludleys – Simon with the particular anguish felt by a man who sees the woman he loves retire to bed with her husband.

The weather the next morning was so fine that Simon, when he came down, took his coffee and croissant out into the garden. Being the first he had claimed the copy of *Nice-Matin* and saw with some satisfaction that it was cold and wet in the rest of Europe.

Priss was the next to appear. She blushed when she saw Simon, and he too looked confused. She was not yet dressed, but wore a white silk dressing-gown over her nightdress, and the very intimacy and informality of these clothes only reminded Simon of what was not his. Ever since Priss had so blithely suggested that Willy should father a child by Helen, Simon had felt obliged to abandon his hypothesis that Willy was impotent, and he imagined now that she had made love with Willy the night before, or even that morning — perhaps only minutes before.

'Did you sleep well?' Priss asked solicitously with just that admixture of intimacy and embarrassment shown by a woman to a man who is and yet is not her lover.

'Yes,' he said curtly — as if it was none of her business. 'What about you?'

She blushed again. 'Well enough,' she said — and then, as if in reply to the question he had not put to her, she added: 'Willy always goes out like a light and sleeps like a log.' As she spoke she sat down on a chair beside his. 'We're being very lucky with the weather,' she went on. 'I thought it might be an idea to go out on the boat today.'

Simon said nothing.

'Would you like that?' she asked.

'Yes. Why not?'

'Some people hate sailing, and I don't want to force you out on expeditions if you'd rather stay here and read . . .'

'No. I should like to go on the boat.'

'Then I'd better go and wake the others,' she said. 'We don't want to leave too late.'

Willy was captain of the *Clöe*, Simon, Helen and Carmen were the passengers, and Charlie and Priss were the crew. As they unpacked the sails and prepared the boat for sea, Willy became agitated: he pranced around the boat, shouting at Priss to do this and Charlie to do that; but while the crew appeared to obey his orders, it soon became apparent to Simon that they had a will of their own — they cast off, started the engine and raised the sails only after muttered discussions among themselves, not in obedience to the captain's orders.

Willy either did not notice this insubordination or did not care. He was, it seemed, playing out his role as 'Ludley man of action', his profile proffered to his guests like that of an actor posing for the camera. Thus with Priss at the tiller and Charlie raising the sails, they passed out of the harbour and turned to the West across the bay. The sea was quite calm but there was a slight breeze from the south: they set course for the Iles de Lerins.

It was not easy to talk against the crackle of the canvas and the slapping sound of the prow hitting the water. They therefore remained silent, content with the spectacle before them – the blue sky, the mountains and beneath them the whole length of the city of Nice lit by the silvery sunlight. Willy and Helen sat forward, leaning against one another and trying to spot the Villa Golitsyn through a pair of binoculars. Every now and then a Boeing or an Airbus would fly over them as it made its approach to the airport. They passed close to where these landed – to the spit of silt formed by the Var where now huge lorries were emptying earth into the sea – extending the land on which the runways had been built to make room for a new port for the Côte d'Azur. They then altered course towards the Napoleonic fortress at Antibes, rounded the Cap d'Antibes, and came in sight of the Iles de Lerins.

They docked the boat at the first – the Ile Sainte Marguerite – and ate lunch at a restaurant near the jetty. Ferries from Cannes came and went with their sparse cargoes of late-season tourists. The sun shone. They drank wine as they waited for the food, and then more wine as the food was served.

'This is great,' said Carmen with a guttural sigh. 'It's really beautiful here. I mean, I can see why all those rich guys come out here. There are other nice places, I guess, but this scenery and this weather in *October* . . .'

'I'm so glad you like it,' said Willy. 'I thought you might be homesick for Malibu beach.'

'My God, why should I be homesick for Malibu beach?'

'Or Venice,' said Willy. 'Isn't there a charming little port, rather like Villefranche, near Los Angeles called Venice? With lots of handsome homosexuals dressed in leather . . .'

'Have you been to Venice?' asked Carmen.

'No, alas. I've been to the other Venice, but only I assure you because it was nearer. Given the chance, I'd much rather have one of those beefy buggers in *your* Venice than a weedy gondolier from *ours*.'

Carmen looked a little confused. She glanced at Charlie but

Charlie only smiled. She then looked at Priss, but Priss was paying no attention to their conversation. She therefore leaned across the table and said quietly to Willy: 'You're not, er, gay, are you?'

'Bisexual, dear girl, bisexual. Everyone's both these days.'

'Well, great, that's great,' said Carmen. 'I'm certainly glad you're not, well . . . I was afraid you might be a little uptight about that sort of thing.'

'And a friend of Charlie's? Not at all. We're upper-class, you see, and the British upper classes have always been awfully broad-minded. We leave morality to the bourgeoisie, don't we, Priss dear? They're the ones who disapprove.'

Priss still paid no attention.

'Well, that's great,' said Carmen, 'just great.'

After lunch they went back to the boat and sailed to the other side of the island. There they dropped anchor and – taking turns to change in the cabin – dived into the sea and swam ashore. Willy led the way. He swam in an eccentric style, somewhat like a frog, with his neck craning out of the water, and when he reached the shore lay down on his back on the sand with his eyes closed in ironic appreciation of the sun. Priss, who came after him, placed her long, elegant body next to his – its health and colour a marked contrast to the pallor of Willy's limbs and torso, and the way the skin hung loosely over his ribs.

After Priss came Helen, who set herself down at Willy's other side, giggling at his parody of a sunbathing man. Then came Simon, Charlie and last of all Carmen, who reached the shore and pulled herself out of the water just as Willy opened his eyes.

He screamed. Priss and Simon who had been lying on their stom-achs both spun round to see what was wrong and were confronted as Willy had been with Carmen's two enormous naked breasts.

'Am I the only one topless?' she asked with disingenuous cheerful-ness. 'I thought everyone went topless in the South of France.'

'Yes, well, a lot of people do,' said Priss, rearranging herself on the sand.

Willy had closed his eyes again: indeed he clenched them shut.

'Well,' said Carmen, lying down quite close to her host, 'I just hate constrictions of *any* kind.'

Willy groaned.

'Why don't you go topless?' Carmen asked Priss.

'Oh, I'm too old.'

'*You* should,' Carmen said to Helen.

'No, I . . . er . . . I just couldn't.'

Willy opened one eye. Carmen was lying on her back, her head propped up against the rubber flippers she had worn to swim from the boat. Her breasts, which while she was standing had hung like overripe fruit from a tree, now in obedience to gravity retreated like well-set blancmange. Only the pigmented flesh around the nipples, and the nipples themselves, protruded from the fluid mass of white flesh as if ginger biscuits surmounted by *glacé* cherries had been placed on top of the puddings.

'It appears,' said Willy, comparing the whiteness of her breasts with the brown colour of her stomach, 'that you don't indulge this freedom in California.'

She laughed. 'Sure I don't. You'd be arrested if you went topless on Malibu.'

'So the Land of the Free is not as free as all that?'

'I guess not.'

'And all the women in California have brown bodies with white tits?'

'I guess so.'

'I wonder if it will pass into their genes,' Willy asked rhetorically, 'producing a race of skewbald women.'

'And boys with white asses,' said Carmen with a laugh.

'Yes. Quite right.' Willy turned to Charlie. 'Charlie-boy, you'd better bare your buttocks.'

'After you, Willy.'

'It doesn't matter about me. I'm not likely to father any children. And anyway, my balls are brown already.'

'Shut up, Will,' said Priss. 'You're going too far.'

'But Carmen doesn't mind that sort of talk, do you, Carmen?'

'I don't mind *anything*.'

'Then think of Helen,' said Priss.

'Oh, *I* don't mind,' said Helen quickly.

'Then think of me,' said Priss.

'But Priss, my dear,' said Willy, 'we can't keep our conversation clean just for a prude like you. I mean to say, what was the point of all that rebellion in the sixties if we can't say fuck and shit and balls and cunt and that sort of thing.'

'Right,' said Carmen.

'You agree with me, don't you?' said Willy, turning to Carmen as if for support.

'Sure I do,' said Carmen.

'Isn't that what 1968 was all about – smoking what you liked, sniffing what you like, bare breasts, bare bums, fucking here, there and everywhere?'

'It *was*,' said Carmen.

'Fucking men, women, girls, boys . . .'

'Anything.'

'Straights, gays, animals, vegetables . . .'

'Wow.'

'Wouldn't you agree,' said Willy to Carmen in a tone of great sincerity, 'that if you – tonight – were to go to bed with a cucumber, and I with a goat, we would be affirming the values of the age in which we live?'

'Sure,' said Carmen, 'only . . .'

'Only what?'

'Well, I'd prefer Charlie to a cucumber.'

'Oh quite,' said Willy, 'and I'd prefer Charlie to a goat.'

He laughed, lay back and closed his eyes again. The others said nothing. Only Carmen, either because she came from another country or because she knew him less well, had failed to catch the exasperated irony in Willy's tone of voice. Charlie, who must have realized what was going on, lay with an impassive expression on his face, as if indifferent to the fate of his fiancée at the hands of his friend.

'Do you know what would be nice?' said Carmen suddenly.

'Tell us,' said Willy. 'What would be nice?'

'France without the French.'

'France without the French,' Willy repeated after her. 'I had never thought of that. How would you like to see it. Depopulated altogether? Or colonized by Americans?'

'And the British too.'

'We're doing our best down here,' said Willy, 'but you I take it would like to see hot dog stands and pubs instead of restaurants and cafés all over the country?'

'Well . . .'

'And cups of tea and iced water replacing claret and Burgundy?'

'No, well, I guess I'd like to keep their wine and food, but not the people. I mean, they're so rude . . .'

'They may be a little touchy,' said Willy, 'but that's because they feel themselves to be a beleaguered nation – a chosen people, their civilization the Ark of the Covenant – surrounded by hordes of Slav and Anglo-Saxon Philistines. And can you blame them?'

'You can blame them,' said Simon, 'for not accepting that their civilization, like ours, has had its day.'

'What? Like the old Venice and the new one? Europe has had its day?'

'Hasn't it?' asked Simon. 'Hasn't the torch been passed to Russia and America?'

'Not at all,' said Willy. 'They have more powerful armies, that's all.'

'What is a nation, anyway?' said Charlie. 'Just a group of people living on the same piece of land.'

'No,' said Willy, 'it's more. Much more. That's the mistake made by Marx. Because he was a Jew, and the Jews were scattered all over the world, he underestimated men's natural ties to their tribes and nations.'

'But look at you,' said Simon. 'Do you think of yourself as English any more?'

'More than ever.'

'But you've lived abroad for seventeen years. You have more in common now with other expatriates in the South of France than you do with the kind of people who inhabit the British Isles.'

'No,' said Willy forcefully. 'It's only when you do live abroad that you realize how much you belong to your native land.'

'But the English you used to know – the sort who played cricket on the village green – don't exist any more.'

'You're much the same as you used to be.'

'I'm an anachronism.'

'Someone must still live there,' said Priss.

'Oh yes,' said Simon. 'There are fifty million or so, but you wouldn't recognize them and they wouldn't recognize you. They wear anoraks and donkey-jackets, and their heads are full of half-digested Marx and Freud.'

'I don't mind what they think or what they wear,' said Willy. 'I still feel I'm English, that England is my home, that I belong there in a way I have never belonged anywhere else.'

'Then why don't you live there?' asked Carmen.

Willy turned and glared at her. 'Because the girls don't bare their breasts,' he said. 'I'm hooked on tits, and this is the only place where I can get a regular fix.'

Five

Aware that it would soon grow cold, they swam back to the boat after only an hour on the beach and set sail for Nice. Once again they took it in turns to change back from their bathing suits into their clothes, and once again Carmen was the last – remaining for most of the voyage at the front of the boat, proffering her naked bust to the wind like the figurehead on the prow of an old clipper.

They were back at the Villa Golitsyn by six. Once in his room, Simon rinsed the salt water out of his bathing trunks, hung them over the bath, took a shower and changed. He came down again soon after eight to find Willy drinking by the sideboard in the drawing-room, making up for his relative abstemiousness earlier in the day by throwing one glass of wine after another down his throat.

'I can't stand that stupid bitch much longer,' he said to Simon as he came in.

'She's not too bad,' said Simon.

'She gets on my nerves.'

'Think of Charlie.'

'How can he stand her? Those bloody great tits . . .'

'Perhaps that's what he always wanted.'

'Impossible.' Willy emptied another glass. 'She must have some sort of hold over him.'

Simon shook his head. 'He's probably happy to have found a woman who accepts him as he is.'

'I hate that kind of compromise,' said Willy vehemently.

'It's probably the best he could do – in women.'

'Then he should stick to men.'

Helen came down next, wearing black slacks and a white blouse, followed by Priss from the kitchen, where she had put the finishing touches to a supper prepared by Aisha. 'We can eat whenever you're ready,' she said.

'Priss,' said Willy – his speech now slurred – 'We've got to get rid of that woman. She's got to go.'

'Hush,' said Priss.

'If I see those bloody great udders once again, I'll be sick,' said

116

Willy. 'I swear it, I'll chuck up.'

'The weather's turning,' said Priss. 'We won't be sunbathing much more.'

'Her voice,' said Willy, putting his hands to his ears. 'And her vacuous opinions. I can't bear it.'

'You must. For Charlie's sake.'

'He can't like that cow.'

'She may be the only girl he'll ever get,' said Priss.

'You women are always the same,' said Willy. 'You think that marriage is paradise when it mostly turns out to be hell.'

Priss made no rejoinder. 'Where are they, anyway?' he asked.

'I don't know.' Priss looked at her watch. 'It's quite late. Perhaps I'd better call them.' She rose, went into the hall and shouted for Charlie and Carmen. Her soft voice could hardly have carried to the attic, but a few moments later, as the others made their way to the table, they appeared looking flushed and embarrassed.

'Sorry to be late,' said Charlie.

'Been fucking?' asked Willy.

'Shut up, Will,' said Priss.

'What's wrong?' he asked with mock innocence. 'There's nothing wrong with an engaged couple jumping the gun, is there, dear? After all, we did.'

'That's not what I meant,' said Priss.

'Oh, I see,' he drawled. 'You mean one shouldn't talk about fucking at table.'

'I'd rather you didn't.'

'Like crapping and pissing?'

'Yes.'

'What do you think?' He turned to Carmen, who had just sat down at his right hand. 'Do you think that fucking and crapping come into the same category?'

'Oh no,' said Carmen coyly. 'I think it's wonderful.'

'Crapping?'

She laughed. 'No. Fucking.'

'So why not talk about it?'

'*I* don't mind.'

'Well I do,' said Priss irritably.

'Priss is very odd,' said Willy – still facing Carmen, and talking to her quietly as if no one else could hear their conversation. 'On the one hand she says that copulation is like eating – the simple fulfilment of a natural appetite – and of course she's not embarrassed to talk about food in bed; but on the other hand she is embarrassed, and thinks it's bad taste, to talk about sex at table.'

'Well, they are kind of different,' said Carmen.

'Of course,' said Willy. 'The holes are at different ends of the body.'

Carmen laughed again, but with a little less certainty. 'Sure,' she said with affected irony. 'That's the only difference.'

'*You* don't have complexes and neurosis about sex, do you?' Willy asked.

'I hope not,' said Carmen.

'It's quite extraordinary that *in this day and age*' – he pronounced those five words with exaggerated emphasis – 'people's sexual behaviour is still inhibited by the old-fashioned values of a superstitious age.'

'Extraordinary,' said Carmen.

' "Where the bee sucks, there suck I," ' said Willy. 'That's my motto.'

'Mine too.'

'And buggery,' said Willy. 'All our complexes about buggery stem from our overzealous nannies who to persuade us to sit on a potty taught us that shit was nasty and naughty . . .'

'I didn't have a nanny,' said Carmen.

'Lucky Charlie,' said Willy.

'It was the sort of people who did have nannies,' said Simon, 'who later turned out to be queer.'

'Then my theory has a reverse validity,' said Willy. 'It was just because the nannies were so strict that the bum was made to seem sinful and exciting.'

'That's more like it,' said Simon. 'It explains why all those Cambridge spies were queer as well. They were irresistibly drawn by the excitement of doing what was forbidden.'

'That's nonsense too,' said Priss, frowning, as if reluctant to be drawn into the conversation. 'It was just that they all went to boys' boarding schools and had nowhere else to go.'

'But up the bums of the fourth-formers,' said Willy. 'Was that all it was, *Carlo mio*? I like to think it was something more.'

Charlie blushed.

'Cut it out, Willy,' said Simon.

'Cut what out?' asked Willy in a tone of sweet reason. 'The past? Are we ashamed of our past?'

118

'I'm not ashamed of anything,' said Charlie.

'Quite right,' said Willy.

'All the same, it's a little tasteless,' said Simon.

'Tasteless?' Again, the pose of innocence.

'It's not very nice for Carmen,' said Priss.

'But Carmen doesn't mind, do you my dear?' Willy turned to give Carmen an open, trusting smile.

She looked baffled. 'Well, I guess not.'

'There are such things as privacy and discretion,' said Priss.

'Pfui,' said Willy. 'Bourgeois hangups. Don't you think so, Carmen?'

'I guess I do.'

'I'm so glad,' said Willy. He raised his head and rolled his blood-shot eyes. His face had gone a mottled red and the pitch of his voice grew higher as he spoke. 'What I like about you is your Californian candour. These English girls . . .' – he waved his hand towards Priss and Helen – 'are so inhibited. Priss knew about Charlie and me. She always knew, and she didn't mind, but she never liked to *talk* about it . . .'

Carmen looked baffled. 'About what?'

'About Charlie and me,' he repeated.

'What about Charlie and you?'

'Didn't you know? We had an affair. We were lovers.'

She blushed. 'Yes, well, I sort of knew that Charlie was gay – I mean, that he used to be.'

'I seduced him,' said Willy in a sweet, high-pitched hiss. 'I was his first lover.'

Carmen now looked dark. 'Sure, well, I don't mind.'

'And neither does Priss, do you dear?'

Priss did not answer. She stood, picked up some plates, and went through the green baize door into the kitchen.

'And neither does Charlie,' said Willy. He too now got to his feet. He went to Charlie and – standing behind his chair – embraced him. 'You remember, don't you, *Carlito mio*? Lying on the scratchy bracken? The dead leaves tickling your little bum?' He put his mouth to Charlie's ear and said in an audible whisper: 'Let's do it again, Charlie. Let's do it now. Come on . . . away from these ghastly women. Come on, come upstairs with me.'

Carmen sat dumbfounded.

'Willy,' said Charlie in a strange, choking voice. 'Willy, please, cut it out.'

'Come on, *Carlito*,' Willy went on in the same coaxing, high-pitched whisper. 'She won't mind, that old bag of yours. She said so. She can watch us if she likes, if she feels left out . . .'

'No, Willy,' said Charlie – his voice still gurgling, not with anger but with an attempt to suppress tears.

Carmen's wide eyes narrowed at last. 'For God's sake, Charlie,' she shouted. 'Get rid of this creep. Push him away.' She stood and grabbed at Willy's arm but Willy only hugged harder and buried his face in Charlie's neck while Charlie merely held on to Willy's wrists as if taking his pulse: he made no attempt to break his embrace.

Priss came back into the room. 'What the hell's going on?' she said.

Willy raised his head. 'Here she comes,' he shouted triumphantly. 'Here comes . . .'

He did not finish his sentence. He stopped. His eyes moved back into his skull, and then slowly like a collapsing chimney stack, he fell to the floor.

For a moment no one moved. They thought it was a further display of Willy's tomfoolery – the exit line for an awkward scene; but then Simon and Charlie looked down and saw that he was helpless on the floor. He was not unconscious. His eyes were open and he tried to rise of his own accord, but he could not, so the two other men took hold of his arms and lifted him to his feet.

They carried him upstairs and laid him on the large four-poster bed. Then, while Charlie went down to see to the wounded feelings of his fiancée, Simon helped Priss remove the clothes from Willy's emaciated body. It had now become difficult to tell whether he was conscious or not. Every now and then his eyes opened and he struggled feebly, as if humiliated to be treated in this way. Red blotches had appeared on his face, and when they covered him with sheets and blankets he tried to kick them off. Only when they left him uncovered would he lie still.

'Would you ask Helen to make him some warm milk?' Priss whispered to Simon as she sat by the bed holding Willy's bony hand.

He went down and delivered this request to Helen, who sat alone in the large drawing-room. He followed her into the kitchen and watched as she cut open the cardboard container and emptied milk into a saucepan.

'Where's Charlie?' he asked.

'He took Carmen down to the town.' She scratched her nose.

'Was she upset by what Willy said?'

'She was a bit. She was being very mean to Charlie.'

'Willy wasn't very nice to her.'

She stirred the milk with her finger. 'With any luck she'll go, then.'

'Don't you like her?'

'No.'

'But you like Willy?'

'Yes.'

'Can he do no wrong?'

She looked up at him with open, empty eyes. 'What do you mean?'

'Is there nothing he might do which you wouldn't like?'

'Such as what?'

'Make a pass . . .'

She blushed. 'I wouldn't mind.'

'You'd let him?'

'What?'

'Sleep with you.'

'He wouldn't want to.'

'Why not?'

'I'm too young.' She took the pan off the flame.

'And he's too old.'

'Oh no.' She poured the milk into a mug.

'Are you in love with Willy?'

She nodded, quite casually, as if he had merely asked whether she was tired or hungry. Then she added: 'But he doesn't love me. He loves Priss.'

'Perhaps he loves you both.'

'I wish he did.'

'You'd accept a *ménage à trois*?'

'What's that?'

'A man living with two women, or a woman with two men.'

'Yes.' She looked down at the mug. 'Do you think he'd like honey in this?'

'Brandy, perhaps.'

She smiled.

'He's much older than you are.'

'I know, but he's special.'

Simon shrugged his shoulders. 'I'm surprised that you find him attractive.'

She smiled to herself – a secret smile. 'I certainly never thought I'd

121

fall for someone like that.'

'You're looking for a father.'

'That's what Willy said.'

'But he doesn't mind the incestuous role?'

'He said that all marriages are based on family relationships; that you always end up with your father or your brother or your mother or your sister . . .'

Simon laughed. 'And what's Priss? His mother?'

'No. His sister.'

'So there's room for a mother and a daughter. A convenient philosophy for a man who wants three wives.'

She looked at the mug again. 'I'd better take this up before it gets cold.'

Six

Simon waited alone in the living-room for Helen to come down again. The admission she had just made – that she loved the decrepit drunk lying in bed upstairs – left him bemused; but he was equally stupefied by his own reactions to the bizarre intrigues of his hostess at the Villa Golitsyn, for instead of feeling disgusted by her schemes to revive her husband with the young flesh of this English schoolgirl, he found that it only fed his obsession. He had recovered from the smarting of his hurt pride to find that the somewhat old-fashioned English woman he had loved before had now taken on the tints of a Transylvanian countess who bathes in the blood of virgins by the light of the full moon.

Despite his obsession with Priss, he still felt some sort of responsibility for Helen, but he realized now that if she was to move into Willy's bed, then Priss was more likely to come to his, and his avuncular concern for another man's daughter was no match for his cold passion for his friend's wife. He had indeed reached that raging stage of love when all his desires and aspirations were contained in her single person; when delirious pleasure and total despair depended upon her inclinations. Cold by nature, and grudging of his emotions, he sensed that this might be his last chance to come out of the prison in which his emotional parsimony had placed him. All his other affections – for his children or for his friends – were largely forgotten; or if remembered, were dim and feebly felt. He could cash them all in if in doing so he could purchase Priss.

He heard footsteps in the hall and Priss, not Helen, came into the room.

'He's asleep,' she said. 'Helen says that she'll stay with him. I'm going out to find Charlie and Carmen.'

'I'll come with you.'

They walked down the steps in the dark, Priss going first and holding her hands in front of her face to protect it from the sharp low-growing leaves of the palm trees. They walked down the Boulevard in silence, past the entrance of Les Grands Cèdres and under the bridge to the two cafés at the corner. Because it was now cold, no one sat on the tables outside. They went into the first one and then the second, searching fruitlessly for Charlie and Carmen. They then walked on down the Avenue de la Californie towards Magnan.

'Will is such a *bore*,' said Priss, shivering from the cold. 'I don't just mean the drinking, which is tiresome enough but all that play-acting which tramples over people's feelings.'

'It's a little cruel.'

'*We* can all take it, because we know him, but Carmen . . . well, the trouble is that Americans don't understand irony, so they certainly can't see the point of someone like Will, who is almost all irony.'

'*I* find it hard enough to judge when he means what he says and when he doesn't,' said Simon.

'I only wish he *did* mean what he said,' said Priss. 'I'd far rather he went to bed with Charlie than felt so guilty about that kind of thing.'

'What kind of thing?'

'Oh, you know . . .' She squeezed between a building and a car that had been parked on the pavement.

'He seems to have led a blameless life since he married you,' said Simon.

'He reads the Bible – I told you, didn't I? – and that can make you feel guilty about *anything*.'

The cafe at Magnan was filled with students from the university. There was no sign of Charlie and Carmen.

'Let's have a drink anyway,' said Priss, sitting down at an empty table. 'They must have gone right into town.'

'I'm sure they'll sort things out,' said Simon.

She frowned. 'I think I could convince Carmen better than Charlie that it was all a charade because Charlie, well, he is still half in love with Will, and if Will really wanted to go to bed with him, I dare say that Charlie wouldn't say no.'

'Why do you call him Will?' asked Simon, 'when everyone else calls him Willy?'

'He was always Will at home,' said Priss, brushing a strand of hair away from her face. 'He was only called Willy by the friends he made at school.'

'You knew him as long ago as that?'

'Yes.' She frowned as if irritated. 'I told you, didn't I? I was the girl next door.'

'If you hadn't known him for quite so long,' said Simon, 'you might find it easier to conceive of life with someone else.'

There must have been something sad in his tone of voice, because Priss laid her hand on his and her frown changed to a smile. 'If I saw him settled,' she said, 'happy, that is, with Helen or someone like Helen, then I'd come to you, if you still wanted me.'

'I'll wait,' said Simon, looking down at the heavy ashtray on the small table, and at her brown hand on his.

'You know how I feel about Will,' she said. 'That won't change, but it doesn't matter, does it? Because you love him too.'

'It doesn't matter, no.'

'I now think,' she said, 'that perhaps I'm not good for him; that he blames me for what's gone wrong in his life, and that if he lived with someone else he might stop drinking and do something.'

'I talked to Helen just now,' said Simon. 'She seems to be game.'

'For a baby?'

'For anything. She's under the Ludley spell.'

Priss smiled. 'Like you?'

'Like me.'

'Well tonight's not the night,' she said, biting her lower lip. 'In fact it's going to be tricky to get them together. He can't sleep with her if he's drunk, and he won't if he's sober.'

'Why not?'

'He just won't.'

'But he likes her, doesn't he?'

'Oh yes.'

'He fancies her?'

'A lot.'

'He must know she's willing.'

'Yes.'

'And he knows you won't mind?'

'Only too well.'

'So what stops him?'

She laughed. 'I think he thinks it would be wrong.'

'Why? Because of her age?'

'I suppose so. I don't really know.'

'Perhaps he's afraid he won't make it.'

She shook her head. 'No. He may be weak but he's nervous, and nervousness and lechery go together, don't they?'

'You should know.'

She blushed. 'He certainly could if he wanted to.'

'Then perhaps he will.'

'We must push him along.' She smiled. 'He's like an old bull with a young heifer. He needs a bit of help.'

'I'll do what I can but . . .' He hesitated.

'What?'

'I'm not altogether surprised that Willy hesitates before fathering a child by a runaway schoolgirl.'

'That's a very predictable opinion,' she snapped. 'Of course conventionally it might be thought wrong. I'm sure her parents would be appalled. But if Will doesn't sleep with her, someone else will – probably one of those students who sleep on the beach. She's longing to lose her virginity. I know. I can remember how I felt at that age. She's longing to and she will, so she may as well lose it to Will and save his life at the same time.'

She stood. Simon paid for the drinks; and then they both set off back to the Villa Golitsyn.

They could hear screams from the bottom of the steps like those of an angry baby, only deep and hoarse. Simon, being ahead of Priss, reached the house before she did. He ran up the stairs and into the Ludleys' bedroom. The bed was empty. For a moment he could see no one in the gloomy light, and the loud cries seemed to come from all four corners of the room. Then he caught sight of Helen's white blouse, and as he came nearer he saw her dishevelled hair and the tears streaming down her face. She was sobbing and saying soothing words into a dark space between a painted linen chest and the wall. Simon came closer still and saw Willy cowering in this confined space, screaming, shaking and kicking – not at Helen, who kept her distance, but at something which seemed to be attacking him on the floor.

So convincing was his terror that Simon thought he must have fallen into a nest of ants, and was about to pull him clear when Priss came up behind him. She pushed past and stood for a moment next to Helen. Willy showed no sign of recognizing her: his eyes stared straight ahead and his face was twisted with disgust as if he saw only too clearly what they could not see crawling towards him on the floor. He kicked at them with his bare feet, crashing his heels onto the hard parquet, apparently unconscious of the pain it must have caused him.

'Shall I pick him up?' asked Simon.

'No,' said Priss.

'He's being bitten by something . . .'

'There's nothing there,' said Helen.

'Just watch him,' said Priss. 'I'll get the doctor.' She started towards the door, then turned to Helen. 'Are you all right?' she asked.

'Yes,' Helen sniffed, 'but Willy . . .'

'He'll be all right. It's DTs.'

'Oh.' She did not understand.

'He thinks he's being attacked by rats,' said Simon. 'It's what happens when you drink too much.'

Helen burst into tears. 'It's all my fault,' she said. 'He asked for some brandy so I brought up the bottle.'

Priss left the room to call the doctor.

Charlie had returned with Carmen by the time the doctor came, and together with Simon he held Willy still on his bed while the doctor stuck a syringe into his pale, flabby buttock. In only a few seconds the drug took effect: Willy was calm and soon slept.

They left Priss with the doctor and went down to the drawing-room. Charlie was shaking; he went to the sideboard to pour himself a drink, but put down the bottle of wine before filling his glass as if Willy's troubles had put him off. He went to the sofa and sat down next to Carmen, who still wore a sulky expression on her face as if afraid that Willy's delirium tremens would upstage her wounded pride.

'What the hell are we going to do?' asked Charlie.

Simon was uninhibited by the example of his friend, and had poured himself a glass of whisky. 'We've got to stop him drinking,' he said.

'But how?'

'Keep him here. Hide the wine. Throw it all out.'

'It wouldn't work. He'd climb out of his room and go down to the café.'

'What else can we do? Everything else has been tried.'

'I don't know why you don't just let him kill himself,' said Carmen.

'No . . .' Charlie raised his hand in a gesture of exasperation. 'I know it's difficult for you to believe it, but he used to be a wonderful guy . . .'

'He sure isn't now.'

'But he could be again.'

Carmen shrugged her shoulders. 'Well, I'm not going to stay around until he is.'

'Perhaps in America,' said Helen quietly from the corner where she was sitting on an upright chair, 'you don't have friends in the same way as we do.'

'Of course we have friends,' said Carmen.

'And don't you stick by them?'

'Not if they try and break up your relationship with your man.'

Charlie sighed. 'I don't think he wants to break up our relationship, Carmen.'

'Of course he does,' said Carmen. 'He's still crazy about you and deeply resentful of me. Can't you see that?'

Charlie gave a snort – half laugh, half sigh – and rolled his head from side to side on the back of the spinach-green sofa. 'Believe me,' he said, 'he isn't crazy about me. He isn't even gay. He never was.'

'Except at school.'

'That wasn't serious.'

'He was your first guy, wasn't he?'

'He was my first anything.'

'Would you have gone gay if it wasn't for Willy?' she asked.

Charlie stopped rolling his head. 'Probably not.'

'There you are, then.'

'Willy isn't queer,' Simon said to Carmen. 'He doesn't fancy Charlie.'

She turned on him fiercely. 'How do you know? And how do I know that you're telling the truth? You're probably gay too. I don't know where I am with any of you British.'

'He doesn't fancy Charlie,' said Simon, 'because he fancies Helen.'

'Huh.' Carmen seemed reluctant to believe what he said.

'He does, doesn't he?' Simon said to Helen.

'Yes,' she said quietly.

'Well, that's pretty disgusting, too. A man of his age with a little girl like that.'

'But it has nothing to do with you,' said Helen.

'I don't care if it does or not,' said Carmen, 'and I don't care if Willy does or doesn't fancy Charlie. I'm not staying in this madhouse. I didn't come all the way to Europe to spend my time with drunks.'

'We can't go,' said Charlie. 'We can't leave them in the lurch.'

'Of course we can,' said Carmen. 'Simon and Helen will stay on. You've done your bit.'

'You don't understand,' said Charlie.

'Oh fuck you, I *do* understand,' Carmen screamed at him. '*You're* the one who's crazy about *him*. Well it's him or me. You'll have to choose.' She stood. 'If you won't come with me, then I'll go on my own.' She flounced (theatrically) out of the room.

Simon looked at Charlie. He had not moved his head from the back of the sofa. 'Perhaps you'd better go with her,' Simon said. 'Helen and I will stay on.'

Charlie sighed. 'The trouble is that in a way she's right. Old Willy, really, means more to me than she does. After all, there are other people like Carmen, and like me, and like you, Simon, but there's no one else like Willy, is there?'

'None that I know,' said Simon.

They heard the front door close as the doctor left, and then saw Priss come in from the hall.

'What did he say?' asked Simon.

She shrugged her shoulders and sat down. 'He said what you might expect him to say, that if Will goes on drinking he'll die; that his liver is likely to pack up at any minute; that his brain is half-pickled already; that his heart is weak.' She looked drawn, tired and sad. The end of her nose was red: she sniffed and wiped it with her hand.

'What did he suggest?' Simon asked.

'A clinic.'

'Did you tell him what happened before?'

'Yes.'

'What did he say?'

'He shrugged his shoulders in the usual French way.'

'What could he say?' said Charlie.

'Not much, I suppose,' said Simon. 'The diagnosis is clear enough: alcoholism. The cure is simple: no alcohol. How the cure is administered is up to us.'

'He gave me some tranquillizers,' said Priss, showing them a carton she held in her hand.

'That'll help,' said Charlie.

'Up to a point,' said Simon.

'What else can we do?' said Priss. 'We'll just have to watch him, but I warn you – it's a terrible bore.'

'We don't mind,' said Charlie. 'That's why we're here.'

'It won't be much fun for Carmen.'

'She's leaving.'

'Oh.' Priss paused as if taking in an unspoken explanation; then she added: 'I'm sorry.'

Charlie shrugged his shoulders. '*C'est la vie*,' he said with a weak smile.

Simon stood up and walked across the room. His civil servant's mind was drawing up a memorandum which he spoke aloud. 'The beast we have to deal with,' he said, standing with his back to the desk, 'has two horns. There's Willy's physical addiction to alcohol, which can be dealt with by keeping him away from drink: and there is the second addiction – the psychological propensity to seek oblivion in drunkenness. Why does he hate to be sober? We haven't really tackled that problem, have we?'

'He thinks he's a failure – a *raté*,' said Charlie.

'Yes,' said Priss. 'He thinks he's wasted his life.'

'Are you sure that that is the explanation?' asked Simon.

'Isn't it enough?' said Priss.

'We all feel at times – at our age, at any rate – that we've wasted our lives. Whether we have or not depends upon our expectations. Now if Willy had wanted to be prime minister and now found himself twenty years later still on the back benches; or if he had been a writer and still couldn't get his books published; then I would understand that he might feel that he had wasted his life. But that

129

isn't the case. At the age of twenty-four or so, Willy chose to become an expatriate, and one couldn't say that he had failed at that.'

'Perhaps he regrets the choice he made at twenty-four,' said Charlie.

'Then why doesn't he go back to England? Or why didn't he ten years ago?'

'He couldn't, could he?' Charlie looked at Priss, who as they were talking had started to grip the hand which held the tranquillizers with the other, and twist them together. 'No he couldn't,' she said simply.

'Why not?' asked Simon.

She said nothing: there was no particular expression on her face.

'You should tell us,' said Simon. 'It might help.'

She shook her head. 'I can't.'

Simon came and stood in front of her. 'If I told you that I knew, and that it didn't matter, and that after so long no one cared any more, would that make a difference?'

She looked up at him. Their eyes met — hers tired and sad, his bright with a devious, bureaucratic benevolence. 'How can you know?' she said. 'No one knows.'

'We've known for a long time.' Simon turned to Charlie and Helen. 'Willy was a traitor,' he said. 'In Djakarta, while second secretary at the Embassy, he photographed a map and gave it to the Indonesian Communists. It led to an ambush of a British patrol in Borneo, and the death of one of his friends.'

'No,' said Priss quietly. 'That's not it. He isn't a traitor. He's my brother, my older brother. That's why we can't go back to England.'

Part Three

One

At breakfast the next morning they all drank their coffee and ate
their bread and jam with lowered eyes. No one spoke. Carmen sat
with arched eyebrows looking out of the window at the olive tree as
if convinced that the silence at table was caused by her dramatic
departure. She may have been waiting for someone to beg her to stay
on, but no one did: indeed the only interruption to the sound of their
sipping and chewing, and the rustling of *Nice-Matin*, was Charlie's
broken French from the hall as he telephoned Air Inter to reserve her
a seat on the next flight to Paris.

At eleven he drove Carmen to the airport. She took her leave of the
others with the same aggrieved expression she had worn since the
previous evening. There was no kissing or shaking hands. Even
Charlie, as he put her suitcase into the boot of the Jaguar, seemed
quite detached about the departure of the girl he had meant to be his
wife, as if he was her chauffeur and nothing more.

Once they had gone, Simon and Priss set to work to get rid of all
the alcohol in the house. They opened and emptied every bottle of
wine they could find, and drained the dregs of those already empty,
before throwing them into the bin. All the cognac, marc and some
duty-free whisky that Simon had brought with him from England
was emptied down the kitchen sink.

At lunch they drank water. Priss sat at her usual place at table
while Helen perched uneasily on Willy's chair. Simon and Charlie sat
between the two women. With Carmen gone, and Willy still asleep in
his room, they all seemed more at ease. Charlie gave a scathing
account of Carmen's histrionic parting at the airport, while Simon
joked about the drunken fish which would be found stranded where
the sewage from the Villa Golitsyn emptied into the sea. Helen
laughed, not just because their jokes were funny, but also because
Carmen's departure had put her in a good mood. Priss too seemed
cheerful. She chatted for a while about their plans, interspersing
what she said with casual references to the recent drama: 'I'm sorry

133

Carmen never saw the Matisse Chapel,' and 'If Will is well enough,' and then finally she seemed to decide that she must mention what no one had referred to that day. 'Look,' she said to Charlie. 'Did Carmen leave because of me and Will – because of what I told you last night?'

'Good heavens, no,' said Charlie. 'I didn't tell her. She just split, that's all.' He glanced at Simon for confirmation.

'Split from here or from you?' asked Priss.

Charlie laughed. 'A bit of both.'

'But what about getting married?'

He looked vaguely towards the Baie des Anges. 'It wouldn't have worked.'

Priss leaned across the table and put her hand on his forearm – on his brown skin covered with golden hairs. 'I'm sorry, Charlie,' she said, 'I really am.'

He sighed. 'In California it seemed different . . . I mean, she seemed different, or I guess I was different.'

'But you could have gone back with her.'

'I never really belonged there,' he said wistfully.

Priss took her hand off his arm and turned to address all three of her guests. 'You're kind to stay,' she said, 'but now that you know about Will and me, you mustn't feel you have to.'

'It makes no difference,' said Helen – quietly, but with a fierce edge to her voice. 'It doesn't matter who people are or what they do . . . if you like them.' She blushed as she spoke: her youthful flesh went pink from her jowls to her nose.

Simon cleared his throat. 'I don't think any of us think worse of you,' he said. 'The problem is, whether Willy thinks worse of himself and drinks as a result.'

'Yes,' said Priss, 'it is perhaps that. When he was younger – well, you can remember what he was like. He wanted his moral values to be his own – to accept nothing from others, particularly not from the conventional moralists whom he despised.'

'I can remember,' said Simon.

'Me too,' said Charlie.

'I adored him,' said Priss. 'I accepted everything he said. I thought he was funny and clever and handsome, and the other boys I met seemed terribly dull compared to Will. Of course a lot of girls feel like that about their brothers and don't sleep with them . . .' She turned to Simon. 'I told you about my father. He slept with anyone and

134

everyone, so we grew up in . . . well, a permissive climate of opinion. One holiday Will came back from school where he'd been trying things out with you boys and it seemed obvious, I suppose, to try things out with me.' She turned to Helen. 'I was about your age when we first slept together. It was terribly risky because in those days there was no such thing as the pill. We had this huge house in Suffolk called Hensfield where as children we'd always been abandoned with our nanny. It had attics filled with old furniture, and there, well, we did it once or twice, just thinking that it was interesting and fun. Then Will went up to Cambridge where he had other girlfriends, and I used to go out with men who'd grope at me in taxis – Guards Officers and stockbrokers and that sort of thing. At Cambridge Will fell in love with a girl – a real bitch as it turned out. He came back and told me that he was going to marry her, which upset me, I suppose, but I accepted it as inevitable. Then, a month before the wedding, he found out that she was sleeping with someone else – a friend of his . . .' She stopped. 'Is this embarrassing?' she asked.

'No,' said Simon. 'Go on.'

'Well, Will was rather disillusioned after that. He came back to Hensfield – that was the house in Suffolk – and that's when we really fell in love. Mother was dead; father was hardly ever there, and we both hated him anyway. It was a wonderful summer. We were alone together for about two months. In the autumn Will went up to London to start at the Foreign Office. I came up too and worked in an art gallery. I still went out with other men for form's sake, and Will went out with girls, but we saw each other at least twice a week all that year. Then he was sent abroad and that was awful.'

She paused with a melancholy expression on her face as if re-membering that period of her life. 'I've never suffered as much as I did then,' she went on. 'Indonesia was so very far away, and although we never spoke about it, we both thought that we ought to use the separation to find someone else. I almost became engaged to a poor old chap called Geoffrey. He was terribly proper and never laid a finger on me, not even in taxis. The only way I could bring myself to smile when I was with him was by imagining the look on his face if I told him about Will and me.

'I broke up with Geoffrey. I couldn't face marrying him or anyone else. I decided quite by myself that if I couldn't live with Will, I'd live alone. I suppose that's why incest is forbidden: if you are close to your brother, you've got so much in common, so many shared

135

experiences and tastes, that adding sex makes it quite exceptional . . .' She stopped again and looked pensive. 'Perhaps,' she added, 'if we had been happier as children, we might have found it easier to get on with other people. As it was, we both felt that only the other could understand that misery which was part of our characters, and that someone outside the family would never comprehend it.'

'Did Willy then send for you?' asked Simon.

'No. I went to live in Morocco. I had some money and wanted to try and be a painter, so I bought a house near Marrakesh. I set myself up as an eccentric English spinster and was going to stay there forever.'

'So what happened?' asked Charlie.

'Father died. Both Will and I came back for the funeral. We just looked at one another over the grave and both knew that it was no good. We couldn't go on without being together.'

'So you flew to Singapore?' said Simon.

'Yes. More or less.'

'But weren't there aunts and uncles and cousins who wondered what had happened to you?'

'I didn't go straight to Singapore. I went back to Marrakesh and lived there for four and a half months. It's still my address so far as people like the solicitors are concerned. One friend from school came out to see me there, but after that, no one.'

'No relatives? No cousins?'

'I think I told you,' said Priss, 'that my father was an exceptionally unpleasant man. We had cousins on both sides of the family, but we never saw them. He thought they were a waste of time. Anyway,' she added, 'it's surprising how quickly people forget you when you go abroad.'

Remembering how quickly he had forgotten Willy, Simon did not disagree. 'Were you married in Singapore?' he asked.

'No. How could we marry? We arranged a sort of blessing by a Buddhist monk who Will had found in a sidestreet somewhere. He didn't know, of course. I think he thought we were marrying without our parents' consent.'

'Then you sailed away . . .'

'Yes.'

'And how long did this idyll last?' Simon asked in a drawl.

Priss glanced at him sharply to see how much sarcasm he had intended. 'It *was* an idyll,' she said. 'We met in Singapore and then

136

sailed away from everything – from our wretched childhood, from the stupid conventions of the middle classes, from a country that was finished – and for months, no for years, we were completely happy.'

'What went wrong?'

She shook her head. 'I don't know. It happened so slowly. I think Will was bored: that was one of the problems. He tried ranching but wasn't much good at it, and he hated the Argentinians – all that *maté* and *machismo*. He had nothing in common with them; there were no theatres or cinemas, and anyway he couldn't speak Spanish, so he used to read – novels, and then philosophy, and finally the Bible.' She said this last word with great contempt.

'Why the Bible?' asked Charlie.

'He pretended it was only curiosity, but the more he read it the more gloomy he became. I tried to get him onto P.G. Wodehouse and Raymond Chandler, which are the sort of books I like, but he said they were superficial, and that he didn't read to amuse himself but to learn. Yet all this so-called learning just made him more and more depressed, and the only way out of his depression was drink.'

'Do you think he feels remorse?'

'Remorse? I don't know. What is remorse? I think that once you've made your bed, you must sleep in it.'

'With no second thoughts?'

'What's the point? The reasons we had at the beginning for rejecting the conventional view of the rights and wrongs of incest still hold good, so it's particularly stupid to read books like the Bible which can only make you feel guilty.'

'Perhaps Willy's a sort of spiritual masochist?' said Charlie.

'Then he wouldn't drink to dull the pain,' said Priss.

'That's true.'

'Do you ever discuss his state of mind with him?' asked Simon. She shook her head. 'No.'

'Why not?'

She frowned. 'He knows that I think any guilt or remorse is self-indulgent.'

'You're exceptionally confident of your point of view.'

'To do wrong,' said Priss, 'you have to harm others. Whom have we harmed?'

Simon shrugged his shoulders. 'No one, certainly, other than yourselves.'

'We haven't harmed ourselves,' she said firmly.

'You have had to make sacrifices.'

'What sacrifices?'

'Well, you can't live in England or have a child. Perhaps Willy now regrets that you have had to give up one or the other of those?'

'Both those problems could be solved,' said Priss, looking at Simon with an expression in her eye which referred him to their earlier conversation.

'You could adopt a child,' said Charlie blithely.

'Or Will could have one by someone else,' said Priss. 'I wouldn't mind.' She glanced at Helen and Helen smiled.

'Or you could have a child by another man,' Simon said to Priss with a trace of mockery in his voice.

'I can't,' she said flatly. 'It's too late for that now.'

Two

Willy slept until mid-afternoon, when Priss and Helen fed him some soup. He then slept again, for an hour or so, and when he woke asked for Simon and some tea.

When Simon entered he was sitting up in the four-poster bed, dressed in a blue and white striped nightshirt. His face was strikingly pale, and Helen was brushing his hair almost as if she was dressing a corpse. He turned his head slowly as Simon came into the room and lifted his hand off the counterpane as a sign of greeting.

'I hear the cat's out of the bag,' he said in a slow, weak voice, 'but that none of you have fled the den of iniquity except for Charlie's American . . .'

'She didn't leave because of that.'

'I know. She left because of me. I was such a swine . . .' His chin sank onto his chest as he pondered his behaviour of the night before.

Simon came and sat on a chair which Helen, like a competent nurse, had placed by his bedside.

'Isn't she enchanting, my angel of mercy?' said Willy, looking up at

Helen who, with a serene and selfconsciously responsible expression, hovered next to his bedhead. 'But you must leave us, dearest Grächen. Simon and I must talk *business*.' He smiled at the idea that he should have any business to discuss.

Helen glanced at Simon as if to say – as nurses always say in films – that he must not tire the patient, but then seemed to decide against it and left the room with only a smile for the two men.

As soon as she had shut the door, Willy clutched Simon by the hand. 'You know what Priss will do next?' he whispered. 'She'll put her in a uniform. She knows my weakness for girls in uniforms . . .'

'I should wait until you're a little stronger,' said Simon.

Willy grinned. 'One gets exceptionally lecherous on the brink of death,' he said. 'It's the life force asserting itself. I'll need all my strength to stop myself . . .'

'Why stop yourself?' asked Simon.

Willy sighed. 'Ah, why indeed. That's really what I want to talk to you about. You see, I love that girl with two contradictory passions – one a benevolent, paternal solicitude, the other a ravenous lechery like Faust's passion for Margareta. Now while I'm sober, I wish her well – that is, I want her to get out of here and get married to some nice, dull fellow, and live happily ever after. But it won't last. I'll forget my good intentions, and with Priss pimping like Mephistopheles . . .'

'She thinks Helen should bear you a child.'

Willy winced. 'I know. A delightful child, I dare say – a little girl like herself, and when *she's* ripe Priss will be pushing *her* into my bed saying: "What's wrong? It's just a bourgeois convention . . ." ' He sank back on his pillows.

'I'm sure she won't do that,' said Simon.

'No, dear boy. Don't take me so literally. I'll be dead long before there's any danger of me sleeping with my daughter. But to keep to the point. I need your help. You brought the girl here. You must take her away. Take her home, Simon. Take her back to her parents – ghastly as they sound, poor child. Because if she stays, I'll corrupt her just as I've corrupted everyone else – Priss, Charlie . . .' He sat up and gripped Simon's hand again. 'But not you, Simon. You, my good fellow, you've proved yourself incorruptible. You were always too English to fall for my Continental speculations, weren't you? You are the branch that will bear fruit, whereas we are the dead wood that will burn for all eternity.'

'No one is going to burn for all eternity,' said Simon.

Willy laughed. 'Don't be so sure.'

'It's the alcohol,' said Simon. 'You've been suffering from halluc-inations.'

'That's what Priss says,' said Willy, 'but I know the difference between the rats and the devils because the devils come after me when I'm sober and they are worse, Simon, far worse . . .' He sank back. 'They are coming for me,' he said, 'just as they came for poor Judas.'

Simon watched his friend, uncertain as to what extent he was still affected by the delirium of the night before. 'I think,' he began cautiously, 'that you are exaggerating your own wickedness. The taboo against incest comes from more primitive societies . . .'

'That's vanity,' said Willy, 'to think that our age is somehow different from other ages.'

'You once believed in Progress,' said Simon, 'so you must have thought that society in the future would be different from society in the past.'

'Yes,' said Willy. 'I did, didn't I?'

'Better.'

'Yes.'

'And don't you believe that now?'

Willy sighed. 'I don't even believe in society. There is no society. There are only people who agree among themselves certain rules for the convenience of living together. And then, perhaps, there is a God – a capricious, possessive, jealous, unreasonable God who sets little tests for men to see if they love Him or not.'

'If there is a God,' said Simon, 'He can't be unreasonable.'

'Why not?'

'Because He has made us in His own image and likeness, and men are reasonable . . .'

'You may be reasonable, Simon, but most men don't know why they do what they do, and only use reason to justify it afterwards.'

'But if you abandon reason,' said Simon, 'what is left?'

'Conscience,' said Willy.

'What did your conscience tell you about marrying your sister?'

'I used reason to persuade myself that I was doing something brave, but I knew, I think, that I was acting from weakness. The other girl – do you remember? After that I was afraid of women. That's why I went off with Priss.'

'And your political convictions? Were they an expression of weakness?'

'In a way, yes.' He hesitated: a mischievous look came into his eye. 'That reminds me. I hear you think that I was responsible for what happened to poor Hamish in Borneo.'

Simon blushed. 'I only suggested that your convictions at the time might have led you to . . .' He floundered. 'To cooperate with the Communists in Indonesia.'

'You were absolutely right.'

Simon looked up with the sharp glance of a cat in sight of its prey. 'You mean you did?'

'I only mean,' said Willy with a taunting smile, 'that you were right to think that the things I believed in at the time might have led me to sacrifice poor old Hamish on the altar of World Revolution. He was a friend, of course, and it is normally thought swinish to betray a friend: but good Communists are always doing that sort of thing, aren't they? The Party comes first. And even old father Abraham was ready to cut the throat of his own son for *his* God.'

'No one would think the worse of you, Willy,' said Simon in a quiet, confidential tone of voice. 'In fact I have been given the authority to reassure you that there's no question now of arrest or prosecution.'

'That's why you came out here, isn't it?' said Willy with an expression of slight sadness on his face. 'To find out if I was a traitor?'

Simon looked away from Willy's eyes. 'It wasn't just that,' he said, 'but they know – they always knew – that the map came from someone inside the Embassy; that it could only have been photographed in Labuan. It had to be you or that other man, Baldwin.'

'Les Baldwin? Yes. I remember him. He was plump and had ginger hair and told jokes.'

'Could he have been the traitor?'

Willy smiled. 'Possibly, yes. Despite the jokes, he had no sense of humour. But he's a less likely candidate than me.'

'Was he a Communist?'

Will shrugged his shoulders. 'He certainly didn't admit to it, but it was difficult to tell what he believed. He hid his thoughts and feelings behind his bluff, jovial north-country act. He was ambitious, I remember, and ashamed at the same time of doing so well and leaving Leeds behind him. I used to call him Les Miserables which he

141

didn't find funny. And certainly, for all his northern charm, I don't think he took to Hamish. I should never have brought him along to Labuan, but then if I was capable of sending old Hamish to a nasty death in the jungle, I would hardly hesitate to spoil his last days on earth with the company of a Yorkshire bore like Baldwin.' He laughed, coughed, and lay back on his pillows.

'You were capable of it, weren't you?' said Simon.

'In those days,' said Willy, 'I was capable of anything.'

'They only thought it was you because you ran off to Argentina.'

'And now that you have an alternative explanation for that,' said Willy – again with a mocking smile – 'you don't know who it was.'

'And we have to know,' said Simon. 'Baldwin is going to Washington.'

Willy sighed and smiled. 'But if I tell you it wasn't me, I might still be lying.'

'I know, but I think I would believe you.'

'It's even possible that Baldwin and I were in it together.'

'Were you?'

'It seems to me the most likely explanation. If I was working on my own, I would hardly have taken Baldwin along to Labuan. And Baldwin on his own couldn't have known that the old Cambridge friend of his colleague in the Embassy was about to be dropped into the jungle. Unless, of course, he acted on the spur of the moment.'

'Won't you tell me, Willy?'

'Why do you need to know?'

'Baldwin, in his new post, will see all the classified documents on both sides of the Atlantic.'

'Secrets, secrets,' Willy murmured. 'What difference does it make in the long run?'

'Please tell me,' said Simon.

'I will,' said Willy, 'if you do something for me.'

'Yes. What? Anything.'

'Get rid of the girl.'

'I'll try.'

'When she's gone, I'll tell you.'

Simon looked sour. He walked to the window and looked out at the balconies of the large block of flats which stood between the villa and the sea.

'I rely on you, Simon,' said Willy from his bed. 'You're the only one I can trust because you're my only failure. You didn't succumb,

142

did you? Whereas Charlie – he's my creation. If it wasn't for me he wouldn't be an ineffectual little pansy, unable to make up his own mind about anything at all. He'd be married with children . . . And Priss, too – I moulded her. I told her that there was no God – no right and wrong, no morals, no convention – so how can I expect her to understand me now? I read her Nietzsche just as I read him to you, and she lapped it up, and then we saw each other by the grave – his grave – the earth going down onto his coffin. Ha, what a swine he was! If he had been only halfway decent, I wouldn't have been in such a hurry to hate God, to hate Him by denying Him, and deny Him by fucking my sister . . .'

Again he sank back on his pillows, panting to recover his breath; but quickly sat up again to speak in an urgent, feverish tone of voice. 'But you should have seen her, Simon, behind her black veil at the churchyard at Hensfield – her blue eyes and little nose, and her two plump lips, neither sour nor smiling but waiting, hoping – like the eyes. She was lovely, Simon, she was always lovely – and even now, this other girl is nothing next to Priss. She has a young body, that's all. But Priss – I've been watching her now for twenty years for some blemish on which to build a revulsion; but there isn't one, Simon. She's flawless and lovely, while the girl is only fresh and young.' He paused again, panting. Simon waited for him to go on. 'You must take her away, Simon. Take her back to England now, while I'm strong. She's so passive and willing, as women always are. They make you feel that you *must* come to them, that that is what they are for – to be kissed and touched – but I won't, I can't. Not another . . .'

He stopped and stretched out his hand – so thin it already seemed like that of a skeleton – towards his cup of tea. It was empty. Simon came back from the window to his bedside, filled the cup, and handed it to his friend.

'Real tea, this time?' said Willy with a smile.

'Real tea,' said Simon.

'Washes out the liver.'

'Yes.'

'Or what's left of it.'

'Yes.'

'Can the liver renew itself?'

'I should think so.'

'The brain can't. Once it's dead, it's dead.'

'So they say.'

'And the soul?'

'I don't believe in the soul.'

'No you don't, do you. You can't if you don't believe in God.' He sighed and looked with some pathos at his friend. 'But if there was a God, Simon, He could forgive . . .'

'Yes. You could go down to Sainte Hélène and confess. It would provide a little excitement for the parish priest.'

'But I should have to repent to be forgiven, wouldn't I? I should have to leave this bed and never again have her body next to mine.'

Simon shrugged his shoulders. 'You would be free to marry Helen. A white wedding, and then you could have *her* body next to you in bed.'

'And her conversation at breakfast!'

'You could talk to Priss at breakfast.'

'She could stay, could she?'

'Yes, so long as you lived together like . . . brother and sister.' He laughed.

'I couldn't do that,' said Willy.

'Why not?'

'She sacrificed everything to become my wife.'

'No more than you sacrificed to become her husband.'

'Oh yes, much more,' said Willy. 'You see I could still have children, but she can't.'

'That isn't your fault.'

'Oh yes it is,' said Willy. 'You see, before she came out to Singapore, when she knew we were going to live together for the rest of our lives, she had herself sterilized in Tangier.'

Three

Priss was in the drawing-room when Simon came down, and before she noticed his presence he studied her face, trying to imagine what she had been like as a girl, looking from beneath her veil at her brother across the open grave. Plumper, perhaps, with pinker cheeks – but with the same inscrutable expression.

She heard his footsteps and turned to meet his eyes with a questioning look in hers. 'What do you think?' she asked.

'He's quite calm.'

'By tomorrow he'll be screaming for a drink.'

'He wants Helen to go.'

'I know.'

'I said I'd try to persuade her.'

'I don't think she'll go unless . . . unless *I* insist.'

'And will you insist?'

Priss looked into her glass. 'No.'

'Your plans for her haven't changed?'

'No.'

Simon sat down on an armchair next to Priss. 'He certainly suffers from remorse,' he said in the voice of a doctor who has been called in to give a second opinion. 'Almost, I would say, from religious belief.'

She shook her head. 'I don't understand it. Is it middle age? The fear of death?'

'I don't know,' said Simon. 'He may have just got bored with scepticism.'

'Or bored with me,' said Priss, 'and he now needs religion to justify dumping me.'

'No,' said Simon. 'He isn't bored with you. I only wish he was.'

She blushed. 'Bored in general, then?'

'Yes.'

'I think you're right. I underestimated the effect idleness would have on him. Love isn't enough. A man should have a job.'

'There's his play . . .'

'It isn't serious. I dare say it might have been if he had started writing before he had started drinking.'

'Even if this relapse into religiosity is caused by boredom,' said Simon, 'we must still treat it seriously.'

A twisted, almost ugly expression came onto Priss's face. 'How can one treat it seriously? It's bunk, isn't it?'

'Yes, of course,' said Simon. 'That's to say, *I* don't believe in it, but Willy does, or so it would seem.'

She now looked merely stubborn. 'My mother was Church of England,' she said, 'and my father was an aggressive atheist. I went to an Anglican Convent school, and believed more or less until I was fifteen or sixteen. I was confirmed. Then Will seduced me. I was willing enough, but he made the move. He said there wasn't a God, and that since there wasn't a God there couldn't be absolute right or wrong. I believed it then and I believe it now. Nothing I have seen or heard since has ever tempted me to go back on what I decided at seventeen. On the contrary. All the superstition in Argentina and Mexico convinced me that I was right.'

'So how do you account for Willy's change of heart?'

She sighed. 'You see Will has a weakness – he always had – for drama. To put it bluntly, he was always a bit of a show-off.'

'I remember.'

'He was frightfully good at arguing. He'd convince you of something, then argue that the opposite was true until you were forced to agree with him; then he'd argue the first proposition all over again. He told me that he'd once made Charlie change his mind on the same subject seven times.'

'I can believe it.'

'Now this sudden faith, this remorse – if you ask me – is a stunt. After all, not everyone marries their sister, but what's the point of doing something *outrageous* if you haven't got an audience.'

'He has us.'

'But you aren't astounded, are you? No one would be, nowadays. They might think it a bit odd, but they wouldn't see it as a cosmic drama like the rebellion of Lucifer in Milton.'

'No, but if Willy was insincere he wouldn't suffer.'

'Oh, he isn't insincere,' she said. 'He's like an actor who lives the role he's playing; or a barrister convinced of his brief. But an actor can change roles, and the barrister can prosecute the same man he has defended with equal conviction; and Willy, if we humour him, will switch back from religion to scepticism again.' She smiled to herself. 'What he would really like would be to convince us all that he is right; to have us down there at Sainte Hélène murmuring the rosary in front of the statue of the Virgin Mary. Then he'd laugh at us for being such gullible, superstitious fools.'

Simon shook his head. 'You think, then, that the whole thing is just showing off?'

'He loves the drama.'

'A drama that could kill him.'

'Climbing a mountain can kill the mountaineer.'

'Is it unreasonable,' asked Simon – choosing his words carefully, and speaking in the most tactful and judicious tone he could manage – 'to have second thoughts, later in life, about marrying one's sister?'

She looked almost angrily into his eyes. 'Do you think that what we did was wrong?'

Simon hesitated. 'I don't much like my sister.'

'That doesn't answer the question.'

'Certainly,' he said, 'by the criteria by which we have come to judge these things these days, I can see no argument against it.'

Her expression changed to one of triumph. 'So you don't think it is wrong?'

'No. I don't see how I can.'

'If you don't, then why does Will?'

'Only because of the Bible, because of Leviticus: "Thou shalt not uncover the nakedness of thy sister." '

'How absurd,' she said with a snort, 'to suffer so much because of something scribbled by an old Jew thousands of years ago.'

It was growing dark. Charlie, who had been with Willy, came down to the drawing-room.

'How is he?' asked Priss.

'Not too bad.'

'I'd better go up and see if he wants anything to eat.'

'Would you mind,' Charlie asked Priss, 'if I went down town for supper this evening?'

'Not at all. There's nothing much here.'

'I'll come with you,' said Simon.

Charlie frowned – an unusual expression for his bland face. 'All right,' he said. He tugged at the lapel of his shirt, as if to draw attention to his slightly altered appearance. He had brushed his hair in a different way: whereas before a lock of soft, blonde hair had flopped over his face, it was now brushed straight back and held in place by water or oil to expose his forehead. He wore a newly laundered blue shirt, but despite the coolness of the evening the buttons were undone halfway to his waist, exposing a large part of his sunburnt chest. The trousers were trousers he had worn before – tight black denim – but they were held in place by a thick, black belt with a heavy brass buckle.

'Are you sure you want me along?' Simon asked, as if inferring from Charlie's appearance that he was going to a party to which Simon had not been asked.

'Of course,' said Charlie without conviction.

'Do go,' said Priss. 'It'll be very boring here.'

Charlie stood and went towards the hall. Simon hesitated for a moment, but unable to think of a convincing excuse for changing his mind, followed Charlie out through the front door to the Jaguar.

'Where shall we go?' Charlie asked as they drove around the loop of the Boulevard de Cambrai.

'I don't mind,' said Simon. 'I just wanted to get out of the house for a while.'

'Yes,' said Charlie. 'Me too.'

They went to the Old Town, parked near the Prefecture and ate at a small restaurant on the market place. Charlie was silent, even sour, which was unusual for someone who was usually so eager to please. 'I find one gets kind of exhausted just being in Villa Golitsyn,' he said with a trace of an American accent back in his voice.

'I know.'

'It's so claustrophobic.'

'Yes.'

'And I'm beginning to doubt whether any of us can really do anything to help.'

'We can try, can't we?'

Charlie sighed. 'What I'm trying to say,' he said, 'is that perhaps it might be as well to let Willy drink himself to death if he feels so awful when he's sober.'

'Were you shocked to realize that Priss was his sister?'

Charlie shrugged his shoulders. 'It's strange. I mean, I thought I'd come across most kinds of strange sex, but never a brother and a sister.'

'What do you make of it?'

Again he shrugged his shoulders. 'I wasn't shocked but I was kind of irritated.'

'Why?'

'Well, Willy could have told us. And I feel sorry for Priss. Willy has this great idea when they're young – a sort of Lord Byron stunt – and he leads her into it because he's been through every other kind of sex; but now he goes into reverse and says it's wrong and sinful, and makes Priss out to be a kind of Eve who tempted him with the forbidden fruit.' He shook his head sadly. 'He always used to do that – to convince us of one thing, then the other, then the first again.'

'I remember.'

'Which is OK with intellectual arguments, but not with a whole life.'

'What about you?' asked Simon. 'Do you feel that you've been manipulated?'

'How?'

'Well, he more or less drove Carmen away.'

'I know, but it wouldn't have worked out between Carmen and me. Willy saw that before I did.'

'Why wouldn't it have worked out?'

Charlie looked away. 'Because I'm gay, I guess.'

'But you must have thought . . .'

'I liked the idea of marriage, of a home and children and all that. Carmen seemed a way out of the gay ghetto, because she knew what I was and didn't care. We slept together, which was OK.' He sounded dubious. 'Except that women are sort of bulgy, aren't they?'

'They're not all as bulgy as Carmen.'

'And they don't seem to like sex for its own sake. There's always some emotional tie-in. They want to be flattered or reassured. It's a lot of hard work. Whereas with men, well, they usually want what you want – sex without strings.'

'I can see the attraction,' said Simon. Then he quickly added: 'If, that is, you find other men attractive.'

'It's better than wanking,' said Charlie.

'I suppose it is,' said Simon doubtfully. 'I've just never fancied the idea.'

'You're indelibly straight,' said Charlie.

'It goes with the pin-striped suit.'

'I know some guys in pin-striped suits,' Charlie began; then he stopped. 'Never mind. It's good to have one sane person around.'

'Thank you.'

'And Willy's pleased you're here, too. He's counting on you, isn't he, to take Helen back to England?'

'Yes, he is.'

'Will you?'

'I don't think she'll come.'

'No.'

'Unless Priss tells her to.'

'And Priss won't?'

'No.'

'Why not?'

'She still thinks that Willy must have a child.'

'It's bizarre, isn't it?' said Charlie.

'It all seems quite reasonable to her.'

'You're attached to Priss, aren't you?' Charlie asked.

Simon half-laughed. 'That's putting it mildly.'

'And what does she feel about you?'

'What do you think?'

'I don't know.' He grinned. 'I wasn't with you on that walk in the woods.'

'We didn't go very far.'

'No,' said Charlie. 'I didn't think you would.'

'She'll never leave him, will she?' Simon's voice faltered as he asked this.

Charlie turned to him with a look of great sympathy. 'I'm afraid not,' he said. 'I'd say that she was fond of you – as fond of you as she can be of anyone else – but that none of us count beside Willy.'

Simon sighed. 'It's a nuisance,' he said. 'She's more or less taken all the love I had left.'

'Forget love,' said Charlie. 'Stick with lust. At least you know where you are.'

'Is that what you're going to do?'

'Yes.'

'What about Carmen?'

'Lost and gone forever.'

'And you?'

'Back to the gay ghetto, I guess.'

'Here in Nice?'

'Sure. There are bars . . . There's one on the Rue Hôtel des Postes.'

'Like a consulate of Sodom and Gomorrah.'

'Yes.' He hesitated, then asked: 'Do you want to come along?'

'I don't think so.'

Charlie looked at him. 'You don't seem to have any vices.'

Simon smiled. ' "If we resist our passions, it is not through our strength but their weakness." '

'Who said that?'

'La Rochefoucauld.'

'Passions aren't vices.'

'They often come to the same thing.'

They parted outside the restaurant. Charlie offered to drive Simon back to the Villa Golitsyn, but Simon preferred to walk. The air was now cold but he wore a pullover as well as a jacket and kept off the sea front to avoid the wind. The prostitutes in the doorways along the Rue de France and the Avenue de la Californie smiled and winked and softly suggested their services; but even though some of them were young and pretty, Simon looked neither to his left nor to his right – an image of British rectitude.

It was almost midnight when he got back to the house. As he crossed the garden from the gate at the top of the steps he saw a dim light come through the drawn curtains of the drawing-room. He came into the hall, closed the front door behind him and then paused to listen to any sound which might tell him whether anyone was still awake. There was none. He went into the drawing-room to turn off the light but saw as soon as he entered that Priss lay asleep on the green sofa. She was wearing her old-fashioned, dark-blue dressing-gown with twisted piping down the side and huge tassels at each end of the cord. Her mouth was half-open and her face seemed small in repose. This, and the white lace of her nightdress, made her seem vulnerable like a child – not the adolescent child who had been seduced by her brother, but the much younger child who had suffered from things she could not understand.

Simon went back to the hall, took a travelling rug from the cupboard under the stairs and returned with it to cover Priss. He then switched off the lamp and left her to sleep.

He climbed the stairs to the landing and wondering if Willy too might be lying uncovered on his bed he opened the door to the Ludleys' room and went in. Here too a lamp had been left on in the far corner of the room. The bed itself was lit by the dim light reflected from the ceiling – enough to show Simon that Helen lay at Willy's side.

He went nearer to study the two sleeping bodies. Willy was on his back, more or less in the centre of the bed, covered by the sheet and blankets. Helen lay not in the bed but on it, curled up like a cat at his side. It seemed as if she had come to him when he was already asleep, had sat down beside him, leaning against the bedhead, and had then fallen asleep. Her body must then have slipped down the mattress: her short nightdress of white embroidered cotton had ridden up to uncover the length of her legs and the base of her buttocks.

Simon stood there for some time, studying the smooth skin of her uncovered body. He then took up the counterpane from the back of the chair, unfolded it, and spread it gently over her.

Four

Simon was woken the next morning when Willy, fully dressed, burst into the room. 'Did you arrange it?' he asked sharply. 'What time is your plane?'

Simon lifted himself up off the pillows, rubbed his eyes and looked at his watch. It was a quarter to seven. 'The airline offices won't be open yet,' he said.

'You could have arranged it yesterday, couldn't you? They're open in the evening.' Never, since Simon had been at the Villa Golitsyn, had Willy spoken to him so sharply, or showed himself so shamelessly in a bad mood. He sat down on the end of Simon's mahogany bed and started to pick dirt from under the fingernails of his right hand.

'There may be a problem . . .' Simon began.

'You promised you would,' Willy interrupted.

'I didn't promise.'

'You brought her here. You must get rid of her.'

'I can't see why it's so urgent,' said Simon.

'Then you're a fool. No. I'm sorry.' Willy looked up, his face showing that panic had replaced irritation as his dominant emotion. 'Look, it's urgent because they're closing in on me.'

'How do you mean?'

'When I woke up this morning, the girl was lying next to me.'

'Where was Priss?'

'She spent the night on the sofa. She wanted the girl to be there on the off chance I'd just roll over . . .'

'And father a child?'

'You must help me, Simon.'

'Just tell them that you don't fancy her.'

'But I do, and they both know it. Women always know. They can tell. And this morning, if I hadn't been feeling so ghastly and sober, God knows what might have happened.' He stood up and went to the window. 'They don't understand how important it is to me not to sleep with Helen. It's the only thing I can offer to propitiate God. Isn't that the word – propitiate?'

'You may be making too much of it all,' said Simon. 'If you don't want to sleep with her, don't sleep with her.'

'But I do.'

'Then do so. If you don't, someone else will soon enough.'

'That's not the point,' said Willy – snapping again and then seeming to regret it. 'I'm not responsible for what she does, or what is done to her by others, but I am responsible for what *I* do . . .'

'I'll talk to her again, if you like,' said Simon, 'but if Priss wants her to stay, then she won't pay much attention to me.'

'She will, Simon. She respects you. We all do.'

'I'll talk to Helen,' said Simon, 'but you must talk to Priss.'

'I will, I will.' He stood and went to the door. 'You see, I've got to have a drink soon – very soon – and if I have one drink I'll have another and then, if she comes to me like that . . .'

'I'll talk to her.'

'I hope it works, because if it doesn't, well, I'll have to think of something else.'

He left the room. Simon lay back on his bed, calculating what he should do. He did not wonder what, in this mess of muddled feelings, would be best for all – or what would be best for one or other of his friends. He only asked himself what course of action would be most likely to get him what he wanted. Certainly he thought of his mission: he wanted to go back to London sure of the truth about the Djakarta leak. But his mission was now of only secondary importance: his passion for Priss came first. If Helen stayed and Willy gave in and slept with her; if she became the mother of his child and, in some sense, his second wife; if the birth of the child gave Willy a reason for living, led him to temper his drinking; if the girl nursed him back to health: how would all that affect Simon's chances with Priss? When she saw that her brother was well, would she then come to London and marry Simon? Or would she, as she had said, get rid of the girl and remain where she was as Willy's wife and the child's adoptive mother?

The latter was more likely. As long as Willy was alive, there was little chance that Priss would ever leave him. On the other hand if the girl left then not only would Willy tell Simon about the Djakarta leak, he would also go back to the bottle. In a matter of months he would die – and as Charlie had said, why should he not die if he wanted to?

What would happen after his death? Next to Willy, Priss had said, she loved Simon more than anyone else. Once Willy had gone, she would be left with only him. She would marry him, *faute de mieux*.

He would be rich with the Ludleys' money. They would have a flat in London and the country house in Suffolk. What would Sarah and her little geologist make of that?

When Simon came down for breakfast there was no one at the dining table. He went into the kitchen, helped himself to some coffee and then returned to sit at his usual place like a long-standing guest at a boarding house. Soon afterwards Helen came down and having fetched herself some breakfast from the kitchen she sat down at the table opposite Simon.

'Where's Priss?' he asked her.

'She went to the market.'

'Willy?'

'In his room, in a foul mood.'

'Charlie?'

She shrugged her shoulders. 'Still in bed, I think.'

'Good, because I want to talk to you.'

She looked at him with an uneasy expression on her face. 'What about?'

'I think the time has come to leave,' said Simon.

She blushed. 'I can't.'

'Why not?'

'They need me.'

'Listen,' said Simon, leaning forward and speaking in a low but urgent tone of voice. 'You're grown up and basically sensible, but there are things – particularly things about marriage – which you can't understand because they're the sort of thing you can only learn from experience. Priss and Willy don't need you, or me, or Charlie. They are wholly obsessed with one another, and if given the chance they'll use you, or me, or Charlie, to revive their own relationship.'

He paused. Helen had taken on a sullen expression and looked down at the table as if she might not even be listening to what he said. He continued nonetheless: 'Priss wants you to have a child, which may sound simple enough but it's not. It takes nine months out of your life. You have to carry around a great weight in your stomach. It exhausts you; it's very painful when the baby's born; it spoils your figure; and for months afterwards you never get a good night's sleep.'

'I'm prepared to put up with all that,' said Helen, 'if it saves Willy from dying.'

'That's sweet and commendable,' saide Simon, 'but it won't save Willy. He's a chronic alcoholic, and while a man may start to drink to drown some sorrow or some remorse, once it has reached the stage that Willy is at, it is a physical addiction. Only months of careful medical care can save him.'

'If he had a baby, he'd have some reason to do that.'

'And if he does come through, and a child is born? What will happen to you? Priss may be happy to use you now. You're almost a child. You don't threaten her. But in a year or two you'll be a woman like her – the mother of Willy's child, a rival for his affection.'

'When she wants me to go, I'll go.'

'And the child?'

She shrugged her shoulders. 'I don't want a baby. It'd be for them.'

Simon gave a short snort – almost a sneeze – of exasperation. 'But don't you see that Willy doesn't want a baby either?'

'He does really.'

'He doesn't want to sleep with you.'

'Only because he thinks he shouldn't.'

'And you think he should?'

She looked at him with the same stubborn expression as before. 'I don't see what would be wrong about it.'

'You should at least respect his feelings.'

'If he was well, he'd want to. He only doesn't because he's ill and dreams about devils.'

'Willy wants you to go home.'

'I know.'

'So will you go?'

She shook her head. 'No. Priss wants me to stay.'

'Then will you tell Willy?'

Priss came into the room from the kitchen carrying a bag filled with peaches. 'Tell Will what?'

'That she won't go home.'

Priss frowned. 'Of course she won't go home. This is her home.'

'Willy wants her to.'

'I know.'

'You should respect his wishes.'

'Don't be absurd. He's delirious . . .'

'Everything he says makes sense to me.'

She laughed – a false laugh – and turned to Helen. 'They do fancy themselves, these gentlemen, don't they? If the roles were reversed it might make some sense, but for Willy to want Helen out of the house in case she might rape him is really a little ridiculous.'

'It's not quite that.'

Priss turned and looked sharply at Simon. 'I thought you were on my side.'

He blushed. 'I only want what's best for Willy.'

'Well, you're doing the worst possible thing for his condition,' she said. 'You're pandering to his paranoia and feeding his delusions. Helen, the baby – it was an idea, that's all. If Will doesn't like it, then we'll drop it and that's that.' She emptied the peaches into a bowl.

The air was sticky and close. Simon left the table to read *Nice-Matin* on the sofa. A few minutes later Charlie came down followed by Willy, whose mood seemed to have improved. 'Give Charlie some coffee, quick,' he said. 'It's the morning after the night before.'

'Please, Willy, it's too early,' said Charlie.

'He's black and blue after some particularly *rough* rough trade,' Willy said to the others. 'I warned you Charlie, Corsican S and M is not for the faint-hearted.' He laughed, and then swung round to face Helen. 'Now then, young lady, what time is your train?'

Helen looked at Priss.

'She's not going,' said Priss.

'She must go,' said Willy.

'Nonsense,' said Priss. She seemed to avoid meeting his eyes.

'This is my house,' Willy said, his voice loud and firm, 'and I say that she must go.' He turned to Simon. 'You'll take her back, won't you, Simon? You'll take her back to England?'

Simon shrugged his shoulders. 'If she'll come.'

'I need her here,' said Priss in a dull, stubborn tone of voice.

'Need her for what?' asked Willy.

'To help look after you.'

'Nurses don't usually sleep in the beds of their patients.'

'I . . . I just fell asleep,' said Helen. Her voice was hoarse, as if she was close to tears.

'You're so bloody ungrateful,' said Priss to Willy. 'Here the two of us work day and night to look after you, to *nurse* you as you so aptly put it, and Helen – who spent all of yesterday at your beck and call – happens to fall asleep on our bed, and you react with the outraged modesty of a nun who's been surprised in her bath by the window-cleaner.'

Willy did not laugh. 'Why weren't *you* in my bed?' he asked. 'Why did you sleep on the sofa down here?'

'I was tired too,' said Priss with somewhat less conviction.

'You're lying,' said Willy, turning away from her. 'You're lying and scheming and treating me like a senile fool.'

'Only because you're behaving like a senile fool.'

'Why, why?' he shouted at her. 'Is it a sign of senility that I now believe in a soul, a God and a Judgement?'

'Yes,' she replied with equal vehemence. 'It's the sign of an unbalanced mind.'

Willy wheeled round to face Charlie. 'Do you think I'm mad, Charlie?'

Charlie glanced uneasily at Priss. 'No, Willy, I mean I shouldn't have thought so. Not mad.'

'But strange?'

'You were always different, Willy.'

'What about you, Simon?'

'No, Willy. I don't think you're mad, but I think you sometimes exaggerate things.'

'What things?'

'You seem a little paranoid, but that's only to be expected.'

'You think I'm imagining things, do you? You think that I've dreamed up the schemes of these two women?'

'No, Willy. I know you haven't. But I think you exaggerate their importance.'

Willy brought his pale face close to his friend's. 'Don't you see, Simon? This is my last chance. At the eleventh hour I've been called to labour in the vineyard. God has given me Faith, and with Faith the knowledge of good and evil. The act – the simple seduction of a willing girl – what significance has that beside all the wickedness and injustice, the cruelty and suffering in the world? None. None at all. But my choice? My acquiescence? That is what matters to God. With my own sister as my Mephistopheles He has let Lucifer set me a simple test so that when, quite soon, I come before Him I can say that among all my many, many sins there was one – one small sin – which I might have committed but for His sake did not.'

'If no one suffers,' said Simon, 'how can it be much of a sin?'

'God suffers,' said Willy. 'When a man acts like an animal, He winces.'

'Man is an animal,' said Priss.

'No,' said Willy, turning with contempt on his sister. 'Woman is

157

the animal – women like Eve, like Jezebel, the Scarlet Woman of the Apocalypse – always belittling the spirit, always peddling your sexual oblivion as a substitute nirvana.'

'Never again,' said Priss.

'No, never again,' said Willy, and with that left the room.

For some minutes after they had heard Willy climb the stairs and close the door to his room, the other four sat in silence. Priss then looked at Simon. She opened her mouth, as if about to speak, but closed it again and turned to Helen. 'Has he eaten anything today?' she asked.

'I don't think so,' Helen replied.

'He must have something.'

'I'll take him some coffee,' said Simon, rising from the sofa and throwing *Nice-Matin* onto the table.

'He ought to have something more nourishing,' said Priss.

'I'll make him some soup,' said Helen.

'No, I will,' said Priss. 'There's a tin of consommé.' She left the table and went towards the green baize door. 'I warned you,' she said to Simon. 'He's bad when he's drunk, but he's worse when he's sober.'

She went into the kitchen. Simon went to the table again and looked at Charlie, who sat leaning on his two elbows, staring down into his cup, which was half-filled with cold coffee. 'Are you feeling rough?' he asked.

Charlie looked up. His eyes were bleary and bloodshot. 'A bit down,' he said.

'Wasn't it fun?'

'It was at the time,' he said, 'but this morning . . .' He shook his head as if trying not to remember the night before.

'We all have something of Dr Jekyll and Mr Hyde in us,' said Simon.

'Except you.'

'Even me.'

Charlie laughed. 'Your Mr Hyde is never let out of the cellar.'

'He's there all the same.'

'I'm sick of them both,' said Charlie. 'The one's a bore and the other's a brute.'

'You have to live with them.'

'Yes,' said Charlie. 'I suppose I do.'

Priss came back from the kitchen carrying a mug of consommé and some biscuits on a tray. 'Will you take it up?' she asked Simon. 'I'm afraid we girls are *persona non grata* this morning.'

'Yes, of course.'

Simon took the tray and carried it carefully across the hall and up the stairs, watching the brim of the large blue mug for fear any of the steaming brown soup should spill out. He balanced the tray on his knee and opened the door to the Ludleys' bedroom, where Willy lay fully dressed on the large four-poster bed.

'So my angel of mercy daren't show her face?' he said.

'She's afraid you'll shout "rape",' said Simon.

Willy did not smile. 'Will she go?'

Simon put down the tray. 'No, I don't think so.'

'You've joined the conspiracy against me.'

'No,' Simon protested. 'I tried to persuade her but . . . well, she seems to feel at home here. You're her family now.'

'Children don't adopt parents,' said Willy.

'Oh, but they do. And anyway, she isn't a child.'

'No,' said Willy. 'Unfortunately she isn't.'

Simon pointed to the mug of consommé. 'Drink up,' he said, 'before it gets cold.'

Willy picked up the mug, sniffed it and then sipped some of the soup. 'Did you make this?' he asked.

'No. Priss did.'

'I thought so.'

'Is anything wrong with it?'

'No. It's excellent.' He drank from the mug. '*You* want to go back, don't you, Simon?'

'There's no hurry. I've another two weeks of leave.'

Willy smiled. 'And you still have to find out about Djakarta.'

'There's no hurry about that, either.'

'But you can't be enjoying it here. I'm being such a bore.'

'You're not a bore – especially if you keep off the drink.'

'But I can't, Simon. I know it and Priss knows it too.'

'You'll kill yourself.'

'If I wanted to do that,' said Willy, 'I'd jump off the top of that block of flats.' He nodded at Les Grands Cèdres. 'But that sin would simply set the seal on all the others. I'll never despair.'

'If you go on drinking, you'll die just as certainly . . .'

159

'It's not a sin to shorten the odds, is it? To want to die is not suicide?'

Simon shrugged his shoulders. 'I don't know. I'm not a theologian.'

'The problem is,' said Willy, looking down at his empty mug, 'how can one shorten them still further?'

'Why shorten them at all? If you can stay off the wine, get better and grow strong, then you can master those women . . .'

'No.' Willy shook his head. 'I'm like Samson,' he said. 'My Delilah has cut off my lock of hair. I'm chained to the pillars of the Philistine fortress. All I can hope for now is one last moment of strength . . .'

'It seems to me,' said Simon, noticing that some colour had returned to Willy's face, 'that you're looking much better already.'

'It's this excellent soup,' said Willy.

'Shall I get you some more?'

'Would you? That would be kind. And tell the others that I'll be down for lunch, and that after lunch we might improvise a new scene from my *Herzen*.'

'We'll have to do something indoors,' said Simon, looking out over the balcony at the darkening sky. 'It looks as if we're in for a storm.'

Simon went downstairs with the empty mug, and finding no one else around passed through from the drawing-room into the kitchen. He found an open tin of consommé by the stove and scraped what remained of the brown jelly into a saucepan. He lit the gas, and then doubting that there would be enough soup to fill the mug, he looked away from the stove for a second tin. Instead of a tin of consommé, however, his eyes settled on a bottle of sherry. He frowned because he had made himself responsible for the removal of all alcohol from the house, yet here in the kitchen was an open, half-full bottle of sherry with its cork lying beside it on the counter. He picked it up and emptied it into the basin, threw the empty bottle into the bin and returned to the stove where the consommé was now hot. He poured it into the mug and took it back up stairs.

'It doesn't taste quite the same,' said Willy.

'I'm sorry,' said Simon.

'Rather too meaty. The last lot had a certain *je ne sais quoi*.'

'This lot came from the bottom of the tin.'

'That must be it.' He sighed. 'Well, I dare say it will do me good.'

160

Five

When Helen came to fetch Willy for lunch she found that the room was empty. She called for him, looked in the other rooms and then came down to tell the others that he had absconded.

Simon and Charlie set off immediately in the Jaguar but did not have far to go. Willy was sitting alone at a table on the pavement outside one of the bars at the corner of the Boulevard de la Californie drinking his third pastis. The other customers were all crowded inside behind the glass doors, looking up at the overcast sky, then down at the eccentric Englishman who seemed quite careless of the impending storm.

'I was remembering those lines of Oscar Wilde,' he said sheepishly to his friends. 'You know – "Yet each man kills the thing he loves . . ." – and the thought of all that absinthe he put down in Dieppe rather got the better of me.' He followed them obediently to the car.

Back at the Villa Golitsyn Priss pretended to be angry with Willy, but the pastis had made him so amiable and benign that she gave up being angry, saying: 'Just don't drink so much, Will. Stick to a glass of wine at lunch.'

'Certainly, my dear, certainly,' he said meekly. 'I'll do anything you say.'

While waiting for lunch to be brought to the table, Willy put on a record of a tango, took hold of Helen, and pranced ineptly around the room in time to the music saying: 'I learned to tango on the *rambla* in Buenos Aires. Just follow me and you'll learn it too.'

Pâté, ham and salad was laid on the table for their midday meal. Priss apologized for the cold food. 'On a day like this,' she said, 'we should have had Irish stew, but it's Aisha's day off and I had so many other things to do.'

'We can warm up with the wine,' said Willy, drawing the corks from the two bottles of the usual Provençal rosé which had miraculously appeared on the table. He filled the glasses of his friends, but when it came to his own he left it empty and only towards the end of lunch drank what was now his ration.

Their conversation was general: there was no reference to Helen's staying or going, none to sin. Even Charlie came out of the hard,

161

melancholy mood in which his experiences of the night before seemed to have put him, but the amiability of the talk was like the closeness of the air – it presaged a storm. Willy's jollity, though not forced, was measured; and Priss appeared apprehensive because of the very ease with which she had dispelled Willy's medieval mood.

When lunch was over, Willy got to his feet and suggested an expedition. 'There's going to be a spectacular storm,' he said. 'I want to watch it. I want to be enveloped by it.'

'I thought we were going to act a scene from *Herzen*,' said Simon.

'It will be a scene from *Herzen*,' said Willy. 'It's just the sort of thing they did in the nineteenth century. *Sturm und Drang*. Let's drive up into the mountains, to the *Saut des Français* or to the *grande corniche* above Eze. We'll stand on the cliff tops and commune with the spirits of Herzen and Nietzsche.' He went towards the hall. 'Come on.'

Priss glanced uneasily at Simon, then at Charlie. 'What do you think?'

'Why not?' said Charlie.

'Do let's,' said Helen. 'I love thunder and lightning.'

Priss stood up to follow her brother. 'It is rather spectacular when there's a storm here,' she said to Simon.

'Come on,' Willy shouted from the hall.

'We'd better take some umbrellas,' said Simon.

'The car's sure to break down,' said Charlie. 'If it even drizzles, she gets water on the distributor.'

'Then we'll walk and get wet,' said Willy.

'Rather you than me,' said Simon.

'Don't be so feeble,' said Willy in just the tone of voice he had used at school.

They left the dishes stacked but unwashed in the kitchen and piled into the Jaguar. Helen sat in the middle of the back seat between Simon and Charlie, and Priss in the front next to Willy, who insisted upon driving himself. 'I'm the only one who can drive,' he said, 'because I'm the only one who knows where we're going.'

'A mystery tour,' said Charlie.

'A mystery tour – exactly,' said Willy. 'Even I don't know where we'll end up.'

He drove out of the gates of the Villa Golitsyn and down the Boulevard de Cambrai to the Promenade: here he turned left so that they knew at least that they were not going up the valley of the Var.

Nor did he turn off at Rhul's Casino – the route towards the *grande corniche*. Instead Willy continued along the Promenade, round beneath the castle, past the Hôtel Suisse and the pretty colonnades of the Old Port to the Quai des deux Emmanuels, where he stopped the car by the boat *Clöe*.

'Time to change our mode of conveyance,' he said in a jocular yet hard tone of voice.

'For what?' asked Priss.

'We'll go out in *Clöe*,' he said, 'and watch the whole coast illuminated by the lightning.'

'Don't be ridiculous,' said Priss. 'The boat will never stand up to the storm.'

'Of course she will,' said Willy, opening his door and climbing out of the car.

Priss turned and glanced at Simon and Charlie. Her habitually inexpressive eyes now flickered with panic. 'Stop him,' she muttered.

Charlie shrugged his shoulders. They all got out of the car. Willy was already standing by the boat: he put the index finger of his right hand into his mouth and then held it up in the air.

'Not a puff of wind,' he said. 'Safe as houses.'

'The calm before the storm,' said Charlie.

Willy leaped onto the boat and pulled back the tarpaulin which covered the entrance to the cabin. 'If you could just help me get the engine going,' he said to Charlie.

Charlie hesitated.

'Don't,' said Priss.

'Come on, Charlie,' said Willy. 'Don't hang about.'

Without looking back, Charlie jumped onto the boat, lifted the wooden cover from the engine and began to work on the choke.

'This is madness, Will,' said Priss.

'You needn't come,' said Willy, looking across at her with a mocking expression on his face. 'Charlie will come with me.'

'He can't sail the boat alone.' She turned to look at Simon, as if appealing to him to stop the expedition.

'Look, Willy,' said Simon. 'I think this mystery tour has gone far enough.'

'For you, perhaps. You always played it safe.'

'It's crazy, Willy. You'll drown.'

'Nothing ventured, nothing gained, Milson.'

'We're grown-up now, Willy. We're not boys at school any more.'

'You're as old as you feel, Milson, and you were always middle-aged.'

'I'll come,' said Helen moving towards the boat.

'No,' said Willy. 'Not you. You're to stay with Simon.'

'But I want to come,' said Helen.

'You can't sail,' said Willy. 'You'll only get in the way.'

Charlie tugged at the string of the starting motor. The engine turned two or three times and then stopped.

'Stay with Simon,' Priss said to Helen, pushing the girl towards the older man.

'Don't go,' said Simon, catching hold of Priss's arm.

She looked into his eyes. 'I must,' she said. 'They haven't got a chance without me.'

Charlie tugged at the rope again; again the engine turned and died.

'We won't be long,' said Priss, gently removing Simon's hand which had clutched at her coat. 'Go to the Old Town and get some gnocchi or ravioli for supper.'

She jumped onto the boat. Charlie tugged at the rope for the third time. The engine turned, faltered, then came to life.

'Cast off,' Willy shouted, standing by the rudder.

Simon went to untie the rope from the bollard. Charlie put the boat into reverse gear and it slowly moved back from its mooring.

'Take care,' Simon shouted.

Helen started to cry.

'We won't be long,' said Priss again.

Once they were clear of the other boats, Charlie changed from reverse into forward gear. The boat hesitated and then slowly moved towards the entrance to the harbour. Priss waved at the two who were still on shore but Charlie remained crouching by the engine and Willy, standing by the rudder, did not turn to look at either Helen or Simon but stared straight out to sea.

Simon and Helen watched the boat until it was lost to view behind the shop front of a ships' chandler.

'Will they be all right?' Helen asked Simon, still sniffing from the tears which had now stopped.

Simon looked to the east, where the sky was a dark grey, then to the west, where it changed to a greenish yellow – the colour of split-pea soup. 'It depends how long they stay out,' he said. 'And then perhaps there won't be a storm. It sometimes stays like this for several days . . .' But as he spoke there came the first sounds of thunder from the mountains above Monaco. He glanced at Helen. She had a timid expression on her face as if embarrassed to be left alone with him.

'Let's get the gnocchi anyway,' he said.

They drove around the back of the castle and parked the car near the Place St François. They were in the narrow streets of the Old Town when it started to rain. One by one huge drops began to fall as if children were spitting from the top windows of the tall houses. They both looked up: the last lines of washing were drawn in. Beneath, in the street, the boxes of fruit and vegetables displayed outside the shops were hauled in by the shopkeepers. The rain began to fall more rapidly and Simon, with Helen at his side, walked faster to reach the shop where Priss liked to buy the home-made pasta. There was a crack of thunder as they opened the glass-fronted door and squeezed into the small shop.

The shopkeeper, a middle-aged woman, stood at the window watching the rain. She returned to her post behind the counter as Simon ordered first the gnocchi and then a kilo of the multicoloured ravioli which was a speciality of Nice. Helen suggested that they buy a bag of grated Parmesan cheese: again she smiled at him timidly when she proposed this, as if Simon might be angry with her for not taking his advice to leave Nice.

They waited in the shop for ten or fifteen minutes to see if the rain might fall with less force, but it went on relentlessly, and feeling an unspoken impatience to get back to the port from his young companion, Simon decided at last to go back to the car. By keeping to the sides of the buildings they remained more or less sheltered and only got wet as they came out into the Place St François and ran to the car. There they sat for a moment in the two front seats, both puffing to regain their breath. Helen brushed her wet hair from where it had stuck to her face, and wiped the water off her cheek and nose.

They parked the car in the same place on the quai and sat facing the empty space left by the absent *Clöe*. The other boats bobbed up and down because now there was a wind as well as rain and even in the port the water was whisked up into little waves. The swell in the Baie des Anges was greater: from where they sat they could see the spray thrown up by the waves which crashed onto the rocks beneath the castle.

They were both silent. Helen's hair now stuck to her head like the sheeny skin of a mole: her small nose quivered when she sniffed.

'We had better go back,' said Simon. 'They've probably beached the boat on the other side of the bay.'

'Let's go to the Promenade,' said Helen. 'We might be able to see them.'

Simon started the engine and drove the car back towards the Villa Golitsyn. The wind was now strong: the palm trees on the Promenade were bent over by the force of the wind, and tables and chairs had been blown over. He drove slowly past the hotels, and Helen looked out over the turbulent water for *Clöe*, but such was the spray and the mingling greyness of both sky and sea, that nothing was visible at all.

'I want to get out,' she said.

He stopped the car and she ran in the rain to the edge of the pavement by the beach. Simon remained in the car, watching the wind blow her dress against her body. She stood there in the storm for three or four minutes looking out to sea. Then there came a wide flash of lightning which lit up the whole horizon, and a loud crash and crackle of thunder. She turned, and dodging the cars which crawled along the Promenade in the rain, came back to the car.

'They're not there,' she said, sniffing from the cold, the wet, and fresh tears. 'There isn't a boat in sight.'

'Don't worry,' said Simon. 'They may have beached the boat already, or have taken shelter in Villefranche.'

They drove back to the Villa Golitsyn. Helen ran ahead of Simon into the house as if the others might be already there. Simon followed with the gnocchi and ravioli. He closed the front door behind him and saw Helen's anxious face framed in the arch into the drawing-room. 'They're not back,' she said.

'No. They're probably in Villefranche. They'll telephone.'

While Helen went upstairs to change out of her soaking clothes, Simon lit a fire in the drawing-room. As he crouched, fanning the flames, he could hear the hiss of hot water running through the old pipes as Helen took a shower. When the fire was alight he too went up to his room. The rain had abated but the wind was still strong. One of the shutters to his window had again broken loose from the clip which normally held it fast. It was banging against the wall. Simon opened the window and stretched around in the wind and rain to secure it. He then took a bath and changed his clothes.

Helen was kneeling in front of the fire when he came down again. She was drying her hair at the blaze, her neck bent as if waiting for the executioner's axe. She leaned on her elbows and fluffed her hair with her hands. Simon stood watching her, studying the two girlish calves sticking out from beneath the hem of her red dressing-gown, and the two hockey-playing heels jutting up from the half-worn slippers.

It was now around six. The black clouds blocked out the mellow light they could usually expect at that time of day so Simon turned on the lights and Helen, who had not realized he was there, gave a start. She lifted her head and clutched at the front of her dressing-gown.

'Are they there?' she asked.

'No.'

Simon poured himself a drink from a half-empty bottle of wine and sat down by the fire.

'I hope nothing's happened to them,' said Helen.

'I'm sure they'll be all right.'

She sat back on her heels – the hockey-playing heels – and with a puzzled, wistful expression said: 'You know, it occurred to me that Willy might want the boat to be wrecked or capsize or something like that.'

'Why?'

She shrugged her shoulders. 'For the excitement, I suppose.'

'Yes. Priss said he liked drama.'

'It would be terribly dangerous, though, wouldn't it? In a storm like this?'

'Priss is a good sailor.'

'I know. And so is Charlie. But it is a bit mad, isn't it, going out like this just before a storm?'

'Crazy.'

She smiled. 'He is mad, isn't he?'

'Completely.'

'I know I don't know many people, but I don't think I'll ever meet anyone else like Willy.' Again she smiled but not at Simon: she was smiling to herself.

Later she went upstairs and changed into jeans and a jersey while Simon washed up lunchtime's dishes. At nine he cooked the gnocchi, made a sauce and a salad dressing. 'We may as well eat,' he said to Helen.

'What can have happened to them?' she asked, chewing the skin from around the nail of her thumb. 'I mean, if they were in Ville-franche they'd have telephoned, surely?'

'They may have had to land on the Iles de Lerins.'

'Isn't there a telephone there?'

'I shouldn't think so.'

'Shouldn't we wait for them?'

'They may have supper there.'

'OK, then. Let's eat. I'm starving.'

Neither went to bed. They sat playing Scrabble until one in the morning, when Helen, without a word, curled up on the sofa and fell asleep. Simon turned out some of the lights, put some new logs on the fire, then went back to his armchair, where he too dozed off.

Six

He was woken by the harsh bell of the telephone. It was light, and when he looked at his watch he saw that it was four in the morning.

He stood and stumbled across the room to answer the telephone. It was the gendarmes in Antibes asking if anyone knew a certain William Ludley.

'Yes,' said Simon in muddled French. 'Why? Is he there? Is he drunk?'

No, the gendarmes replied. He was not drunk. He was dead.

The storm had passed but the air was still soggy and drops of rain slipped off the palm trees onto the ground. The Jaguar would not start. The sound of the motor, growing weaker at each attempt, was – with the drip and patter of this residual rain – the only sound in the early morning air.

Simon abandoned the car and with the frightened, bleary-eyed child stumbling behind him he walked out through the gates in search of a taxi. They found one only when they reached the Boulevard de la Californie, and it took them along the empty roads to the Gendarmerie in Antibes.

They were first shown Willy's sodden passport, and were asked if the photograph was that of the man they knew. Simon asked if any other bodies had been recovered from the sea.

Several people had been drowned that night, the gendarme told him, but some had been found without their papers. He spoke as if this was something they would have to answer for in the next world.

'But there were only two others on the boat,' said Simon.

'The tidal wave,' said the gendarme. 'It took at least a dozen.'

Simon did not understand what the gendarme meant, but did not question him further. He and Helen followed him to the police car.

When they reached the morgue Simon — imagining that Willy's features might be horrifying to see — suggested to Helen that she wait in the car. She had shown no signs of emotion until that moment, but now she clung to his arm and said: 'Please let me come'; so together they followed the gendarme down a passage to a small cold room where seven bodies lay on trolleys covered by sheets.

A man in a white coat talked for a moment to the gendarme and then led Simon and Helen to the third trolley. He pulled back the sheet. Simon need not have been concerned about his friend's appearance because Willy's face in death looked much as it had done when he had lain next to Helen on his own bed. No one had combed his hair, as Helen had done, but the salt water had stiffened and whitened the wisps which were usually swept back over his scalp and now lay awry over his forehead.

'Is it Ludley?' the gendarme asked him.

'Yes,' said Simon.

'Yes,' Helen repeated softly.

'Why did you ask if he was drunk?' the gendarme asked.

'For no particular reason.'

'Did he drink?'

'From time to time.'

'Only a fool or a drunkard would have gone out in weather like that.'

Simon made no rejoinder. He was led back to the first of the covered corpses, and again the sheet was drawn back from the face. The fine but swarthy face of an Arab looked up at him, the mouth and eyes both open. Helen gripped his arm. Simon shook his head. 'No, I don't know who he is.'

They moved on to the second trolley and again the sheet was drawn back, this time to reveal poor Charlie, his mouth and eyes closed, his face set in the same bland expression it had worn in life.

'He was called Hope,' said Simon. 'Charles Hope. He was also on the boat.'

They passed by the third trolley which held Willy's corpse and moved on to the fourth. The face here was of an older man, thin and pinched but with tough skin and bushy eyebrows. Simon shook his head. They moved on to the fifth.

'No,' said the man in white. 'These are motor accidents.' And he led Simon and Helen on to the end of the line of bodies. 'This is a woman,' he said. 'She's the last of the drowned ones for the moment.' He drew back the sheet and Simon looked down on the exact, almost expressionless face that he had loved so much when she was alive. Her mouth was open a little – the lips a centimetre apart. Her eyes were closed. Her skin had already taken on the shine of a corpse: her features were like those of a life-sized doll.

'Do you know her?' asked the gendarme.

'Yes.'

'Was she one of your friends?'

'Yes.'

'What was she called?'

'Priscilla Ludley.'

'The wife of the Ludley there?'

'Yes. Or rather, no. No. She was his sister.'

They returned to the Gendarmerie. The fact that the Ludleys had lived in France for some years without a visa or a *permis de séjour* made Simon too an object of suspicion until he had established that he worked for the Foreign Office in London. The attitude of the gendarme then changed. He seemed to feel an automatic respect for a fellow official, even an official of a foreign government. In his heavy, Provençal accent he even expressed some sympathy for the death of Simon's friends.

It was nine in the morning when they came out of the Gendarmerie into the weak sunshine. They walked towards the sea and stopped at a café to eat breakfast. Simon bought a copy of *Nice-Matin*, which gave a dramatic account of the tidal wave which had killed their friends. The torrent of water rushing down the Var into the Baie des Anges had dislodged the earth emptied into the sea by the airport. This massive subsidence beneath the surface had sucked down the sea, leading to a huge tidal wave which had swept back and forth across the bay, smashing the sailing boats moored in the harbour of Antibes on the one side, and sweeping into the sea nine labourers on the site of the new port on the other. A sailing boat had also been caught in its path: three English tourists had been drowned.

As he translated this story from the paper for Helen, Simon glanced at her every now and then to see if she was about to cry, but she still held the same expression on her face of wide-eyed shock. Only when he had finished reading did she say: 'Was it an accident?'

'Yes.'

'I thought, perhaps, that he wanted to die because of me and Priss and that business about the baby.'

'No,' said Simon. 'I'm sure that if it hadn't been for the tidal wave, the boat would have survived the storm.'

They took a cab from Antibes back to the Villa Golitsyn. There they were both so tired, after an almost sleepless night, that they went to their rooms to sleep.

Simon was woken by hunger at three in the afternoon. He went down to the kitchen and made himself a sandwich with a piece of stale baguette and some Emmenthal cheese. He did not sit down to eat it. The house seemed hollow without its owners: he felt ill-at-ease – a trespasser. He walked through from the kitchen into the living-room, wondering if there was any reason why he should not leave for London that night, or at the latest the next morning. The three dead bodies could either be buried in Nice or sent back to England: in either case it was a matter for solicitors and the police. It had nothing to do with him.

He frowned as he munched his sandwich. He was inwardly embarrassed that he felt no grief over the death of his three friends. When he thought of the two Ludleys lying in the morgue, he was overwhelmed not by sorrow but by frustration and annoyance. It irritated him that his holiday in the South of France should have ended like this. He felt cheated by them both – by Willy of the solution to the Djakarta leak; by Priss of her love and her body.

He wished that Priss was with him there in the room. The sight of her corpse had not doused his desire; indeed the very certainty that it was now impossible to consummate it exacerbated his frustration. His sexual hunger, quiescent for so long after his divorce, had returned with a ravenous force, yet the warm and supple body to which he had looked for its satisfaction was now cold and rotting on a trolley in Antibes. The only woman he wanted could not be his.

He turned and looked out of the window, remembering the agreeable prostitutes who always stood on the pavements of the Boulevard de la Californie. Before it would have seemed brutish to go to one of them, but desire still gnawed at his groin. How absurd to be fastidious about where one sends one's sperm, he thought to himself, his eyes on the box hedge outside the kitchen window. That was Willy's mistake. He died to escape from his own desire for a girl he did not love. But how could he love her? There was nothing there to love. He should have just had her and let it go at that.

Simon pushed the last morsel of bread and cheese into his mouth and wiped some butter from his fingers onto a dishcloth. Sex can be sublime, he thought, but it is also a natural function, like crapping. Willy was constipated and it killed him.

He left the kitchen and went upstairs to return to his room. He stopped on the landing by the door to the Prince's dressing-room. He should wake Helen. She should get ready to go back to England. He knocked at the door to her room. There was no answer. He opened the door and as he did so the memory returned to him of how he had seen her before – once in her blue schoolgirl's bloomers, and later with her nightdress hitched round her waist.

· The room was dark – the shutters closed. He peered at her bed and saw that although the blankets and sheets were disarranged, no one lay in it. He thought that she might have got up before him, and had perhaps gone down to the town, but as he turned to go back onto the landing he remembered the passage between this, the Prince's dressing-room, and the Prince's bedroom where the Ludleys had slept. He crossed the room, passed by the open wardrobes containing Priss and Willy's clothes, and entered the large bedroom near to the window which led onto the balcony. The shutters here were ajar; he could see that Helen was asleep on their bed.

He went closer. She lay on her back, her head and one shoulder all that showed above the line of sheets and blankets. There was a mark on the shoulder where it had been creased by the strap of her slip. The skin around her eyes was red, as if she had cried herself to sleep. Methodically he took off his clothes, laying them neatly on the chair by the bed. Last of all he removed his wristwatch: the metal strap clicked on the glass top of the bedside table. It was a quarter to four. Helen shifted slightly and murmured in her sleep. He watched her, waiting, and when she lay still again carefully raised the blankets and slid in beside her. She moved drowsily as he embraced her but became only properly conscious when her virginity was gone.

Part Four

One

On the pretext of seeing to the Ludleys' affairs, Simon stayed on at the Villa Golitsyn. Helen stayed with him, and apart from the time he spent at the Prefecture in Old Nice, or in talking on the telephone to the Ludleys' solicitor in London, Simon kept the company of his callow mistress.

As Priss had predicted, Helen had seemed happy enough to lose her virginity, and on the evening after Simon had seduced her she cooked supper for him as if that too was part of her new adult role. She put the ravioli they had bought in the old town into a pan of boiling water but cooked it for too short a time. His teeth stuck into the hard lumps of pasta which she had crowned with warmed but otherwise untreated tomatoes.

After that, in the evening, they ate out. The food was better in the restaurants but the making of conversation was an ordeal. Willy too had been right: Helen had the body of a woman but the mind of an uninteresting child. Simon could think of nothing to say to her, and when she talked to him – about her parents, her school or her pony – he found it difficult to listen. The only two things they had in common were sex and the Ludleys, and as if by an unspoken agreement the Ludleys were forbidden as a topic of conversation.

They therefore returned to sex, and certainly Helen was interested enough in that. They talked about it at table and practised it back at the Villa Golitsyn. In the absence of her *hors catégorie* lover, she made the most of the five-star, and Simon did what he could to live up to his rating. He stimulated his flagging appetite by varying the ways in which he made love to her, and went on to enact pantomimes of his own invention. He called her his 'pet', tied a poodle's collar around her neck and led her naked on all fours around the Ludleys' bedroom. Helen accepted everything he suggested, as if she was being taught the rules of a new game: when he brought her champagne in a saucer she lapped it up like a cat while Simon stood back to admire the tableau he had created – the naked girl crouching by the open window, pink in the light of the setting sun.

Quite soon, however, he tired of these games with her body and became impatient to get back to England but it was not until the tenth day after the drowning that the formalities were completed for the return of the corpses to England. It would have been done sooner had not the heir to the Ludley estate, a second cousin, asked to have them buried in Nice – by doing so he hoped to avoid Transfer Tax on the Ludley assets outside the United Kingdom. But both Willy and Priss, soon after leaving England, had made wills which stated quite clearly that wherever they should happen to die, their bodies should be buried in the churchyard at Hensfield, their family home in Suffolk. And so, at the solicitor's request, Simon dispatched the sealed coffins to London and followed with Helen the next day.

Already at the airport he felt embarrassed to have Helen at his side. He was annoyed at having to pay for her ticket, and at the way in which she seemed to cling to him – not touching him but placing herself next to him as if they were a couple. The sounds and smells of the airport reminded Simon of the many times he had flown abroad on Foreign Office business, and for the first time he began to worry that someone who knew him might see him with Helen and imagine that he had picked her up on the Riviera. Certainly she now looked more like the mistress of a middle-aged man than a runaway schoolgirl. She had short, well-cut hair and wore the elegant, grown-up clothes that Priss had bought for her. She was thinner, too, and had an older look on her face. Only her mind remained that of a child, and it was well concealed by her sophisticated appearance.

Their plane took off over the Baie des Anges and Helen, who sat by the window, looked down in silence through the scratched Perspex of the windows at the water which had killed their friends. Then, when the Airbus had climbed high enough to fly north over the mountains, she turned her attention to the safety instructions and the flight magazine in the pocket in front of her.

Simon, who had been reading an English newspaper, turned and asked her what she planned to do when they got to London. He put the question in a solicitous tone of voice, as if anxious about her future; but it was firmly phrased to emphasize that he would play no part in it.

For a while she did not answer. Then, without taking her eyes off the magazine, she said: 'What do *you* think I should do?'

'Sooner or later, you'll have to go home.'

'I suppose I will.' She sounded as though she thought she could avoid it.

'I should get it over and done with.'

She turned to face him. 'Can't we stay together?'

Quickly and without meeting her eyes he said: 'Not really, no.'

She sniffed and looked back at her magazine.

'You can stay in my flat tonight, if you like,' said Simon. 'But tomorrow you'd better go home.'

'Can't I go to the funeral.'

'I'd rather you didn't.'

She seemed to accept his decision. 'Won't we see each other again, then?'

'Of course. Every now and then.' He turned and forced himself to smile.

She smiled back. 'You can come and take me out from school.'

'I'm sure they won't send you back to boarding school.'

'I hope not.'

'The school is unlikely to take you back.'

'Then perhaps they'll send me to a crammer's in London.'

'That would make more sense.'

'Then it would be easy.'

'What?'

'To see you.'

'Yes.'

The stewardess handed them each a plastic cup of fruit juice.

'The only problem is,' said Simon shiftily, 'that I'm often abroad, and when I'm in England I'm usually very busy.'

She seemed embarrassed by his excuses. 'Have you really travelled a lot?' she asked. 'Can I look at your passport?'

He took it out from the inside pocket of his jacket. She took it and turned the pages, looking at the different visas. 'You've been almost everywhere,' she said.

'It's part of my job.'

'And all I've got,' she said, taking her shining new passport from her bag, 'is a tiny little stamp from Calais.'

He took her passport and opened it at the photograph of Helen. It was unrecognizable. She was dressed in her school uniform and her hair was tied in plaits.

'It's awful,' said Helen, trying to snatch the passport back from him.

'When was it taken?'

'Years ago.'

'But the passport is new.' He turned the pages to see the date of issue; then glanced back to her date of birth. 'Is this right?' he asked. 'Were you born on 10 November 1963?'

'Yes. Why?'

'It means that you're only fifteen years old.'

'Nearly sixteen.'

'You said you were seventeen.'

'I wanted you to think I was older.'

He drew in his breath. 'It's against the law in England to sleep with a girl under the age of sixteen.'

'Is it in France?'

'I don't know, but if anyone knew it could get me into a lot of trouble.'

'Good,' said Helen with a smile. 'Now I'll be able to blackmail you.'

Two

At Heathrow Simon persuaded Helen to stand ahead of him in the queue of passengers waiting to pass through immigration controls. He watched as the official who looked at her passport seemed to make some joke about the photograph, but she was not detained and a few minutes later the two stood together again waiting for their suitcases to come from the plane.

They took a taxi into London. The sight of the red, double-decker buses and the ugly Edwardian houses which lined the road brought home to Simon the risks he had run in seducing the girl beside him. He could not understand why he had done it: he tried to remember the state of mind which had led him to act as he did, but all he could remember was his longing for Priss. What if Helen told her parents? He quickly rehearsed in his mind the explanation he would present if ever he was accused of what he had done. He would deny that he had slept with her. He would deny taking her to the Ludleys. He would say that Charlie had picked her up at the station, and that he could not have reported her presence in the Villa Golitsyn without jeopardizing his investigation into the Djakarta leak. *Raison d'état* was the best excuse for everything.

He turned to look at Helen, almost in a rage. Her eyes were not directed at him, but flickered back and forth as she studied the people on the pavement. He wished he had not said that she could spend the night in his flat, for he now saw how dangerous that was; he opened his mouth to tell her that it was impossible, but then realized that what she had said on the plane was true. She could indeed blackmail him: she alone was a witness to what he had done.

They reached his small flat in Pimlico. The woman who had cleaned it had come in the day after he had left but appeared not to have been there since. The rooms had that particular smell of London dust: they seemed mean and squalid after the Villa Golitsyn. Simon went into the little kitchen to put on a kettle to make some tea while Helen – still wearing her St Laurent raincoat – sat on his sofa reading the colour supplement to an old edition of the *Sunday Times*. She too seemed depressed by the dinginess of his dwelling, and this in turn infuriated him: insignificant though she was, he did not want to sink in her estimation from a suave, urbane lover into a pitiable, middle-aged man.

He took his suitcase into his bedroom and started to unpack his summer clothes. Everything which met his eye – particularly the row of grey, pin-striped suits in his wardrobe – reminded him of his earlier persona and position. Helen, who had gone to make the tea when the kettle had boiled, seemed like part of a concupiscent nightmare of the night before: she should have been gone with the dawn.

Like a child on the last days of the holidays, Helen expected some sort of treat before going home: they therefore went to a film in the West End, and after that had supper in a restaurant in Chelsea. The others dining there seemed mostly to be off-duty stockbrokers and their girlfriends – fading roses from Surrey and Hampshire – so Simon, at least, felt inconspicuous with Helen; but her very similarity to these other girls in the restaurant, and the continuing banality of her conversation, only emphasized the absence of any real affinity between them. She had ceased to be a neutral embodiment of animal youth and beauty, and was turning before his eyes into the kind of woman her mother must be.

All this did not prevent him from making love to her that night but it prevented him from enjoying it. He had done it because he had thought it was expected of him on their last night together, and so it appeared had she; for as soon as they had finished she got out of bed and went into the living-room to watch a late-night film on television. When at last she came to bed she slept soundly, but Simon stayed awake, twitching every now and then as he imagined the police hammering at his door.

The next morning he put on a grey suit and a black tie, and after a hurried breakfast drove Helen to Waterloo to catch a train back to Ascot.

'Are you dressed like that for the funeral?' she asked.

'Yes.' He glanced at his watch.

'It makes you look older.'

'I am older.'

When they reached the station she said: 'You can leave me here, if you like. You don't have to see me off.'

'I want to make sure you don't get the boat train to Southampton,' said Simon, 'and run off to New York.' He parked the car and took her case from the boot.

'Don't worry,' she said, skipping along beside him as they walked into the station. 'I won't do a bunk again.'

'Do you feel you can face them?'

'Yes,' she said. 'I feel older too.'

'They may not know who you are.'

She laughed and ran ahead to buy a magazine.

'If there's any trouble,' said Simon as he closed the door to her compartment, 'you can always ring me – either at the office or at the flat.'

'I'll ring you tomorrow anyway,' she said, leaning through the open window, 'to tell you what happens.' The train started to move. 'Oh, and thanks,' she said – the child remembering her good manners. 'Thanks for everything.'

Three

There were few mourners at the Ludleys' funeral in the parish church at Hensfield. The church itself, built no doubt by prosperous wool-merchants in the thirteenth century, was larger than was warranted by the size of the village. What congregation there was had gathered in the pews near to the altar. Simon, who had driven up from London and had lost his way in the country lanes, arrived late. The ceremony had started, so he slipped into a pew near the back of the church, and to distract himself from the tedium of the service he tried to guess from the view of their backs who the others might be.

There was an old lady wearing a veil and a threadbare but elegant coat, whom he thought to be an aunt – perhaps their mother's sister – and there was a tall man in a grey check suit with blonde hair curling over his collar whom Simon took to be the land agent for the Hensfield estate. Most of the others had the look of tenant farmers and their wives, or workers from the estate – foresters, gardeners or gamekeepers.

Only two other men besides Simon were wearing city clothes: one, he thought, might be the cousin who had inherited the house, and the other someone from the firm of solicitors who dealt with the Ludleys' affairs. They were sitting apart: the first was a thin man in a dark blue suit holding a black coat tightly over his arm. He might also be the village doctor. The second was bulkier and still wore his well-cut, velvet-collared overcoat.

The vicar spoke well. Neither he nor anyone else in the village had seen the Ludleys for thirteen years, so he limited himself to fond recollections of 'William and Priscilla' as children. 'Of course we would all have preferred them to have lived at home,' said the old man from the pulpit, 'but both chose to live and die abroad.' He shrugged his shoulders. 'Who knows what drives a man or a woman to do this or that? Only Gòd. What might have seemed to some a dereliction of duty may have been quite the opposite in the eyes of the Almighty. We must judge not that we be not judged.'

The estate workers and tenant farmers carried the two coffins to the single grave which had been dug next to that of their parents. Simon walked behind with the other mourners. Nothing in their faces told him more than he had inferred from the sight of their backs. He was also distracted from his guessing game by the sight of the open grave, for he remembered how Willy had stood by this very same plot so many years before, watching his father's body lowered into the ground, then raising his eyes to see the expectant, open mouth and plump, unsmiling lips of his only sister.

Simon looked up at the sky. Was it the same season, he wondered. The trees now had no leaves, but they were the same trees: the church tower, the telegraph poles, the roofs of the barns beyond the wall to the graveyard – all these would have been the same. He looked down again at the coffins. How he would like to have told them that he had been there, that he had seen the village where they had lived as children; and suddenly, for the first time since they had drowned, Simon was overwhelmed by sadness and wished that they were both still alive. He wanted to say to Willy how ashamed he felt about Helen – ashamed because he had been her first lover without loving her, had debauched her without affection.

'Yet how could I love her when I loved you?' he asked the first of the two coffins as it was lowered into the ground. 'I loved you, Priss,' he repeated soundlessly, mouthing the words on his lips: but then he became confused over which of the two coffins contained her body. The straps went under the second. He wanted to ask but dared not, and inwardly became frantic because no one would ever know which body was above and which below.

As they walked towards the gate of the churchyard, the man in the grey check suit introduced himself as the Ludleys' estate agent and invited all the mourners back to Hensfield House for lunch.

Simon, driving his own car, followed the others down the village and through the open gates into the park. Between the trees, and across the open grassland, he could see a large, symmetrical building which he took to be the Ludleys' home. It dated, he thought, from the end of the eighteenth century, but when he came closer he could see that it had been maintained in such good condition that it might have been built yesterday. Already, from the outside, one could tell that it was no one's home: the hedges were too well clipped; the lawns too trim. There was no evidence of human habitation, only human pride.

The inside too was chill – not in a literal sense, because the rooms were well heated against the damp autumn air, but by the cleanliness and order in each of the formal rooms. In the large, impersonal dining-room, three women in aprons stood beside a sideboard ready to serve the mourners with soup, ham, grouse, cold beef and tongue – all of which had been laid out on a white cloth. Their faces showed the kind of shy excitement that a gardener's wife might feel when called upon to act outside the usual routine of her life. Great trouble had been taken with the food, and there was vastly too much for the few who were there. Simon imagined that the agent had ordered a shooting lunch, and that the staff, dormant for fifteen years, had risen to the occasion as a final obeisance to their dead employer.

The table was set with twenty places, but only six sat down – the agent and his wife; the thinner of the two men in city suits who had introduced himself as the solicitor responsible for the Ludleys' affairs; the old lady, who was indeed an aunt – a sister of their mother; Simon; and the second man in a city suit, who smiled at Simon as if he knew him from beneath thick, ill-kempt eyebrows.

'Is that the cousin who will inherit the house?' Simon asked the solicitor, nodding towards this, the last of the unidentified mourners.

'Tristram Bailey-Jones?' the solicitor replied. 'No, no, alas, he wanted to come but he couldn't get away. He's something in the City, you know. Always flying off to the Middle East.'

The aunt, who sat on Simon's other side, suddenly turned to him and asked: 'Are you the one who was there?'

'Where?'

'In France. Where they drowned.'

'Yes.'

'Tell me what happened,' she said.

'They were out on their boat with another friend, Charlie Hope. There was a tidal wave.'

'In the Mediterranean? A tidal wave?'

Simon explained about the building of the new port.

'But wasn't it a funny time to take a holiday?' the aunt asked.

'They weren't on holiday,' said Simon. 'They – that is Willy – lived there.'

'In Nice? I thought he lived in Brazil.'

'He used to live in Argentina but he had settled in Nice.'

'And she lived in Africa, didn't she?'

'Yes. In Morocco.'

She sighed. 'I never understood why they didn't live in England.'

'I think it was the tax,' said Simon.

'Yes,' said the old lady sharply. 'That would account for Will living abroad, but Priscilla had no money of her own. None to speak of, anyway. She could have lived in England.'

'The light,' said Simon. 'She liked the light in Morocco – for her painting.'

They moved through to the drawing-room, where they drank coffee – some sitting, some standing around a great log fire. Simon, as the only one there who had known the Ludleys in their later years, was cross-questioned by the agent's wife and then trapped by the solicitor, who while unctuously thanking him for the trouble he had saved him in Nice, also tried to discover the amount of money they should expect from the sale of the Villa Golitsyn.

As soon as he had finished his coffee, Simon took his leave. He was accompanied to the door by the agent, and the thickset man with the bushy eyebrows left the house at the same time. They walked across the gravel towards their cars and this fellow-guest, who now wore his velvet-collared overcoat, asked Simon if he would like a lift back to London.

He asked in a bluff, familiar way – speaking with the touch of a northern accent – and Simon was surprised at the question, since the man must surely know that he had a car of his own. He turned and declined the offer, noticing as he did so in the bright, horizontal light of the winter sun the red hair mixed with the grey.

'You're Milson, aren't you?' the man said as he pulled on a pair of leather gloves.

'Yes.'

'I'm Baldwin, Leslie Baldwin. We work for the same firm.'

'Yes,' said Simon.

'So did Ludley, of course. That's where I knew him.'

'In Djakarta,' said Simon.

'That's right.' The man's jovial face turned hard for a moment. 'So you know about me?' he said.

Simon blushed in confusion. 'Well, Willy mentioned that you'd been with him in Djakarta.'

'What else did he say?'

Simon hesitated. He tried to remember what it was that Willy had said about Baldwin but could only remember 'Les Miserables'. He hesitated, then smiled at Baldwin, opened his mouth to speak but could think of nothing to say.

Baldwin's face took on the hard expression it had worn a moment before. 'Never mind what he said,' he said sharply, taking his gloved hand out of his pocket and reaching inside his coat. 'I know why you went out there, and I dare say you have come back somewhat better informed. But before you go to see Fowler, you had better look at these.'

He took a brown envelope from his inside pocket and handed it to Simon. It was not sealed, and for a moment Simon thought it contained money, but when he reached inside he found a collection of photographs, almost all of himself with Helen. They had been arranged in sequence. The first showed them arriving at the station in Nice, Helen still wearing her school uniform. There were then several on the Promenade des Anglais, and others on the beach. One or two had been taken at Sospel, where they had stopped on their way to the chapel in the mountains, and all had the grainy texture of pictures taken with a telephoto lens. The last in the series were more than a dozen blurred but unmistakable photographs of the two of them naked in the Ludleys' bedroom – including one of Helen wearing only a poodle's collar, drinking from the saucer of champagne.

Simon stood there stunned, unable to understand how anyone could have taken such photographs, but then he remembered the block of flats between the house and the sea – Les Grands Cèdres – and the window opening out onto the balcony of the Villa Golitsyn.

'You know she's under age, don't you?' said Baldwin.

'Yes,' said Simon sourly. He looked down at the photographs again. In one of those taken on the beach, Priss sat next to Helen: she seemed to be staring at him, a slight smile on her face.

'I'm sorry about this,' said Baldwin in a dispassionate tone of voice. 'I find it distasteful, but my friends are quite convinced that every Englishman has his sexual perversion and in your case, I'm afraid, it turned out to be true.'

'What do you intend to do?' Simon asked.

'We don't know what Ludley told you,' said Baldwin, 'but we know why Fowler sent you out there and have no reason to suppose that you didn't get what you wanted.'

'How do you know I haven't spoken to Fowler already?'

'Because you haven't been to the office, and Fowler doesn't believe in the telephone.'

'These photographs,' said Simon, 'are better proof than anything

Willy may have said . . .'

'But you won't show them to Fowler, will you?' said Baldwin. 'I'm afraid they know you, Milson – not personally, perhaps, but they know your type. You don't really care who wins the cold war or runs this country.'

Simon opened his mouth to protest, but Baldwin interrupted him. 'Don't misunderstand me,' he said. 'I'm glad you are as you are, because people like you make it easier for people like me. We can always count on you to take the path of least resistance.'

He laughed – the empty laugh of a man with no sense of humour. 'Mind you, I'm not the idealist I once was.'

'Why are you so sure that I won't tell Fowler everything that you've told me?'

'Because I know you're not a fool. Remember that whatever Ludley may have told you, and you may tell Fowler, they'll never be able to prove anything against me. The worst they can do is shunt me off into some cosy little embassy. It won't be quite what I wanted, but I'll be rather more comfortable in Copenhagen or Vienna than you will be in Wormwood Scrubs.'

Simon said nothing: he looked down at the toes of his shoes and kicked the gravel.

'No need to answer me now,' said Baldwin. 'If I don't go to Washington, I'll know why – and the snaps, I'm afraid, will go to the police and *Private Eye*.' Baldwin got into his car. 'Keep the prints,' he said. 'The negatives will do me. Show them to your little friend. They might even turn her on.' He laughed. 'We won't meet again,' he said. 'I'll know what you've decided by what happens to me.'

Four

It was sleeting as Simon drove back to London. The half-formed flakes of snow landed on his windscreen as a constellation of crystals and then were either swept away by the monotonous movement of the wipers, or melted into small drops of water and trickled down the glass.

Simon drove with scrupulous care, fighting an impulse to drive headlong into a car or lorry coming in the opposite direction. Never in his life before had he felt so desolate – abandoned by everyone who had ever loved him, and now faced with the choice of betraying his country or ruining himself.

Behind this overwhelming misery his thoughts darted around like eels in stagnant water, searching for some channel to escape. Only one seemed clear – to give in to blackmail, to tell Fowler that Willy had confessed his treason before he died. It was simple and safe: no one could ever refute him. Even if Baldwin was discovered later in his career, that would only signify that perhaps both had been traitors. Nothing could ever be proved against Simon.

The alternative – to tell Fowler everything that had happened – would certainly lead to dismissal and disgrace. Even if Fowler could control the police, nothing could hold back the pack of scavenging journalists, hungry for rich scandals in high places. He would be lampooned as a pervert and sent to prison. There would follow the humiliating search for some other employment; the embarrassment of his friends; the shame of his children; the smug satisfaction of his wife. He would prefer to kill himself than suffer such indignities, but rather than kill himself he would overcome his scruples and lie to Fowler and go on living as before.

What if that made him a traitor in his turn? What did it signify? 'Traitor' was an old-fashioned word from the world of Shakespeare's plays. One could betray governments, perhaps, but not one's country; and even the zeal for secrecy among governments was an exaggerated fetish of politicians and civil servants. What difference would it make if Baldwin did now pass the secrets of the British and American governments to the governments of China or the Soviet Union? There was never going to be a war because both sides already knew all they needed to know – that their enemies could destroy them many times over. All the rest was a charade. What difference was made to the destinies of the Western nations by the treason of Maclean, Philby or Blake? None. None at all. And Baldwin's espionage would do as little as theirs had done, so why should Simon destroy his life to unmask it?

The knot of nerves in his stomach had loosened. He drove faster on the open road. What was England anyway? he asked himself. He conjured up a collage of images and memories – the Queen, the Horseguards, Hensfield House, Helen in her school uniform, the Houses of Parliament, his wife's mother, the Ludleys' land agent, Fowler . . . So what if lying about Baldwin did in some obscure way hasten the day when all these would be swept away? What did he care if there was a Communist Revolution? The weather would not change. The beer would taste the same. He would enjoy the expropriation of his parents-in-law's estates in Dorset: he would be glad to see Hensfield House seized from the smug heir who was 'something in the City'. Simon would not suffer from a change in regime: Popular Democracies needed Civil Servants just as much as Parliamentary Democracies. Either would give him a job and pay him a pension.

He reached the outskirts of London, still angry that he faced such a dilemma but satisfied that he had reached the right decision.

It was six by the time he reached home. He went from his car to a supermarket, bought some groceries and climbed the stairs to his flat. He was happy that at last he was alone with his own books, pictures and furniture. He turned up the heating and took a bath, then dressed in jeans and a jersey, made himself supper – shrimps mixed with scrambled eggs on toast, salad, blackcurrant yogurt and half a bottle of white Burgundy – and ate what he had made in front of the television.

He remained absorbed in the drama he was watching until he dropped a blob of yogurt onto his lap. He licked the spoon and scooped it off the denim of his jeans, but in doing so noticed another stain beside it. He wondered what it was, and then remembered that a dribble of strawberry jam had dropped from a piece of baguette one morning when he had eaten breakfast in the garden of the Villa Golitsyn. Willy had been sitting next to him.

He looked back at the screen and tried once again to lose himself in the programme, but the memory of Willy, sitting in the sun, was suddenly stronger than the images on the screen. 'What would Willy have done?' he asked himself; and answered almost immediately: 'Willy would have agreed. After all, he knew it was Baldwin. If he had thought it important, he would have told me.'

He looked again at the television but Willy, in the shadow of the cypress tree, would not leave Simon's mind. If anything he seemed to shake his head and say: 'Don't be too sure, Simon, old boy. I'm an unpredictable fellow.'

'Anyway,' Simon thought to himself, 'what do I care what Willy would have thought?' And he concentrated once again on the television; but by now he had lost the thread of the plot, so he stood up, switched it off and poured himself a glass of scotch whisky.

He sat down again with *The Times*, which he had not had time to read that morning, but neither the newsprint nor the whisky were any more successful than the television at dislodging the image of his dead friend. So he thought once again of what Willy's attitude would have been to his predicament. Certainly everything he had argued to himself about the demise of a certain class was in tune with what Willy had learned from E.H. Carr. But Willy would not have cared for Baldwin – the self-righteous bullying of the man. Nor did Simon. Willy would probably have told Fowler the truth and damned the consequences – *pour épater les bourgeois* – but as Willy himself had said, Simon embodied a different kind of Englishman: no extravagant, suicidal gestures, no crazy, Quixotic bursts of patriotic self-sacrifice should be expected of him. He must run true to form: he must save his own skin.

He poured himself another drink and then lit one of his small Dutch cigars. For some odd reason he could not convince himself that Willy would agree with this reasoning. 'But how the hell can I know what Willy would have thought?' he asked himself in an exasperated tone of voice. He had contradicted himself over and over again: he would probably have referred Simon to Moses on Mount Sinai, but which of the Ten Commandments covered the Official Secrets Act? The Eighth, perhaps: Thou shalt not bear false witness against thy neighbour. But why should Willy mind if he was branded posthumously as a traitor? He was dead – past caring about his reputation as a patriot. He had no family in this world to suffer from his dishonour, and there was no other world from which Willy could listen to Simon lie to Fowler; nor any Last Judgement, like that painted on the chapel wall, at which Willy could come forward and bear witness against him.

He poured himself another drink, and repeated to himself that Willy was dead; but the more he insisted upon this rational fact the more real became the phantom of his dead friend until Simon – like Willy at Herzen's tomb – began to talk aloud to his dead friend as if he alone could help him. 'What shall I do?' he asked in a plaintive, desperate voice. 'What the hell shall I do, Willy?'

'Face the music, Milson,' the voice seemed to reply.

'I can't, Willy.'

'Never give in to a bully,' said Willy again – not now the Willy of the Villa Golitsyn but the healthy, heroic figure whom Simon had known at school.

'I must, Willy, don't you see? A man's first duty is not to his country, or even to his friends. It's to himself.'

'But to his soul, Simon. Not to his reputation.'

'I don't believe in the soul, Willy.'

'Then call it self-respect.'

'For God's sake, Willy, let me off,' said Simon, sitting with his face thrust into his hands, his cigar forgotten in the ashtray beside him. 'I can't do what you want. I can't face the consequences.'

'Don't let me down, old boy.'

'But I've already let you down with the girl.'

'Then now is your chance to make up for it.'

'I can't, Willy, I can't,' said Simon again; and then clutching the bottle of whisky with both hands he stood, sobbing, and staggered to bed.

Five

When Simon reached his desk at half past nine the next morning there was already a message from Fowler asking him to report as soon as it was convenient. He went up in the middle of the morning.

'Sit down,' said Fowler – almost curtly. Then he offered him coffee in a softer tone, an offer which Simon declined. 'How did it go, then?' he asked, sitting down behind his desk as before and stirring a mug of coffee which had been placed on his blotting pad. 'I hope at least that you had some decent weather.'

'It was mixed,' said Simon. 'There were some storms . . .'

'Yes. I heard about Ludley.'

'He was with his sister and another friend.'

'Yes,' said Fowler. 'I read about it in the paper.'

'I stayed on for a week or so to see to the repatriation of the bodies.'

'Of course.'

'They were buried yesterday in Suffolk.'

'And our little business?' asked Fowler. 'Did Ludley say anything before he died?'

'We talked about it,' said Simon. 'He knew what I wanted to know but he wouldn't tell me.'

'Did he give a reason? Was he afraid?'

'No. He said he thought it wasn't important. He liked to tease people, you know. He was playing a game.'

'A game, perhaps, to cover up for himself?'

'No,' said Simon in a slow, deliberate tone of voice. 'I have other evidence that it wasn't Ludley.'

Fowler was sipping his coffee. When Simon said this he put down his mug and leaned forward on his desk. 'What evidence?'

'I saw Baldwin yesterday,' said Simon.

'Baldwin? Do you mean our Baldwin? Leslie Baldwin?'

'Yes. He is the other man, I think?'

'I never said so.'

'No.'

'Where did you see him?'

'At Ludley's funeral.'

'What did he say?'

'He seemed to know what you had asked me to do in Nice and . . . he tried to blackmail me.'

'How?'

'In Nice there was a girl – a schoolgirl.'

A look of distaste came onto Fowler's face.

'I had thought she was more than sixteen,' said Simon, 'but it turned out that she was a year younger.'

Fowler's expression relaxed. 'Not a child?'

'No, but they took photographs – compromising photographs.'

'I see.' Fowler paused. 'So he's worried, which must mean that he's still busy.'

'He said that if his appointment is not confirmed, he'll know why and he'll send the photographs to the press and to the police.'

Fowler sat fingering the upper lip where once he had had a moustache. 'Has he still got the photographs on him?' he asked. 'They'd be evidence . . .'

'No. He gave the prints to me, but he must have the negatives.'

'He's not a fool. They'll be held by someone else.'

'I shall resign, of course,' said Simon.

'No,' said Fowler. 'Wait. It's possible, you see, that if Baldwin is still busy then we'll confirm his appointment anyway.'

'I don't understand.'

'It's not my decision,' said Fowler, 'but a spy can be useful if he doesn't know we know.'

'That hadn't occurred to me.'

'And sooner or later they'll come back to you, if they've got those photographs. That could be useful too.'

'So what shall I do?' asked Simon.

'Nothing. Leave it to me.' Fowler got to his feet and came out from behind his desk. 'I appreciate what you've done,' he said, shaking Simon by the hand. 'It couldn't have turned out better.'

'Shouldn't I resign?' asked Simon.

Fowler laughed. 'Good Heavens, no. If all our people resigned over something like that, we wouldn't have much of a Foreign Service. But I should watch your step. All sorts of things go on in the South of France which are best not done at home.'

Simon returned to his desk and began to sift through the papers which had piled up in his absence.

'A girl phoned,' his secretary said. 'She said she'd ring again.'

'Did she give her name?'

'No. She sounded young. It might have been your daughter.'

It had been Helen. She telephoned again after lunch to say that all was well at home. 'I'm going to a sixth-form college in Windsor,' she said.

'That sounds much better than boarding school.'

'Yes. And they haven't sold Pixie.'

'Who's Pixie?'

'My pony.'

'Good.'

'I'll come up and see you if you like?'

'Later on, perhaps.'

'Whenever you like.' She sounded unconcerned. 'Did you see the bit in the paper about Willy and Priss?'

'No.'

'It was in the *Telegraph*.'

'What did it say?'

'Oh, nothing much. Just the facts. But that wasn't the point about them, was it? The facts?'

'No,' said Simon. 'They never are.'

NEW FROM BARD
DISTINGUISHED MODERN FICTION

MULATA
Miguel Angel Asturias   58552-9/$3.50

Nobel Prize winner Miguel Angel Asturias combines the mysterious myth, folklore and fantasy of South and Central America in an ingenious, intoxicating adventure story. "Asturias has a robust vein of humor, a strong predilection for the erotic, and the ability to carry one into the mythic world he creates by oscillating between the real and the mythic."   —*Saturday Review*

FALLING
Susan Fromberg Schaeffer   59006-9/$3.50

After an attempted suicide, Elizabeth Kamen is determined to make a new beginning for herself. With the aid of an analyst, Elizabeth examines her past and realizes that what she thought was "falling" is a journey forward—of maturation, self-acceptance, of the ability to know real love, and of learning to appreciate the fragments of her past that helped form her. "We are engaged with remarkable intensity in this young woman's fight for a life of her own... Susan Fromberg Schaeffer is the finest talent we've seen in a long while."   —*The New York Times Book Review*

THE SHOOTING PARTY
Isabel Colegate   59543-5/$3.50

A "beautifully written" (*London Times*) portrayal of the English gentry living the last moments of a way of life prior to the outbreak of World War I. In the autumn of 1913, Sir Randolph Nettleby assembles a group of friends at his Oxfordshire estate for the biggest pheasant shoot of the season. However, a more significant drama is unfolding, one that will end in tragedy for them all. "A novel of unusual force and flavor."   —*The New Yorker*

THE GIRL IN THE PHOTOGRAPH
Lygia Fagundes Telles   **80716-0/$3.95**

A vibrant novel that follows three days in the lives of three very different women as they face critical events in their lives. This is the first English translation of the bestseller by Brazil's foremost woman writer.

Coming in August
THE WOMAN WHO LIVED IN A PROLOGUE
Nina Schneider   **59881-7/$3.95**

At age 73, Araidne Arkady takes pen in hand to write her autobiography "to discover my own life, whatever that is." Araidne's compelling reflections make sense of meaningless losses, accidental tragedies and unnerving passions. And from it all, she discovers a series of new beginnings. "The achievement of a lifetime...extraordinary...affirms the value of age and experience."
— *Washington Post Book World*

Bard 8   7-82

NEW FROM BARD
DISTINGUISHED MODERN FICTION

CALL IT SLEEP
Henry Roth   60764-6/$3.95

One of the great American novels, it tells the story of the immigrant experience in America. First published in 1934 to critical acclaim, it quickly dropped out of sight. But with its 1964 publication it received the recognition it deserved when *The New York Times Book Review* hailed it as "one of the few genuinely distinguished novels written by a 20th-century American."

KONTINENT 4:
Contemporary Russian Writers
George Bailey, Editor   81182-0/$4.95

A compelling and provocative collection of 23 articles and short stories from *KONTINENT*, the quarterly journal of Russian and Eastern European dissident writers. These powerful works are written both by emigres from the Soviet Union and her satellite countries as well as by dissidents who must smuggle their manuscripts from behind the Iron Curtain. Filled with courage, defiance and surprising humor, these works afford a unique look at contemporary Russian literary, political and social thought.

DAUGHTER OF NIGHT
Lydia Obukhova,
translated by Mirra Ginsburg   61192-9/$2.95

An absorbing fantasy adventure that explores an intriguing possibility: what if human thought were created with the help of alien visitors from technologically advanced planets? "Expertly translated, excites the imagination and should keep a tight grip on any reader...a smashing tale."

Publishers Weekly

QUIN'S SHANGHAI CIRCUS
Edward Whittemore   61200-3/$3.50

A surreal, colorful novel of a young man whose search for his lost parents takes him on a wild odyssey through the Orient. Edward Whittemore "has an incredible imagination. His fantasies could be a combination of such as Borges, Pynchon, Nabokov, Fuentes and Barth."

Pittsburgh Post-Gazette

Bard 11-82